JACQUELINE

By TH. BENTZON
(MME. BLANC)

Crowned by the French Academy

With a Preface by M.
THUREAU-DANGIN
of the French Academy

WILDSIDE PRESS

TH. BENTZON

T is natural that the attention and affection of Americans should be attracted to a woman who has devoted herself assiduously to understanding and to making known the aspirations of our country, especially in introducing the labors and achievements of our women to their sisters in France, of whom we also have much to learn; for simple, homely virtues and the charm of womanliness may still be studied with advantage on the cherished soil of France.

Marie-Thérèse Blanc, née Solms—for this is the name of the author who writes under the *nom de plume* of Madame Bentzon—is considered the greatest of living French female novelists. She was born in an old French château at Seine-Porte (Seine et Oise), September 21, 1840. This château was owned by Madame Bentzon's grandmother, the Marquise de Vitry, who was a woman of great force and energy of character, "a ministering angel" to her country neighborhood. Her grandmother's first marriage was to a Dane, Major-General Adrien-Benjamin de Bentzon, a Governor of the Danish Antilles. By this marriage there was one

PREFACE

daughter, the mother of Thérèse, who in turn married the Comte de Solms. "This mixture of races," Madame Blanc once wrote, "surely explains a kind of moral and intellectual cosmopolitanism which is found in my nature. My father of German descent, my mother of Danish—my *nom de plume* (which was her maiden-name) is Danish—with Protestant ancestors on her side, though she and I were Catholics—my grandmother a sound and witty Parisian, gay, brilliant, lively, with superb physical health and the consequent good spirits—surely these materials could not have produced other than a cosmopolitan being."

Somehow or other, the family became impoverished. Thérèse de Solms took to writing stories. After many refusals, her début took place in the *Revue des Deux Mondes*, and her perseverance was largely due to the encouragement she received from George Sand, although that great woman saw everything through the magnifying glass of her genius. But the person to whom Thérèse Bentzon was most indebted in the matter of literary advice—she says herself—was the late M. Caro, the famous Sorbonne professor of philosophy, himself an admirable writer, "who put me through a course of literature, acting as my guide through a vast amount of solid reading, and criticizing my work with kindly severity." Success was slow. Strange as it may seem, there is a prejudice against female writers in France, a country that has produced so many admirable women-authors. However, the time was to come when M. Becloz found one of her stories in the *Journal des Débats*. It was the one entitled *Un Divorce*, and he

PREFACE

lost no time in engaging the young writer to become one of his staff. From that day to this she has found the pages of the *Revue* always open to her.

Madame Bentzon is a novelist, translator, and writer of literary essays. The list of her works runs as follows: *Le Roman d'un Muet* (1868); *Un Divorce* (1872); *La Grande Saulière* (1877); *Un remords* (1878); *Yette* and *Georgette* (1880); *Le Retour* (1882); *Tête folle* (1883); *Tony,* (1884); *Emancipée* (1887); *Constance* (1891); *Jacqueline* (1893). We need not enter into the merits of style and composition if we mention that *Un remords, Tony,* and *Constance* were crowned by the French Academy, and *Jacqueline* in 1893. Madame Bentzon is likewise the translator of Aldrich, Bret Harte, Dickens, and Ouida. Some of her critical works are: *Litterature et Mœurs etrangères,* 1882, and *Nouveaux romanciers americains,* 1885.

Paul Emmeaudangis

de l'Académie Française.

CONTENTS

CONTENTS

JACQUELINE

CHAPTER I

A PARISIENNE'S "AT HOME"

ESPITE a short frock, checked stockings, wide turned-over collar, and a loose sash around the waist of her blouse—in other words, despite the childish fashion of a dress which seemed to denote that she was not more than thirteen or fourteen years of age, she seemed much older. An observer would have put her down as the oldest of the young girls who on Tuesdays, at Madame de Nailles's afternoons, filled what was called "the young girls' corner" with whispered merriment and low laughter, while, under pretence of drinking tea, the noise went on which is always audible when there is anything to eat.

No doubt the amber tint of this young girl's complexion, the raven blackness of her hair, her marked yet delicate features, and the general impression produced by her dark coloring, were reasons why she seemed older than the rest. It was Jacqueline's privilege to exhibit that style of beauty which comes earliest to perfection, and retains it longest; and, what was an equal privilege, she resembled no one.

THÉO BENTZON

The deep bow-window—her favorite spot—which enabled her to have a reception-day in connection with that of her mamma, seemed like a great basket of roses when all her friends assembled there, seated on low chairs in unstudied attitudes: the white rose of the group was Mademoiselle d'Etaples, a specimen of pale and pensive beauty, frail almost to transparency; the Rose of Bengal was the charming Colette Odinska, a girl of Polish race, but born in Paris; the dark-red rose was Isabelle Ray—Belle she was called triumphantly— whose dimpled cheeks flushed scarlet for almost any cause, some said for very coquetry. Then there were three little girls called Wermant, daughters of an *agent de change*—a spray of May roses, exactly alike in features, manners, and dress, sprightly and charming as little girls could be. A little *pompon* rose was tiny Dorothée d'Avrigny, to whom the pet name Dolly was appropriate, for never had any doll's waxen face been more lovely than her little round one, with its mouth shaped like a little heart—a mouth smaller than her eyes, and these were round eyes, too, but so bright, and blue, and soft, that it was easy to overlook their too frequently startled expression.

Jacqueline had nothing in common with a rose of any kind, but she was not the less charming to look at. Such was the unspoken reflection of a man who was well able to be a judge in such matters. His name was Hubert Marien. He was a great painter, and was now watching the clear-cut, somewhat Arab-like profile of this girl—a profile brought out distinctly against the dark-red silk background of a screen, much as we see

JACQUELINE

a cameo stand out in sharp relief from the glittering stone from which the artist has fashioned it. Marien looked at her from a distance, leaning against the fireplace of the farther salon, whence he could see plainly the corner shaded by green foliage plants where Jacqueline had made her *niche*, as she called it. The two rooms formed practically but one, being separated only by a large recess without folding-doors, or *portières*. Hubert Marien, from his place behind Madame de Nailles's chair, had often before watched Jacqueline as he was watching her at this moment. She had grown up, as it were, under his own eye. He had seen her playing with her dolls, absorbed in her story-books, and crunching sugar-plums, he had paid her visits—for how many years? He did not care to count them.

And little girls bloom fast! How old they make us feel! Who would have supposed the most unpromising of little buds would have transformed itself so soon into what he gazed upon? Marien, as an artist, had great pleasure in studying the delicate outline of that graceful head surmounted by thick tresses, with rebellious ringlets rippling over the brow before they were gathered into the thick braid that hung behind; and Jacqueline, although she appeared to be wholly occupied with her guests, felt the gaze that was fixed upon her, and was conscious of its magnetic influence, from which nothing would have induced her to escape even had she been able. All the young girls were listening attentively (despite their more serious occupation of consuming dainties) to what was going on in the next room among the grown-up people, whose conversation reached them only in detached fragments.

So long as the subject talked about was the last reception at the French Academy, these young girls (comrades in the class-room and at the weekly catechising) had been satisfied to discuss together their own little affairs, but after Colonel de Valdonjon began to talk complete silence reigned among them. One might have heard the buzzing of a fly. Their attention, however, was of little use. Exclamations of oh! and ah! and protests more or less sincere drowned even the loud and somewhat hoarse voice of the Colonel. The girls heard it only through a sort of general murmur, out of which a burst of astonishment or of dissent would occasionally break forth. These outbreaks were all the curious group could hear distinctly. They sniffed, as it were, at the forbidden fruit, but they longed to inhale the full perfume of the scandal that they felt was in the air. That stout officer of cuirassiers, of whom some people spoke as "The Chatterbox," took advantage of his profession to tell many an unsavory story which he had picked up or invented at his club. He had come to Madame de Nailles's reception with a brand-new concoction of falsehood and truth, a story likely to be hawked round Paris with great success for several weeks to come, though ladies on first hearing it would think proper to cry out that they would not even listen to it, and would pretend to look round them for their fans to hide their confusion.

The principal object of interest in this scandalous gossip was a valuable diamond bracelet, one of those priceless bits of jewelry seldom seen except in show-windows on the Rue de la Paix, intended to be bought only for presentation to princesses—of some sort or kind. Well, by an extraordinary chance the Marquise de Versannes—aye, the lovely Georgine de Versannes herself—had picked up this bracelet in the street—by chance, as it were.

"It so happened," said the Colonel, "that I was at her mother-in-law's, where she was going to dine. She came in looking as innocent as you please, with her hand in her pocket. 'Oh, see what I have found!' she cried. 'I stepped upon it almost at your door.' And the bracelet was placed under a lamp, where the diamonds shot out sparkles fit to blind the old Marquise, and make that old fool of a Versannes see a thousand lights. He has long known better than to take all his wife says for gospel—but he tries hard to pretend that he believes her. 'My dear,' he said, 'you must take that to the police.' 'I'll send it to-morrow morning,' says the charming Georgine, 'but I wished to show you my good luck.' Of course nobody came forward to claim the bracelet, and a month later Madame de Versannes appeared at the Cranfords' ball with a brilliant diamond bracelet, worn like the Queen of Sheba's, high up on her arm, near the shoulder, to hide the lack of sleeve. This piece of finery, which drew everybody's attention to the wearer, was the famous bracelet picked up in the street. Clever of her!—wasn't it, now?"

"Horrid! Unlikely! Impossible. . . . What do you mean us to understand about it, Colonel? Could she have . . . ?"

Then the Colonel went on to demonstrate, with many coarse insinuations, that that good Georgine, as he familiarly called her, had done many more things than people gave her credit for. And he went on to add: "Surely, you must have heard of the row about her between Givrac and the Homme-Volant at the Cirque?"

"What, the man that wears stockinet all covered with gold scales? Do tell us, Colonel!"

But here Madame de Nailles gave a dry little cough which was meant to impose silence on the subject. She was not a prude, but she disapproved of anything that was bad form at her receptions. The Colonel's revelations had to be made in a lower tone, while his hostess endeavored to bring back the conversation to the charming reply made by M. Renan to the somewhat insipid address of a member of the Académie.

"We sha'n't hear anything more now," said Colette, with a sigh. "Did you understand it, Jacqueline?"

"Understand—what?"

"Why, that story about the bracelet?"

"No—not all. The Colonel seemed to imply that she had not picked it up, and indeed I don't see how any one could have dropped in the street, in broad daylight, a bracelet meant only to be worn at night—a bracelet worn near the shoulder."

"But if she did not pick it up—she must have stolen it."

"Stolen it?" cried Belle. "Stolen it! What! The Marquise de Versannes? Why, she inherited the finest diamonds in Paris!"

"How do you know?"

JACQUELINE

"Because mamma sometimes takes me to the Opera, and her subscription day is the same as that of the Marquise. People say a good deal of harm of her—in whispers. They say she is barely received now in society, that people turn their backs on her, and so forth, and so on. However, that did not hinder her from being superb the other evening at *Polyeucte.*"

"So you only go to see *Polyeucte?*" said Jacqueline, making a little face as if she despised that opera.

"Yes, I have seen it twice. Mamma lets me go to *Polyeucte* and *Guillaume Tell*, and to the *Prophète*, but she won't take me to see *Faust*—and it is just *Faust* that I want to see. Isn't it provoking that one can't see everything, hear everything, understand everything? You see, we could not half understand that story which seemed to amuse the people so much in the other room. Why did they send back the bracelet from the Prefecture to Madame de Versannes if it was not hers?"

"Yes—why?" said all the little girls, much puzzled.

Meantime, as the hour for closing the exhibition at the neighboring hippodrome had arrived, visitors came pouring into Madame de Nailles's reception—tall, graceful women, dressed with taste and elegance, as befitted ladies who were interested in horsemanship. The tone of the conversation changed. Nothing was talked about but superb horses, leaps over ribbons and other obstacles. The young girls interested themselves in the spring toilettes, which they either praised or criticised as they passed before their eyes.

"Oh! there is Madame Villegry," cried Jacqueline; "how handsome she is! I should like one of these days to be that kind of beauty, so tall and slender. Her waist measure is only twenty-one and two thirds inches. The woman who makes her corsets and my mamma's told us so. She brought us one of her corsets to look at, a love of a corset, in brocatelle, all over many-colored flowers. That material is much more *distingué* than the old satin——"

"But what a queer idea it is to waste all that upon a thing that nobody will ever look at," said Dolly, her round eyes opening wider than before.

"Oh! it is just to please herself, I suppose. I understand that! Besides, nothing is too good for such a figure. But what I admire most is her extraordinary hair."

"Which changes its color now and then," observed the sharpest of the three Wermant sisters. "Extraordinary is just the word for it. At present it is dark red. Henna did that, I suppose. Raoul—our brother—when he was in Africa saw Arab women who used henna. They tied their heads up in a sort of poultice made of little leaves, something like tea-leaves. In twenty-four hours the hair will be dyed red, and will stay red for a year or more. You can try it if you like. I think it is disgusting."

"Oh! look, there is Madame de Sternay. I recognized her by her perfume before I had even seen her. What delightful things good perfumes are!"

"What is it? Is it heliotrope or jessamine?" asked Yvonne d'Etaples, sniffing in the air.

"No—it is only orris-root—nothing but orris-root; but she puts it everywhere about her—in the hem of her petticoat, in the lining of her dress. She lives, one might say, in the middle of a *sachet*. The thing that will please me most when I am married will be to have no limit to my perfumes. Till then I have to satisfy myself with very little," sighed Jacqueline, drawing a little bunch of violets from the loose folds of her blouse, and inhaling their fragrance with delight.

"*Tiens!* here comes somebody who has to be contented with much less," said Yvonne, as a young girl joined their circle. She was small, awkward, timid, and badly dressed. On seeing her Colette whispered: "Oh! that tiresome Giselle. We sha'n't be able to talk another word."

Jacqueline kissed Giselle de Monredon. They were distant cousins, though they saw each other very seldom. Giselle was an orphan, having lost both her father and her mother, and was being educated in a convent from which she was allowed to come out only on great occasions. Her grandmother, whose ideas were those of the old school, had placed her there. The Easter holidays accounted for Giselle's unexpected arrival. Wrapped in a large cloak which covered up her convent uniform, she looked, as compared with the gay girls around her, like a poor sombre night-moth, dazzled by the light, in company with other glittering creatures of the insect race, fluttering with graceful movements, transparent wings and shining corselets.

"Come and have some sandwiches," said Jacqueline, and she drew Giselle to the tea-table, with the kind intention apparently of making her feel more at her ease. But she had another motive. She saw some one who was very interesting to her coming at that moment toward the table. That some one was a man about forty, whose pointed black beard was becoming slightly gray—a man whom some people thought ugly, chiefly because they had never seen his somewhat irregular features illumined by a smile which, spreading from his lips to his eyes, lighted up his face and transformed it. The smile of Hubert Marien was rare, however. He was exclusive in his friendships, often silent, always somewhat unapproachable. He seldom troubled himself to please any one he did not care for. In society he was not seen to advantage, because he was extremely bored, for which reason he was seldom to be seen at the Tuesday receptions of Madame de Nailles; while, on other days, he frequented the house as an intimate friend of the family. Jacqueline had known him all her life, and for her he had always his beautiful smile. He had petted her when she was little, and had been much amused by the sort of adoration she had no hesitation in showing that she felt for him. He used to call her *Mademoiselle ma femme*, and M. de Nailles would speak of him as "my daughter's future husband." This joke had been kept up till the little lady had reached her ninth year, when it ceased, probably by order of Madame de Nailles, who in matters of propriety was very punctilious. Jacqueline, too, became less familiar than she had been with the man she called "my great painter." Indeed, in her heart of hearts, she cherished a grudge against him. She thought he presumed on the right he had assumed of teasing her. The older she grew the more he treated her as if she were a baby, and, in the little passages of arms that continually took place between them, Jacqueline was bitterly conscious that she no longer had the best of it as formerly. She was no longer as droll and lively as she had been. She was easily disconcerted, and took everything *au serieux*, and her wits became paralyzed by an embarrassment that was new to her. And, pained by the sort of sarcasm which Marien kept up in all their intercourse, she was often ready to burst into tears after talking to him. Yet she was never quite satisfied unless he was present. She counted the days from one Wednesday to another, for on Wednesdays he always dined with them, and she greeted any opportunity of seeing him on other days as a great pleasure. This week, for example, would be marked with a white stone. She would have seen him twice. For half an hour Marien had been enduring the bore of the reception, standing silent and self-absorbed in the midst of the gay talk, which did not interest him. He wished to escape, but was always kept from doing so by some word or sign from Madame de Nailles. Jacqueline had been thinking: "Oh! if he would only come and talk to us!" He was now drawing near them, and an instinct made her wish to rush up to him and tell him— what should she tell him? She did not know. A few moments before so many things to tell him had been passing through her brain.

What she said was: "Monsieur Marien, I recommend to you these little spiced cakes." And, with some awkwardness, because her hand was trembling, she held out the plate to him.

"No, thank you, Mademoiselle," he said, affecting a

tone of great ceremony, "I prefer to take this glass of punch, if you will permit me."

"The punch is cold, I fear;—suppose we were to put a little tea in it. Stay—let me help you."

"A thousand thanks; but I like to attend to such little cookeries myself. By the way, it seems to me that Mademoiselle Giselle, in her character of an angel who disapproves of the good things of this life, has not left us much to eat at your table."

"Who—I?" cried the poor schoolgirl, in a tone of injured innocence and astonishment.

"Don't pay any attention to him," said Jacqueline, as if taking her under her protection. "He is nothing but a tease; what he says is only chaff. But I might as well talk Greek to her," she added, shrugging her shoulders. "In the convent they don't know what to make of a joke. Only spare *her* at least, if you please, Monsieur Marien."

"I know by report that Mademoiselle Giselle is worthy of the most profound respect," continued the pitiless painter. "I lay myself at her feet—and at yours. Now I am going to slip away in the English fashion. Good-evening."

"Why do you go so soon? You can't do any more work to-day."

"No, it has been a day lost—that is true."

"That's polite! By the way—" here Jacqueline became very red and she spoke rapidly—"what made you just now stare at me so persistently?"

"I? Impossible that I could have permitted myself to stare at you, Mademoiselle."

JACQUELINE

"That is just what you did, though. I thought you had found something to find fault with. What could it be? I fancied there was something wrong with my hair, something absurd that you were laughing at. You always do laugh, you know."

"Wrong with your hair? It is always wrong. But that is not your fault. You are not responsible for its looking like a hedgehog's."

"Hedgehogs haven't any hair," said Jacqueline, much hurt by the observation.

"True, they have only prickles, which remind me of the susceptibility of your temper. I beg your pardon— I was looking at you critically. Being myself indulgent and kind-hearted, I was only looking at you from an artist's point of view—as is always allowable in my profession. Remember, I see you very rarely by daylight. I am obliged to work as long as the light allows me. Well, in the light of this April sunshine I was saying to myself—excuse my boldness!—that you had reached the right age for a picture."

"For a picture? Were you thinking of painting me?" cried Jacqueline, radiant with pleasure.

"Hold a moment, please. Between a dream and its execution lies a great space. I was only imagining a picture of you."

"But my portrait would be frightful."

"Possibly. But that would depend on the skill of the painter."

"And yet a model should be—I am so thin," said Jacqueline, with confusion and discouragement.

"True; your limbs are like a grasshopper's."

"Oh! you mean my legs—but my arms. . . ."

"Your arms must be like your legs. But, sitting as you were just now, I could see only your head, which is better. So! one has to be accountable for looking at you? Mademoiselle feels herself affronted if any one stares at her! I will remember this in future. There, now! suppose, instead of quarrelling with me, you were to go and cast yourself into the arms of your cousin Fred."

"Fred! Fred d'Argy! Fred is at Brest."

"Where are your eyes, my dear child? He has just come in with his mother."

And at that moment Madame de Nailles, with her pure, clear voice—a voice frequently compared to that of Mademoiselle Reichemberg, called:

"Jacqueline!"

Jacqueline never crossed the imaginary line which divided the two salons unless she was called upon to do so. She was still summoned like a child to speak to certain persons who took an especial interest in her, and who were kind enough to wish to see her—Madame d'Argy, for example, who had been the dearest friend of her dead mother. The death of that mother, who had been long replaced by a stepmother, could hardly be said to be deeply regretted by Jacqueline. She remembered her very indistinctly. The stories of her she had heard from Modeste, her old nurse, probably served her instead of any actual memory. She knew her only as a woman pale and in ill health, always lying on a sofa. The little black frock that had been made for her had been hardly worn out when a new mamma, as gay and fresh as the other had been sick and suffering, had come into the household like a ray of sunshine.

After that time Madame d'Argy and Modeste were the only people who spoke to her of the mother who was gone. Madame d'Argy, indeed, came on certain days to take her to visit the tomb, on which the child read, as she prayed for the departed:

MARIE JACQUELINE ADELAIDE DE VALTIER

BARONNE DE NAILLES

DIED AGED TWENTY-SIX YEARS.

And such filial sentiment as she still retained, concerning the unknown being who had been her mother, was tinged by her association with this melancholy pilgrimage which she was expected to perform at certain intervals. Without exactly knowing the reason why, Jacqueline was conscious of a certain hostility that existed between Madame d'Argy and her stepmother.

The intimate friend of the first Madame de Nailles was a woman with neither elegance nor beauty. She never had left off her widow's weeds, which she had worn since she had lost her husband in early youth. In the eyes of Jacqueline her sombre figure personified austere, exacting Duty, a kind of duty not attractive to her. That very day it seemed as if duty inconveniently stepped in to break up a conversation that was deeply interesting to her. The impatient gesture that she made when her mother called her might have been interpreted into: Bother Madame d'Argy!

[15]

"Jacqueline!" called again the silvery voice that had first summoned her; and a moment after the young girl found herself in the centre of a circle of grown people, saying good-morning, making curtseys, and kissing the withered hand of old Madame de Monredon, as she had been taught to do from infancy. Madame de Monredon was Giselle's grandmother. Jacqueline had been instructed to call her "aunt;" but in her heart she called her *La Fée Grognon*, while Madame d'Argy, pointing to her son, said: "What do you think, darling, of such a surprise? He is home on leave. We came here the first place—naturally."

"It was very nice of you. How do you do, Fred?" said Jacqueline, holding out her hand to a very young man, in a jacket ornamented with gold lace, who stood twisting his cap in his hand with some embarrassment: "It is a long time since we have seen each other. But it does not seem to me that you have grown a great deal."

Fred blushed up to the roots of his hair.

"No one can say that of you, Jacqueline," observed Madame d'Argy.

"No—what a may-pole!—isn't she?" said the Baronne, carelessly.

"If she realizes it," whispered Madame de Monredon, who was sitting beside Madame d'Argy on a *causeuse* shaped like an S, "why does she persist in dressing her like a child six years old? It is absurd!"

"Still, she can have no reason for keeping her thus in order to make herself seem young. She is only a stepmother."

"Of course. But people might make comparisons. Beauty in the bud sometimes blooms out unexpectedly when it is not welcome."

"Yes—she is fading fast. Small women ought not to grow stout."

"Anyhow, I have no patience with her for keeping a girl of fifteen in short skirts."

"You are making her out older than she is."

"How is that?—how is that? She is two years younger than Giselle, who has just entered her eighteenth year."

While the two ladies were exchanging these little remarks, the Baronne de Nailles was saying to the young naval cadet:

"Monsieur Fred, we should be charmed to keep you with us, but possibly you might like to see some of your old friends. Jacqueline can take you to them. They will be glad to see you."

"*Tiens!*—that's true," said Jacqueline. "Dolly and Belle are yonder. You remember Isabelle Ray, who used to take dancing lessons with us."

"Of course I do," said Fred, following his cousin with a feeling of regret that his sword was not knocking against his legs, increasing his importance in the eyes of all the ladies who were present. He was not, however, sorry to leave their imposing circle. Above all, he was glad to escape from the clear-sighted, critical eyes of Madame de Nailles. On the other hand, to be sent off to the girls' corner, after being insulted by being told he had not grown, hurt his sense of self-importance.

Meantime Jacqueline was taking him back to her own corner, where he was greeted by two or three little exclamations of surprise, shaking hands, however, as his former playmates drew their skirts around them, trying to make room for him to sit down.

"Young ladies," said Jacqueline, "I present to you a *bordachien*—a little middy from the practice-ship the *Borda*."

They burst out laughing: "A *bordachien!* A middy from the practice-ship!" they cried.

"I shall not be much longer on the practice-ship," said the young man, with a gesture which seemed as if his hand were feeling for the hilt of his sword, which was not there, "for I am going very soon on my first voyage as an ensign."

"Yes," explained Jacqueline, "he is going to be transferred from the *Borda* to the *Jean-Bart*—which, by the way, is no longer the *Jean-Bart*, only people call her so because they are used to it. Meantime you see before you "C," the great "C," the famous "C," that is, he is the pupil who stands highest on the roll of the naval school at this moment."

There was a vague murmur of applause. Poor Fred was indeed in need of some appreciation on the score of merit, for he was not much to look upon, being at that trying age when a young fellow's moustache is only a light down, an age at which youths always look their worst, and are awkward and unsociable because they are timid.

"Then you are no longer an idle fellow," said Dolly, rather teasingly. "People used to say that you went into the navy to get rid of your lessons. That I can quite understand."

"Oh, he has passed many difficult exams.," cried Giselle, coming to the rescue.

"I thought I had had enough of school," said Fred, without making any defense, "and besides I had other reasons for going into the navy."

His "other reasons" had been a wish to emancipate himself from the excessive solicitude of his mother, who kept him tied to her apron-strings like a little girl. He was impatient to do something for himself, to become a man as soon as possible. But he said nothing of all this, and to escape further questions devoured three or four little cakes that were offered him. Before taking them he removed his gloves and displayed a pair of chapped and horny hands.

"Why—poor Fred!" cried Jacqueline, who remarked them in a moment, "what kind of almond paste do you use?"

Much annoyed, he replied, curtly: "We all have to row, we have also to attend to the machinery. But that is only while we are cadets. Of course, such apprenticeship is very hard. After that we shall get our stripes and be ordered on foreign service, and expect promotion."

"And glory," said Giselle, who found courage to speak.

Fred thanked her with a look of gratitude. She, at least, understood his profession. She entered into his feelings far better than Jacqueline, who had been his first confidante—Jacqueline, to whom he had confided his purposes, his ambition, and his day-dreams. He thought Jacqueline was selfish. She seemed to care only for herself. And yet, selfish or not selfish, she pleased him better than all the other girls he knew—a thousand times more than gentle, sweet Giselle.

"Ah, glory, of course!" repeated Jacqueline. "I understand how much that counts, but there is glory of various kinds, and I know the kind that I prefer," she added in a tone which seemed to imply that it was not that of arms, or of perilous navigation. "We all know," she went on, "that not every man can have genius, but any sailor who has good luck can get to be an admiral."

"Let us hope you will be one soon, Monsieur Fred," said Dolly. "You will have well deserved it, according to the way you have distinguished yourself on board the *Borda*."

This induced Fred to let them understand something of life on board the practice-ship; he told how the masters who resided on shore ascended by a ladder to the gun-deck, which had been turned into a schoolroom; how six cadets occupied the space intended for each gun-carriage, where hammocks hung from hooks served them instead of beds; how the chapel was in a closet opened only on Sundays. He described the gymnastic feats in the rigging, the practice in gunnery, and many other things which, had they been well described, would have been interesting; but Fred was only a poor narrator. The conclusion the young ladies seemed to reach unanimously after hearing his descriptions, was discouraging. They cried almost with one voice:

JACQUELINE

"Think of any woman being willing to marry a sailor."

"Why not?" asked Giselle, very promptly.

"Because, what's the use of a husband who is always out of your reach, as it were, between water and sky? One would better be a widow. Widows, at any rate, can marry again. But you, Giselle, don't understand these things. You are going to be a nun."

"Had I been in your place, Fred," said Isabelle Ray, "I should rather have gone into the cavalry school at Saint Cyr. I should have wanted to be a good huntsman, had I been a man, and they say naval officers are never good horsemen."

Poor Fred! He was not making much progress among the young girls. Almost everything people talked about outside his cadet life was unknown to him; what he could talk about seemed to have no interest for any one, unless indeed it might interest Giselle, who was an adept in the art of sympathetic listening, never having herself anything to say.

Besides this, Fred was by no means at his ease in talking to Jacqueline. They had been told not to *tutoyer* each other, because they were getting too old for such familiarity, and it was he, and not she, who remembered this prohibition. Jacqueline perceived this after a while, and burst out laughing:

"*Tiens!* You call me 'you,'" she cried, "and I ought not to say 'thou' but 'you.' I forgot. It seems so odd, when we have always been accustomed to *tutoyer* each other."

"One ought to give it up after one's first communion," said the eldest Mademoiselle Wermant, sententiously. "We ceased to *tutoyer* our boy cousins after that. I am told nothing annoys a husband so much as to see these little familiarities between his wife and her cousins or her playmates."

Giselle looked very much astonished at this speech, and her air of disapproval amused Belle and Yvonne exceedingly. They began presently to talk of the classes in which they were considered brilliant pupils, and of their success in compositions. They said that sometimes very difficult subjects were given out. A week or two before, each had had to compose a letter purporting to be from Dante in exile to a friend in Florence, describing Paris as it was in his time, especially the manners and customs of its universities, ending by some allusion to the state of matters between the Guelphs and the Ghibellines.

"Good heavens! And could you do it?" said Giselle, whose knowledge of history was limited to what may be found in school abridgments.

It was therefore a great satisfaction to her when Fred declared that he never should have known how to set about it.

"Oh! papa helped me a little," said Isabelle, whose father wrote articles much appreciated by the public in the *Revue des Deux Mondes*. "But he said at the same time that it was horrid to give such crack-brained stuff to us poor girls. Happily, our subject this week is much nicer. We have to make comparisons between *La Tristesse d'Olympio*, *Souvenir*, and *Le Lac*. That will be something interesting."

JACQUELINE

"The *Tristesse d'Olympio?*" repeated Giselle, in a tone of interrogation.

"You know, of course, that it is Victor Hugo's," said Mademoiselle de Wermant, with a touch of pity.

Giselle answered with sincerity and humility, "I only knew that *Le Lac* was by Lamartine."

"Well!—she knows that much," whispered Belle to Yvonne—"just that much, anyhow."

While they were whispering and laughing, Jacqueline recited, in a soft voice, and with feeling that did credit to her instructor in elocution, Mademoiselle X——, of the *Théâtre Français:*

> Que le vent qui gémit, le roseau qui soupire,
> Que les parfums légers de ton air embaumé,
> Que tout ce qu'on entend, l'on voit ou l'on respire,
> Tout dise: Ils ont aimé.

> *May the moan of the wind, the green rushes' soft sighing,*
> *The fragrance that floats in the air you have moved,*
> *May all heard, may all breathed, may all seen, seem but trying*
> *To say: They have loved.*

Then she added, after a pause: "Isn't that beautiful?"

"How dares she say such words?" thought Giselle, whose sense of propriety was outraged by this allusion to love. Fred, too, looked askance and was not comfortable, for he thought that Jacqueline had too much assurance for her age, but that, after all, she was becoming more and more charming.

At that moment Belle and Yvonne were summoned,

[23]

and they departed, full of an intention to spread everywhere the news that Giselle, the little goose, had actually known that *Le Lac* had been written by Lamartine. The Bénédictine Sisters positively had acquired that much knowledge.

These girls were not the only persons that day at the reception who indulged in a little ill-natured talk after going away. Mesdames d'Argy and de Monredon, on their way to the Faubourg St. Germain, criticised Madame de Nailles pretty freely. As they crossed the Parc Monceau to reach their carriage, which was waiting for them on the Boulevard Malesherbes, they made the young people, Giselle and Fred, walk ahead, that they might have an opportunity of expressing themselves freely, the old dowager especially, whose toothless mouth never lost an opportunity of smirching the character and the reputation of her neighbors.

"When I think of the pains my poor cousin de Nailles took to impress upon us all that he was making what is called a *mariage raisonnable!* Well, if a man wants a wife who is going to set up her own notions, her own customs, he had better marry a poor girl without fortune! This one will simply ruin him. My dear, I am continually amazed at the way people are living whose incomes I know to the last *sou.* What an example for Jacqueline! Extravagance, fast living, elegant self-indulgence. . . . Did you observe the Baronne's gown? —of rough woolen stuff. She told some one it was the last creation of Doucet, and you know what that implies! His serge costs more than one of our velvet gowns. . . . And then her artistic tastes, her *bric-à-*

JACQUELINE

brac! Her salon looks like a museum or a bazaar. I
grant you it makes a very pretty setting for her and all
her coquetries. But in my time respectable women
were contented with furniture covered with red or yellow silk damask furnished by their upholsterers. They
didn't go about trying to hunt up the impossible. *On
ne cherche pas midi à quatorze heures.* You hold, as I
do, to the old fashions, though you are not nearly so
old, my dear Elise, and Jacqueline's mother thought as
we think. She would say that her daughter is being
very badly brought up. To be sure, all young creatures
nowadays are the same. Parents, on a plea of tenderness, keep them at home, where they get spoiled among
grown people, when they had much better have the
same kind of education that has succeeded so well with
Giselle; bolts on the garden-gates, wholesome seclusion, the company of girls of their own age, a great reg-
ularity of life, nothing which stimulates either vanity or
imagination. That is the proper way to bring up girls
without notions, girls who will let themselves be married without opposition, and are satisfied with the state
of life to which Providence may be pleased to call them.
For my part, I am enchanted with the ladies in the Rue
de Monsieur, and, what is more, Giselle is very happy
among them; to hear her talk you would suppose she
was quite ready to take the veil. Of course, that is a
mere passing fancy. But fancies of that sort are never
dangerous, they have nothing in common with those
that are passing nowadays through most girls' brains.
Having 'a day!'—what a foolish notion: And then to
let little girls take part in it, even in a corner of the

[25]

room. I'll wager that, though her skirts are half way up her legs, and her hair is dressed like a baby's, that that little de Nailles is less of a child than my granddaughter, who has been brought up by the Bénédictines. You say that she probably does not understand all that goes on around her. Perhaps not, but she breathes it in. It's poison—that's what it is!"

There was a good deal of truth in this harsh picture, although it contained considerable exaggeration.

At this moment, when Madame de Monredon was sitting in judgment on the education given to the little girls brought up in the world, and on the ruinous extravagance of their young stepmothers, Madame de Nailles and Jacqueline—their last visitors having departed—were resting themselves, leaning tenderly against each other, on a sofa. Jacqueline's head lay on her mother's lap. Her mother, without speaking, was stroking the girl's dark hair. Jacqueline, too, was silent, but from time to time she kissed the slender fingers sparkling with rings, as they came within reach of her lips.

When M. de Nailles, about dinner-time, surprised them thus, he said, with satisfaction, as he had often said before, that it would be hard to find a home scene more charming, as they sat under the light of a lamp with a pink shade.

That the stepmother and stepdaughter adored each other was beyond a doubt. And yet, had any one been able to look into their hearts at that moment, he would have discovered with surprise that each was thinking of something that she could not confide to the other.

JACQUELINE

Both were thinking of the same person. Madame de Nailles was occupied with recollections, Jacqueline with hope. She was absorbed in Machiavellian strategy, how to realize a hope that had been formed that very afternoon.

"What are you both thinking of, sitting there so quietly?" said the Baron, stooping over them and kissing first his wife and then his child.

"About nothing," said the wife, with the most innocent of smiles.

"Oh! I am thinking," said Jacqueline, "of many things. I have a secret, papa, that I want to tell you when we are quite alone. Don't be jealous, dear mamma. It is something about a surprise—Oh, a lovely surprise for you."

"Saint Clotilde's day—my *fête*-day is still far off," said Madame de Nailles, refastening, mother-like, the ribbon that was intended to keep in order the rough ripples of Jacqueline's unruly hair, "and usually your whisperings begin as the day approaches my *fête*."

"Oh, dear!—you will go and guess it!" cried Jacqueline in alarm. "Oh! don't guess it, please."

"Well! I will do my best not to guess, then," said the good-natured Clotilde, with a laugh.

"And I assure you, for my part, that I am discretion itself," said M. de Nailles.

So saying, he drew his wife's arm within his own, and the three passed gayly together into the dining-room.

CHAPTER II

A CLEVER STEPMOTHER

O man took more pleasure than M. de Nailles in finding himself in his own home—partly, perhaps, because circumstances compelled him to be very little there. The post of deputy in the French Chamber is no sinecure. He was not often an orator from the tribune, but he was absorbed by work in the committees—"Harnessed to a lot of bothering reports," as Jacqueline used to say to him. He had barely any time to give to those important duties of his position, by which, as is well known, members of the *Corps Législatif* are shamelessly harassed by constituents, who, on pretence that they have helped to place the interests of their district in your hands, feel authorized to worry you with personal matters, such as the choice of agricultural machines, or a place to be found for a wet-nurse.

Besides his public duties, M. de Nailles was occupied by financial speculations—operations that were no doubt made necessary by the style of living commented on by his cousin, Madame de Monredon, who was as stingy as she was bitter of tongue. The elegance that she found fault with was, however, very far from being great when compared with the luxury of the present day. Of course, the Baronne had to have her horses, her opera-box, her fashionable frocks. To supply these very moderate needs, which, however, she never insisted upon, being, so far as words went, most simple in her tastes, M. de Nailles, who had not the temperament which makes men find pleasure in hard work, became more and more fatigued. His days were passed in the Chamber, but he never neglected his interest on the Bourse; in the evening he accompanied his young wife into society, which, she always declared, she did not care for, but which had claims upon her nevertheless. It was therefore not surprising that M. de Nailles's face showed traces of the habitual fatigue that was fast aging him; his tall, thin form had acquired a slight stoop; though only fifty he was evidently in his declining years. He had once been a man of pleasure, it was said, before he entered politics. He had married his first wife late in life. She was a prudent woman who feared to expose him to temptation, and had kept him as far as possible away from Paris.

In the country, having nothing to do, he became interested in agriculture, and in looking after his estate at Grandchaux. He had been made a member of the *Conseil Général*, when unfortunately death too early deprived him of the wise and gentle counsellor for whom he felt, possibly not a very lively love, but certainly a high esteem and affection. After he became a widower he met in the Pyrenees, where, as he was whiling away the time of seclusion proper after his loss, a young lady who appeared to him exactly the person he needed to bring up his little daughter—because she was extremely attractive to himself. Of course M. de Nailles found plenty of other reasons for his choice, which he gave to the world and to himself to justify his second marriage—but this was the true reason and the only one. His friends, however, all of whom had urged on him the desirability of taking another wife, in consideration of the age of Jacqueline, raised many objections as soon as he announced his intention of espousing Mademoiselle Clotilde Hecker, eldest daughter of a man who had been, at one time, a prefect under the Empire, but who had been turned out of office by the Republican Government. He had a large family and many debts; but M. de Nailles had some answer always ready for the objections of his family and friends. He was convinced that Mademoiselle Hecker, having no fortune, would be less exacting than other women and more disposed to lead a quiet life.

She had been almost a mother to her own young brothers and sisters, which was a pledge for motherliness toward Jacqueline, etc., etc. Nevertheless, had she not had eyes as blue as those of the beauties painted by Greuze, plenty of audacious wit, and a delicate complexion, due to her Alsatian origin—had she not possessed a slender waist and a lovely figure, he might have asked himself why a young lady who, in winter, studied painting with the commendable intention of making her own living by art, passed the summers at all the watering-places of France and those of neighboring countries, without any perceptible motive.

But, thanks to the bandage love ties over the eyes of men, he saw only what Mademoiselle Clotilde was willing that he should see. In the first place he saw the great desirability of a talent for painting which, unlike music—so often dangerous to married happiness—gives women who cultivate it sedentary interests. And then he was attracted by the model daughter's filial piety as he beheld her taking care of her mother, who was the victim of an incurable disorder, which required her by turns to reside at Cauterets, or sometimes at Ems, sometimes at Aix in Savoy, and sometimes even at Trouville. The poor girl had assured him that she asked no happier lot than to live eight months of the year in the country, where she would devote herself to teaching Jacqueline, for whom at first sight she had taken a violent fancy (the attraction indeed was mutual). She assured him she would teach her all she knew herself, and her diplomas proved how well educated she had been.

Indeed, it seemed as if only prejudice could find any objection to so prudent and reasonable a marriage, a marriage contracted principally for the good of Jacque line.

It came to pass, however, that the air of Grand chaux, which is situated in the most unhealthful part of Limouzin, proved particularly hurtful to the new Madame de Nailles. She could not live a month on her husband's property without falling into a state of health which she attributed to malaria. M. de Nailles was at first much concerned about the condition of things which seemed likely to upset all his plans for retirement in the country, but, his wife having persuaded him that his position in the *Conseil Général* was only a stepping-stone to a seat in the *Corps Législatif*, where his place ought to be, he presented himself to the electors as a candidate, and was almost unanimously elected deputy, the conservative vote being still all-powerful in that part of the country.

His wife, it was said, had shown rare zeal and activity at the time of the election, employing in her husband's service all those little arts which enable her sex to succeed in politics, as well as in everything else they set their minds to. No lady ever more completely turned the heads of country electors. It was really Madame de Nailles who took her seat in the Left Centre of the Chamber, in the person of her husband.

After that she returned to Limouzin only long enough to keep up her popularity, though, with touching resignation, she frequently offered to spend the summer at Grandchaux, even if the consequences should be her death, like that of Pia in the Maremma. Her husband, of course, peremptorily set his face against such self-sacrifice.

The facilities for Jacqueline's education were increased by their settling down as residents of Paris. Madame de Nailles superintended the instruction of her stepdaughter with motherly solicitude, seconded, however, by a *promeneuse*, or walking-governess, which left her free to fulfil her own engagements in the afternoons. The walking-governess is a singular modern institution, intended to supply the place of the too often inconvenient daily governess of former times. The necessary qualifications of such a person are that she should have sturdy legs, and such knowledge of some foreign language as will enable her during their walks to converse in it with her pupil. Fraulein Schult, who came from one of the German cantons of Switzerland, was an ideal *promeneuse*. She never was tired and she was well-informed. The number of things that could be learned from her during a walk was absolutely incredible.

Madame de Nailles, therefore, after a time, gave up to her, not without apparent regret, the duty of accompanying Jacqueline, while she herself fulfilled those duties to society which the most devoted of mothers can not wholly avoid; but the stepmother and stepdaughter were always to be seen together at mass at one o'clock; together they attended the *Cours* (that system of classes now so much in vogue) and also the weekly instruction given in the catechism; and if Madame de Nailles, when, at night, she told her husband all she had been doing for Jacqueline during the day (she never made any merit of her zeal for the child's welfare), added: "I left Jacqueline in this place or in that, where Mademoiselle Schult was to call for her," M. de Nailles showed no disposition to ask questions, for he well understood that his wife felt a certain delicacy in telling him that she had been to pay a brief visit to her own relatives, who, she knew, were distasteful to him. He had, indeed, very soon discerned in them a love of intrigue, a desire to get the most they could out of him, and a disagreeable propensity to *parasitism*. With the consummate tact she

3 [33]

showed in everything she did, Madame de Nailles kept her own family in the background, though she never neglected them. She was always doing them little services, but she knew well that there were certain things about them that could not but be disagreeable to her husband. M. de Nailles knew all this, too, and respected his wife's affection for her family. He seldom asked her where she had been during the day. If he had she would have answered, with a sigh: "I went to see my mother while Jacqueline was taking her dancing-lesson, and before she went to her singing-master."

That she was passionately attached to Jacqueline was proved by the affection the little girl conceived for her. "We two are friends," both mother and daughter often said of each other. Even Modeste, old Modeste, who had been at first indignant at seeing a stranger take the place of her dead mistress, could not but acknowledge that the usurper was no ordinary stepmother. It might have been truly said that Madame de Nailles had never scolded Jacqueline, and that Jacqueline had never done anything contrary to the wishes of Madame de Nailles. When anything went wrong it was Fraulein Schult who was reproached first; if there was any difficulty in the management of Jacqueline, she alone received complaints. In the eyes of the "two friends," Fraulein Schult was somehow to be blamed for everything that went wrong in the family, but between themselves an observer might have watched in vain for the smallest cloud. Madame de Nailles, when she was first married, could not make enough of the very ugly yet attractive little girl, whose tight black curls and gypsy face made an admirable contrast to her own more delicate style of beauty, which was that of a blonde. She caressed Jacqueline, she dressed her up, she took her about with her like a little dog, and overwhelmed her with demonstrations of affection, which served not only to show off her own graceful attitudes, but gave spectators a high opinion of her kindness of heart.

When from time to time some one, envious of her happiness, pitied her for being childless, Madame de Nailles would say: "What do you mean? I have one daughter; she is enough for me."

It is a pity children grow so fast, and that little girls who were once ugly sometimes develop into beautiful young women. The time came when the model step-mother began to wish that Jacqueline would only de-velop morally, intellectually, and not physically. But she showed nothing of this in her behavior, and re-plied to any compliments addressed to her concerning Jacqueline with as much maternal modesty as if the dawning loveliness of her stepdaughter had been due to herself.

"Her nose is rather too long—don't you think so? And she will always be too dark, I fear." But she used always to add, "She is good enough and pretty enough to pass muster with any critic—poor little pussy-cat!" She became desirous to discover some tendency to ill-health in the plant that was too ready to bloom into beauty and perfection. She would have liked to be able to assert that Jacqueline's health would not per-

mit her to sit up late at night, that fashionable hours
would be injurious to her, that it would be undesirable
to let her go into society as long as she could be kept
from doing so.   But Jacqueline persisted in never being ill, and was calculating with impatience how many
years it would be before she could go to her first ball
—three or four possibly.   Was Madame de Nailles in
three or four years to be reduced to the position of a
chaperon?   The young stepmother thought of such a
possibility with horror.   Her anxiety on this subject,
however, as well as several other anxieties, was so well
concealed that even her husband suspected nothing.

The complete sympathy which existed between the
two beings he most loved made M. de Nailles very
happy.   He had but one thing to complain of in his
wife, and that thing was very small.   Since she had
married she had completely given up her painting.
He had no knowledge of art himself, and had therefore
given her credit for great artistic capacity.   The fact
was that in her days of poverty she had never been
artist enough to make a living, and now that she was
rich she felt inclined to laugh at her own limited ability.
Her practice of art, she said, had only served to give
her a knowledge of outline and of color; a knowledge
she utilized in her dress and in the smallest details of
house decoration and furniture.   Everything she wore,
everything that surrounded her, was arranged to perfection.   She had a genius for decoration, for furniture,
for trifles, and brought her artistic knowledge to bear
even on the tying of a ribbon, or the arrangement of a
nosegay.

JACQUELINE

"This is all I retain of your lessons," she said sometimes to Hubert Marien, when recalling to his memory the days in which she sought his advice as to how to prepare herself for the "struggle for life."

This phrase was amusing when it proceeded from her lips. What!—"struggle for life" with those little delicate, soft, childlike hands? How absurd! She laughed at the idea now, and all those who heard her laughed with her; Marien laughed more than any one. He, who had befriended her in her days of adversity, seemed to retain for the Baroness in her prosperity the same respectful and discreet devotion he had shown her as Mademoiselle Hecker. He had sent a wonderful portrait of her, as the wife of M. de Nailles, to the Salon—a portrait that the richer electors of Grandchaux, who had voted for her husband and who could afford to travel, gazed at with satisfaction, congratulating themselves that they had a deputy who had married so pretty a woman. It even seemed as if the beauty of Madame de Nailles belonged in some sort to the *arrondissement*, so proud were those who lived there of having their share in her charms.

Another portrait—that of M. de Nailles himself—was sent down to Limouzin from Paris, and all the peasants in the country round were invited to come and look at it. That also produced a very favorable impression on the rustic public, and added to the popularity of their deputy. Never had the proprietor of Grandchaux looked so grave, so dignified, so majestic, so absorbed in deep reflection, as he looked standing beside a table covered with papers—papers, no doubt,

THÉO BENTZON

all having relation to local interests, important to the
public and to individuals. It was the very figure of a
statesman destined to high dignities. No one who
gazed on such a deputy could doubt that one day he
would be in the ministry.

It was by such real services that Marien endeavored
to repay the friendship and the kindness always awaiting him in the small house in the Parc Monceau, where
we have just seen Jacqueline eagerly offering him some
spiced cakes. To complete what seemed due to the
household there only remained to paint the curiously
expressive features of the girl at whom he had been
looking that very day with more than ordinary attention. Once already, when Jacqueline was hardly out
of baby-clothes, the great painter had made an admirable sketch of her tousled head, a sketch in which she
looked like a little imp of darkness, and this sketch
Madame de Nailles took pains should always be seen,
but it bore no resemblance to the slender young girl
who was on the eve of becoming, whatever might be
done to arrest her development, a beautiful young
woman. Jacqueline disliked to look at that picture.
It seemed to do her an injury by associating her with
her nursery. Probably that was the reason why she
had been so pleased to hear Hubert Marien say unexpectedly that she was now ready for the portrait which
had been often joked about, every one putting it off
to the period, always remote, when "the may-pole"
should have developed a pretty face and figure.

And now she was disquieted lest the idea of taking
her picture, which she felt was very flattering, should

[38]

remain inoperative in the painter's brain. She wanted
it carried out at once, as soon as possible. Jacqueline
detested waiting, and for some reason, which she never
talked about, the years that seemed so short and swift
to her stepmother seemed to her to be terribly long.
Marien himself had said: "There is a great interval
between a dream and its execution." These words
had thrown cold water on her sudden joy. She wanted
to force him to keep his promise—to paint her portrait
immediately. How to do this was the problem her
little head, reclining on Madame de Nailles's lap after
the departure of their visitors, had been endeavoring
to solve.

Should she communicate her wish to her indulgent
stepmother, who for the most part willed whatever
she wished her to do? A vague instinct—an instinct
of some mysterious danger—warned her that in this
case her father would be her better confidant.

CHAPTER III

WEEK later M. de Nailles said to Hubert Marien, as they were smoking together in the conservatory, after the usual little family dinner on Wednesday was over:

"Well!—when would you like Jacqueline to come to sit for her picture?"

"What! are you thinking about that?" cried the painter, letting his cigar fall in his astonishment.

"She told me that you had proposed to make her portrait."

"The sly little minx!" thought Marien. "I only spoke of painting it some day," he said, with embarrassment.

"Well! she would like that 'some day' to be now, and she has a reason for wanting it at once, which, I hope, will decide you to gratify her. The third of June is Sainte-Clotilde's day, and she has taken it into her head that she would like to give her mamma a magnificent present—a present that, of course, we shall unite to give her. For some time past I have been thinking of asking you to paint a portrait of my daughter," continued M. de Nailles, who had in fact had no more wish for the portrait than he had had to be a deputy, until it had been put into his head. But the women of his household, little or big, could persuade him into anything.

"I really don't think I have the time now," said Marien.

"Bah!—you have whole two months before you. What can absorb you so entirely? I know you have your pictures ready for the Salon."

"Yes—of course—of course—but are you sure that Madame de Nailles would approve of it?"

"She will approve whatever I sanction," said M. de Nailles, with as much assurance as if he had been master in his domestic circle; "besides, we don't intend to ask her. It is to be a surprise. Jacqueline is looking forward to the pleasure it will give her. There is something very touching to me in the affection of that little thing for—for her mother." M. de Nailles usually hesitated a moment before saying that word, as if he were afraid of transferring something still belonging to his dead wife to another—that dead wife he so seldom remembered in any other way. He added, "She is so eager to give her pleasure."

Marien shook his head with an air of uncertainty.

"Are you sure that such a portrait would be really acceptable to Madame de Nailles?"

"How can you doubt it?" said the Baron, with much astonishment. "A portrait of her daughter!—done by a great master? However, of course, if we are putting you to any inconvenience—if you would rather not undertake it, you had better say so."

THÉO BENTZON

"No—of course I will do it, if you wish it," said Marien, quickly, who, although he was anxious to do nothing to displease Madame de Nailles, was equally desirous to stand well with her husband. "Yet I own that all the mystery that must attend on what you propose may put me to some embarrassment. How do you expect Jacqueline will be able to conceal——"

"Oh! easily enough. She walks out every day with Mademoiselle Schult. Well, Mademoiselle Schult will bring her to your studio instead of taking her to the Champs Elysées—or to walk elsewhere."

"But every day there will be concealments, falsehoods, deceptions. I think Madame de Nailles might prefer to be asked for her permission."

"Ask for her permission when I have given mine? *Ah, ça!* my dear Marien, am I, or am I not, the father of Jacqueline? I take upon myself the whole responsibility."

"Then there is nothing more to be said. But do you think that Jacqueline will keep the secret till the picture is done?"

"You don't know little girls; they are all too glad to have something of which they can make a mystery."

"When would you like us to begin?"

Marien had by this time said to himself that for him to hold out longer might seem strange to M. de Nailles. Besides, the matter, though in some respects it gave him cause for anxiety, really excited an interest in him. For some time past, though he had long known women and knew very little of mere girls, he had had his suspicions that a drama was being enacted in Jacqueline's heart, a drama of which he himself was the hero. He amused himself by watching it, though he did nothing to promote it. He was an artist and a keen and penetrating observer; he employed psychology in the service of his art, and probably to that might have been attributed the individual character of his portraits—a quality to be found in an equal degree only in those of Ricard.

What particularly interested him at this moment was the assumed indifference of Jacqueline while her father was conducting the negotiation which was of her suggestion. When they returned to the salon after smoking she pretended not to be the least anxious to know the result of their conversation. She sat sewing near the lamp, giving all her attention to the piece of lace on which she was working. Her father made her a sign which meant "He consents," and then Marien saw that the needle in her fingers trembled, and a slight color rose in her face—but that was all. She did not say a word. He could not know that for a week past she had gone to church every time she took a walk, and had offered a prayer and a candle that her wish might be granted. How very anxious and excited she had been all that week! The famous composition of which she had spoken to Giselle, the subject of which had so astonished the young girl brought up by the Bénédictine nuns, felt the inspiration of her emotion and excitement. Jacqueline was in a frame of mind which made reading those three masterpieces by three great poets, and pondering the meaning of their words, very dangerous. The poems did not affect her with the melancholy they inspire in those who have "lived and loved," but she was attracted by their tenderness and their passion. Certain lines she applied to herself—certain others to another person. The very word *love* so often repeated in the verses sent a thrill through all her frame. She aspired to taste those "intoxicating moments," those "swift delights," those "sublime ecstasies," those "divine transports"—all the beautiful things, in short, of which the poems spoke, and which were as yet unknown to her. How could she know them? How could she, after an experience of sorrow, which seemed to her to be itself enviable, retain such sweet remembrances as the poets described?

"Let us love—love each other! Let us hasten to enjoy the passing hour!" so sang the poet of *Le Lac*. That passing hour of bliss she thought she had already enjoyed. She was sure that for a long time past she had loved. When had that love begun? She hardly knew. But it would last as long as she might live. One loves but once.

These personal emotions, mingling with the literary enchantments of the poets, caused Jacqueline's pen to fly over her paper without effort, and she produced a composition so far superior to anything she usually wrote that it left the lucubrations of her companions far behind. M. Regis, the professor, said so to the class. He was enthusiastic about it, and greatly surprised. Belle, who had been always first in this kind of composition, was far behind Jacqueline, and was so greatly annoyed at her defeat that she would not speak to her for a week. On the other hand Colette and

JACQUELINE

Dolly, who never had aspired to literary triumphs, were moved to tears when the "Study on the comparative merits of Three Poems, *Le Lac, Souvenir,* and *La Tristesse d'Olympio*," signed "Mademoiselle de Nailles," received the honor of being read aloud. This reading was followed by a murmur of applause, mingled with some hisses which may have proceeded from the viper of jealousy. But the paper made a sensation like that of some new scandal. Mothers and governesses whispered together. Many thought that that little de Nailles had expressed sentiments not proper at her age. Some came to the conclusion that M. Regis chose subjects for composition not suited to young girls. A committee waited on the unlucky professor to beg him to be more prudent for the future. He even lost, in consequence of Jacqueline's success, one of his pupils (the most stupid one, be it said, in the class), whose mother took her away, saying, with indignation, "One might as well risk the things they are teaching at the Sorbonne!"

This literary incident greatly alarmed Madame de Nailles! Of all things she dreaded that her daughter should early become dreamy and romantic. But on this point Jacqueline's behavior was calculated to reassure her. She laughed about her composition, she frolicked like a six-year-old child; without any apparent cause, she grew gayer and gayer as the time approached for the execution of her plot.

The evening before the day fixed on for the first sitting, Modeste, the elderly maid of the first Madame de Nailles, who loved her daughter, whom she had known from the moment of her birth, as if she had been her own foster-child, arrived at the studio of Hubert Marien in the Rue de Prony, bearing a box which she said contained all that would be wanted by Mademoiselle. Marien had the curiosity to look into it. It contained a robe of oriental muslin, light as air, diaphanous—and so dazzlingly white that he remarked:

"She will look like a fly in milk in that thing."

"Oh!" replied Modeste, with a laugh of satisfaction, "it is very becoming to her. I altered it to fit her, for it is one of Madame's dresses. Mademoiselle has nothing but short skirts, and she wanted to be painted as a young lady."

"With the approval of her papa?"

"Yes, of course, Monsieur, Monsieur le Baron gave his consent. But for that I certainly should not have minded what the child said to me."

"Then," replied Marien, "I can say nothing," and he made ready for his sitter the next day, by turning two or three studies of the nude, which might have shocked her, with their faces to the wall.

A foreign language can not be properly acquired unless the learner has great opportunities for conversation. It therefore became a fixed habit with Fraulein Schult and Jacqueline to keep up a lively stream of talk during their walks, and their discourse was not always about the rain, the fine weather, the things displayed in the shop-windows, nor the historical monuments of Paris, which they visited conscientiously.

JACQUELINE

What is near the heart is sure to come eventually to the surface in continual *tête-à-tête* intercourse. Fraulein Schult, who was of a sentimental temperament, in spite of her outward resemblance to a grenadier, was very willing to allow her companion to draw from her confessions relating to an intended husband, who was awaiting her at Berne, and whose letters, both in prose and verse, were her comfort in her exile. This future husband was an apothecary, and the idea that he pounded out verses as he pounded his drugs in a mortar, and rolled out rhymes with his pills, sometimes inclined Jacqueline to laugh, but she listened patiently to the plaintive outpourings of her *promeneuse*, because she wished to acquire a right to reciprocate by a few half-confidences of her own. In her turn, therefore, she confided to Fraulein Schult—moved much as Midas had been, when for his own relief he whispered to the reeds—that if she were sometimes idle, inattentive, "away off in the moon," as her instructors told her by way of reproach, it was caused by one ever-present idea, which, ever since she had been able to think or feel, had taken possession of her inmost being—the idea of being loved some day by somebody as she herself loved.

"Was that somebody a boy of her own age?"

Oh, fie!—mere boys—still schoolboys—could only be looked upon as playfellows or comrades. Of course she considered Fred—Fred, for example!—Frédéric d'Argy—as a brother, but how different he was from her ideal. Even young men of fashion—she had seen some of them on Tuesdays—Raoul Wermant, the one

who so distinguished himself as a leader in the german,
or Yvonne's brother, the officer of chasseurs, who had
gained the prize for horsemanship, and others besides
these—seemed to her very commonplace by comparison. No!—he whom she loved was a man in the
prime of life, well known to fame. She didn't care if
he *had* a few white hairs.

"Is he a person of rank?" asked Fraulein Schult,
much puzzled.

"Oh! if you mean of noble birth, no, not at all.
But fame is so superior to birth! There are more
ways than one of acquiring an illustrious name, and
the name that a man makes for himself is the noblest
of all!"

Then Jacqueline begged Fraulein Schult to imagine
something like the passion of Bettina for Goethe—
Fraulein Schult having told her that story simply with
a view of interesting her in German conversation—
only the great man whose name she would not tell was
not nearly so old as Goethe, and she herself was much
less childish than Bettina. But, above all, it was his
genius that attracted her—though his face, too, was very
pleasing. And she went on to describe his appearance
—till suddenly she stopped, burning with indignation;
for she perceived that, notwithstanding the minuteness
of her description, what she said was conveying an
idea of ugliness and not one of the manly beauty she
intended to portray.

"He is not like that at all," she cried. "He has
such a beautiful smile—a smile like no other I ever
saw. And his talk is so amusing—and——" here

JACQUELINE

Jacqueline lowered her voice as if afraid to be over-heard, "and I do think—I think, after all, he does love me—just a little."

On what could she have founded such a notion? Good heaven!—it was on something that had at first deeply grieved her, a sudden coldness and reserve that had come over his manner to her. Not long before she had read an English novel (no others were allowed to come into her hands). It was rather a stupid book, with many tedious passages, but in it she was told how the high-minded hero, not being able, for grave reasons, to aspire to the hand of the heroine, had taken refuge in an icy coldness, much as it cost him, and as soon as possible had gone away. English novels are nothing if not moral.

This story, not otherwise interesting, threw a gleam of light on what, up to that time, had been inexplicable to Jacqueline. *He* was above all things a man of honor. *He* must have perceived that his presence troubled her. *He* had possibly seen her when she stole a half-burned cigarette which he had left upon the table, a prize she had laid up with other relics—an old glove that he had lost, a bunch of violets he had gathered for her in the country. Yes! When she came to think of it, she felt certain he must have seen her furtively lay her hand upon that cigarette; that cigarette had compromised her. Then it was he must have said to himself that it was due to her parents, who had always shown him kindness, to surmount an attachment that could come to nothing—nothing at present. But when she should be old enough for him

4

to ask her hand, would he dare? Might he not rashly think himself too old? She must seek out some way to give him encouragement, to give him to understand that she was not, after all, so far—so very far from being a young lady—old enough to be married. How difficult it all was! All the more difficult because she was exceedingly afraid of him.

It is not surprising that Fraulein Schult, after listening day after day to such recitals, with all the alternations of hope and of discouragement which succeeded one another in the mind of her precocious pupil, guessed, the moment that Jacqueline came to her, in a transport of joy, to ask her to go with her to the Rue de Prony, that the hero of the mysterious love-story was no other than Hubert Marien.

As soon as she understood this, she perceived that she should be placed in a very false position. But she thought to herself there was no possible way of getting out of it, without giving a great deal too much importance to a very innocent piece of childish folly; she therefore determined to say nothing about it, but to keep a strict watch in the mean time. After all, M. de Nailles himself had given her her orders. She was to accompany Jacqueline, and do her crochet-work in one corner of the studio as long as the sitting lasted.

All she could do was to obey.

"And above all not a word to mamma, whatever she may ask you," said Jacqueline.

And her father added, with a laugh, "Not a word." Fraulein Schult felt that she knew what was expected of her. She was naturally compliant, and above all things she was anxious to get paid for as many hours of her time as possible—much like the driver of a *fiacre*, because the more money she could make the sooner she would be in a position to espouse her apothecary.

When Jacqueline, escorted by her Swiss duenna, penetrated almost furtively into Marien's studio, her heart beat as if she had a consciousness of doing something very wrong. In truth, she had pictured to herself so many impossible scenes beforehand, had rehearsed the probable questions and answers in so many strange dialogues, had soothed her fancy with so many extravagant ideas, that she had at last created, bit by bit, a situation very different from the reality, and then threw herself into it, body and soul.

The look of the *atelier*—the first she had ever been in in her life—disappointed her. She had expected to behold a gorgeous collection of *bric-à-brac*, according to accounts she had heard of the studios of several celebrated masters. That of Marien was remarkable only for its vast dimensions and its abundance of light. Studies and sketches hung on the walls, were piled one over another in corners, were scattered about everywhere, attesting the incessant industry of the artist, whose devotion to his calling was so great that his own work never satisfied him.

Only some interesting casts from antique bronzes, brought out into strong relief by a background of tapestry, adorned this lofty hall, which had none of that confusion of decorative objects, in the midst of which some modern artists seem to pose themselves rather than to labor.

[51]

THÉO BENTZON

A fresh canvas stood upon an easel, all ready for the sitter.

"If you please, we will lose no time," said Marien, rather roughly, seeing that Jacqueline was about to explore all the corners of his apartment, and that at that moment, with the tips of her fingers, she was drawing aside the covering he had cast over his *Death of Savonarola*, the picture he was then at work upon. It was not the least of his grudges against Jacqueline for insisting on having her portrait painted that it obliged him to lay aside this really great work, that he might paint a likeness.

"In ten minutes I shall be ready," said Jacqueline, obediently taking off her hat.

"Why can't you stay as you are? That jacket suits you. Let us begin immediately."

"No, indeed! What a horrid suggestion!" she cried, running up to the box which was half open. "You'll see how much better I can look in a moment or two."

"I put no faith in your fancies about your toilette. I certainly don't promise to accept them."

Nevertheless, he left her alone with her Bernese governess, saying: "Call me when you are ready, I shall be in the next room."

A quarter of an hour, and more, passed, and no signal had been given. Marien, getting out of patience, knocked on the door.

"Have you nearly done beautifying yourself?" he asked, in a tone of irony.

"Just done," replied a low voice, which trembled.

He went in, and to the great amusement of Fraulein

JACQUELINE

Schult, who was not too preoccupied to notice everything, he stood confounded—petrified, as a man might
be by some work of magic. What had become of
Jacqueline? What had she in common with that
dazzling vision? Had she been touched by some
fairy's wand? Or, to accomplish such a transformation, had nothing been needed but the substitution of
a woman's dress, fitted to her person, for the short
skirts and loose waists cut in a boyish fashion, which
had made the little girl seem hardly to belong to any
sex, an indefinite being, condemned, as it were, to
childishness? How tall, and slender, and graceful she
looked in that long gown, the folds of which fell from
her waist in flowing lines, a waist as round and flexible
as the branch of a willow; what elegance there was in
her modest *corsage*, which displayed for the first time
her lovely arms and neck, half afraid of their own
exposure. She still was not robust, but the leanness
that she herself had owned to was not brought into
prominence by any bone or angle, her dark skin was
soft and polished, the color of ancient statues which
have been slightly tinted yellow by exposure to the sun.
This girl, a Parisienne, seemed formed on the model
of a figurine of Tanagra. Greek, too, was her small
head, crowned only by her usual braid of hair, which
she had simply gathered up so as to show the nape of
her neck, which was perhaps the most beautiful thing
in all her beautiful person.

"Well!—what do you think of me?" she said to Marien, with a searching glance to see how she impressed
him—a glance strangely like that of a grown woman.

THÉO BENTZON

"Well!—I can't get over it!—Why have you bedizened yourself in that fashion?" he asked, with an affectation of *brusquerie*, as he tried to recover his power of speech.

"Then you don't like me?" she murmured, in a low voice. Tears came into her eyes; her lips trembled.

"I don't see Jacqueline."

"No—I should hope not—but I am better than Jacqueline, am I not?"

"I am accustomed to Jacqueline. This new acquaintance disconcerts me. Give me time to get used to her. But once again let me ask, what possessed you to disguise yourself?"

"I am not disguised. I am disguised when I am forced to wear those things, which do not suit me," said Jacqueline, pointing to her gray jacket and plaid skirt which were hung up on a hat-rack. "Oh, I know why mamma keeps me like that—she is afraid I should get too fond of dress before I have finished my education, and that my mind may be diverted from serious subjects. It is no doubt all intended for my good, but I should not lose much time if I turned up my hair like this, and what harm could there be in lengthening my skirts an inch or two? My picture will show her that I am improved by such little changes, and perhaps it will induce her to let me go to the *Bal Blanc* that Madame d'Etaples is going to give on Yvonne's birthday. Mamma declined for me, saying I was not fit to wear a low-necked *corsage*, but you see she was mistaken."

"Rather," said Marien, smiling in spite of himself.

"Yes—wasn't she?" she went on, delighted at his look. "Of course, I have bones, but they don't show like the great hollows under the collar-bones that Dolly shows, for instance—but Dolly looks stouter than I because her face is so round. Well! Dolly is going to Madame d'Etaples's ball."

"I grant," said Marien, devoting all his attention to the preparation of his palette, that she might not see him laugh, "I grant that you have bones—yes, many bones—but they are not much seen because they are too well placed to be obtrusive."

"I am glad of that," said Jacqueline, delighted.

"But let me ask you one question. Where did you pick up that queer gown? It seems to me that I have seen it somewhere."

"No doubt you have," replied Jacqueline, who had quite recovered from her first shock, and was now ready to talk; "it is the dress mamma had made some time ago when she acted in a comedy."

"So I thought," growled Marien, biting his lips.

The dress recalled to his mind many personal recollections, and for one instant he paused. Madame de Nailles, among other talents, possessed that of amateur acting. On one occasion, several years before, she had asked his advice concerning what dress she should wear in a little play of Scribe's, which was to be given at the house of Madame d'Avrigny—the house in all Paris most addicted to private theatricals. This reproduction of a forgotten play, with its characters attired in the costume of the period in which the play was placed, had had great success, a success due

[55]

largely to the excellence of the costumes. In the comic parts the dressing had been purposely exaggerated, but Madame de Nailles, who played the part of a great coquette, would not have been dressed in character had she not tried to make herself as bewitching as possible.

Marien had shown her pictures of the beauties of 1840, painted by Dubufe, and she had decided on a white gauze embroidered with gold, in which, on that memorable evening, she had captured more than one heart, and which had had its influence on the life and destiny of Marien. This might have been seen in the vague glance of indignation with which he now regarded it.

"Never," he thought, "was it half so pretty when worn by Madame de Nailles as by her stepdaughter."

Jacqueline meantime went on talking.

"You must know—I was rather perplexed what to do—almost all mamma's gowns made me look horribly too old. Modeste tried them on me one after another. We burst out laughing, they seemed so absurd. And then we were afraid mamma might chance to want the one I took. This old thing it was not likely she would ask for. She had worn it only once, and then put it away. The gauze is a little yellow from lying by, don't you think so? But we asked my father, who said it was all right, that I should look less dark in it, and that the dress was of no particular date, which was always an advantage. These Grecian dresses are always in the fashion. Ah! four years ago mamma was much more slender than she is now. But we have taken it in—oh! we took it in a great deal under the arms, but we had to let it down. Would you believe it?—I am taller than mamma—but you can hardly see the seam, it is concealed by the gold embroidery."

"No matter for that. We shall only take a three-quarters' length," said Marien.

"Oh, what a pity! No one will see I have a long skirt on. But I shall be *décolletée*, at any rate. I shall wear a comb. No one would know the picture for me —nobody!—You yourself hardly knew me—did you?"

"Not at first sight. You are much altered."

"Mamma will be amazed," said Jacqueline, clasping her hands. "It was a good idea!"

"Amazed, I do not doubt," said Marien, somewhat anxiously. "But suppose we take our *pose*—Stay!—keep just as you are. Your hands before you, hanging down—so. Your fingers loosely clasped—that's it. Turn your head a little. What a lovely neck!—how well her head is set upon it!" he cried, involuntarily.

Jacqueline glanced at Fraulein Schult, who was at the farther end of the studio, busy with her crochet. "You see," said the look, "that he has found out I am pretty—that I am worth something—all the rest will soon happen."

And, while Marien was sketching in the graceful figure that posed before him, Jacqueline's imagination was investing it with the white robe of a bride. She had a vision of the painter growing more and more resolved to ask her hand in marriage as the portrait grew beneath his brush; of course, her father would say at first: "You are mad—you must wait. I shall not let Jacqueline marry till she is seventeen." But long engagements, she had heard, had great delights, though in France they are not the fashion. At last, after being long entreated, she was sure that M. and Madame de Nailles would end by giving their consent —they were so fond of Marien. Standing there, dreaming this dream, which gave her face an expression of extreme happiness, Jacqueline made a most admirable model. She had not felt in the least fatigued when Marien at last said to her, apologetically: "You must be ready to drop—I forgot you were not made of wood; we will go on to-morrow."

Jacqueline, having put on her gray jacket with as much contempt for it as Cinderella may have felt for her rags after her successes at the ball, departed with the delightful sensation of having made a bold first step, and being eager to make another.

Thus it was with all her sittings, though some left her anxious and unhappy, as for instance when Marien, absorbed in his work, had not paused, except to say, "Turn your head a little—you are losing the *pose*." Or else, "Now you may rest for to-day."

On such occasions she would watch him anxiously as he painted swiftly, his brush making great splashes on the canvas, his dark features wearing a scowl, his chin on his breast, a deep frown upon his forehead, on which the hair grew low. It was evident that at such times he had no thought of pleasing her. Little did she suspect that he was saying to himself: "Fool that I am!—A man of my age to take pleasure in seeing that little head filled with follies and fancies of which

JACQUELINE

I am the object. But can one—let one be ever so old—always act or think reasonably? You are mad, Marien! A child of fourteen! Bah!—they make her out to be fourteen—but she is fifteen—and was not that the age of Juliet? But, you old graybeard, *you* are not Romeo! —*Ma foi!* I am in a pretty scrape. It ought to teach me not to play with fire at my age."

Those words "at my age" were the refrain to all the reflections of Hubert Marien. He had seen enough in his relations with women to have no doubt about Jacqueline's feelings, of which indeed he had watched the rise and progress from the time she had first begun to conceive a passion for him, with a mixture of amusement and conceit. The most cautious of men are not insensible to flattery, whatever form it may take. To be fallen in love with by a child was no doubt absurd —a thing to be laughed at—but Jacqueline seemed no longer a child, since for him she had uncovered her young shoulders and arranged her dark hair on her head with the effect of a queenly diadem. Not only had her dawning loveliness been revealed to him alone, but to him it seemed that he had helped to make her lovely. The innocent tenderness she felt for him had accomplished this miracle. Why should he refuse to inhale an incense so pure, so genuine? How could he help being sensible to its fragrance? Would it not be in his power to put an end to the whole affair whenever he pleased? But till then might he not bask in it, as one does in a warm ray of spring sunshine? He put aside, therefore, all scruples. And when he did this Jacqueline with rapture saw the painter's face, no longer with its scowl, but softened by some secret influence, the lines smoothed from his brow, while the beautiful smile which had fascinated so many women passed like a ray of light over his expressive mobile features; then she would once more fancy that he was making love to her, and indeed he said many things, which, without rousing in himself any scruples of conscience, or alarming the propriety of Fraulein Schult, were well calculated to delude a girl who had had no experience, and who was charmed by the illusions of a love-affair, as she might have been by a fairy-story.

It is true that sometimes, when he fancied he might have gone too far, Marien would grow sarcastic, or stay silent for a time. But this change of behavior produced on Jacqueline only the same effect that the caprices of a coquette produce upon a very young admirer. She grew anxious, she wanted to find out the reason, and finally found some explanation or excuse for him that coincided with her fancies.

The thing that reassured her in such cases was her picture. If she could seem to him as beautiful as he had made her look on canvas she was sure that he must love her.

"Is this really I? Are you sure?" she said to Marien with a laugh of delight. "It seems to me that you have made me too handsome."

"I have hardly done you justice," he replied. "It is not my fault if you are more beautiful than seems natural, like the beauties in the keepsakes. By the way, I hold those English things in horror. What do you say of them?"

JACQUELINE

Then Jacqueline undertook to defend the keepsake beauties with animation, declaring that no one but a hopelessly realistic painter would refuse to do justice to those charming monstrosities.

"Good heavens!" thought Marien, "if she is adding a quick wit to her other charms—that will put the finishing stroke to me."

When the portrait was sufficiently advanced, M. de Nailles came to the studio to judge of the likeness. He was delighted: "Only, my friend, I think," he cried to Marien, endeavoring to soften his one objection to the picture, "that you have given her a look—how can I put it?—an expression very charming no doubt, but which is not that of a child of her age. You know what I mean. It is something tender—intense—profound, too feminine. It may come to her some day, perhaps —but hitherto Jacqueline's expression has been generally that of a merry, mischievous child."

"Oh, papa!" cried the young girl, stung by the insult.

"You may possibly be right," Marien hastened to reply, "it was probably the fatigue of posing that gave her that expression."

"Oh!" repeated Jacqueline, more shocked than ever.

"I can alter it," said the painter, much amused by her extreme despair. But Marien thought that Jacqueline had not in the least that precocious air which her father attributed to her, when standing before him she gave herself up to thoughts the current of which he followed easily, watching on her candid face its changes of expression. How could he have painted her other than she appeared to him? Was what he saw an apparition—or was it a work of magic?

Several times during the sittings M. de Nailles made his appearance in the studio, and after greatly praising the work, persisted in his objection that it made Jacqueline too old. But since the painter saw her thus they must accept his judgment. It was no doubt an effect of the grown-up costume that she had had a fancy to put on.

"After all," he said to Jacqueline, "it is of not much consequence; you will grow up to it some of these days. And I pay you my compliments in advance on your appearance in the future."

She felt like choking with rage. "Oh! is it right," she thought, "for parents to persist in keeping a young girl forever in her cradle, so to speak?"

CHAPTER IV

A DANGEROUS MODEL

IME passed too quickly to please Jacqueline. Her portrait was finished at last, notwithstanding the willingness Marien had shown—or so it seemed to her—to retouch it unnecessarily that she might again and again come back to his *atelier*. But it was done at last. She glided into that dear *atelier* for the last time, her heart big with regret, with no hope that she would ever again put on the fairy robe which had, she thought, transfigured her till she was no longer little Jacqueline.

"I want you only for one moment, and I need only your face," said Marien. "I want to change—a line—I hardly know what to call it, at the corner of your mouth. Your father is right; your mouth is too grave. Think of something amusing—of the Bal Blanc at Madame d'Etaples, or merely, if you like, of the satisfaction it will give you to be done with these everlasting sittings—to be no longer obliged to bear the burden of a secret, in short to get rid of your portrait-painter."

She made him no answer, not daring to trust her voice.

"Come! now, on the contrary you are tightening

[63]

your lips," said Marien, continuing to play with her ᵃs a cat plays with a mouse—provided there ever was a cat who, while playing with its mouse, had no intention of crunching it. "You are not merry, you are sad. That is not at all becoming to you."

"Why do you attribute to me your own thoughts? It is you who will be glad to get rid of all this trouble."

Fraulein Schult, who, while patiently adding stitch after stitch to the long strip of her crochet-work, was often much amused by the dialogues between sitter and painter, pricked up her ears to hear what a Frenchman would say to what was evidently intended to provoke a compliment.

"On the contrary, I shall miss you very much," said Marien, quite simply; "I have grown accustomed to see you here. You have become one of the familiar objects of my studio. Your absence will create a void."

"About as much as if this or that were gone," said Jacqueline, in a hurt tone, pointing first to a Japanese bronze and then to an Etruscan vase; "with only this difference, that you care least for the living object."

"You are bitter, Mademoiselle."

"Because you make me such provoking answers, Monsieur. My feeling is different," she went on impetuously, "I could pass my whole life watching you paint."

"You would get tired of it probably in the long run."

"Never!" she cried, blushing a deep red.

"And you would have to put up with my pipe—that big pipe yonder—a horror."

JACQUELINE

"I should like it," she cried, with conviction.

"But you would not like my bad temper. If you knew how ill I can behave sometimes! I can scold, I can become unbearable, when this, for example," here he pointed with his mahlstick to the *Savonarola*, "does not please me."

"But it is beautiful—so beautiful!"

"It is detestable. I shall have to go back some day and renew my impressions of Florence—see once more the Piazze of the Signora and San Marco—and then I shall begin my picture all over again. Let us go together—will you?"

"Oh!" she cried, fervently, "think of seeing Italy! —and with you!"

"It might not be so great a pleasure as you think. Nothing is such a bore as to travel with people who are pervaded by one idea, and my *idée fixe* is my picture— my great Dominican. He has taken complete possession of me—he overshadows me. I can think of nothing but him."

"Oh! but you think of me sometimes, I suppose," said Jacqueline, softly, "for I share your time with him."

"I think of you to blame you for taking me away from the fifteenth century," replied Hubert Marien, half seriously. "Ouf!—There! it is done at last. That dimple I never could manage I have got in for better or for worse. Now you may fly off. I set you at liberty— you poor little thing!"

She seemed in no hurry to profit by his permission. She stood perfectly still in the middle of the studio.

5   [65]

"Do you think I have posed well, faithfully, and with docility all these weeks?" she asked at last.

"I will give you a certificate to that effect, if you like. No one could have done better."

"And if the certificate is not all I want, will you give me some other present?"

"A beautiful portrait—what can you want more?"

"The picture is for mamma. I ask a favor on my own account."

"I refuse it beforehand. But you can tell me what it is, all the same."

"Well, then—the only part of your house that I have ever been in is this *atelier*. You can imagine I have a curiosity to see the rest."

"I see! you threaten me with a domiciliary visit without warning. Well! certainly, if that would give you any amusement. But my house contains nothing wonderful. I tell you that beforehand."

"One likes to know how one's friends look at home —in their own setting, and I have only seen you here at work in your *atelier*."

"The best point of view, believe me. But I am ready to do your bidding. Do you wish to see where I eat my dinner?" asked Marien, as he took her down the staircase leading to his dining-room."

Fraulein Schult would have liked to go with them— it was, besides, her duty. But she had not been asked to fulfil it. She hesitated a moment, and in that moment Jacqueline had disappeared. After consideration, the *promeneuse* went on with her crochet, with a shrug of her shoulders which meant: "She can't come to much harm."

Seated in the studio, she heard the sound of their voices on the floor below. Jacqueline was lingering in the fencing-room where Marien was in the habit of counteracting by athletic exercises the effects of a too sedentary life. She was amusing herself by fingering the dumb-bells and the foils; she lingered long before some precious suits of armor. Then she was taken up into a small room, communicating with the *atelier*, where there was a fine collection of drawings by the old masters. "My only luxury," said Marien.

Mademoiselle Schult, getting impatient, began to roll up yards and yards of crochet, and coughed, by way of a signal, but remembering how disagreeable it would have been to herself to be interrupted in a *tête-à-tête* with her apothecary, she thought it not worth while to disturb them in these last moments. M. de Nailles's orders had been that she was to sit in the *atelier*. So she continued to sit there, doing what she had been told to do without any qualms of conscience.

When Marien had shown Jacqueline all his drawings he asked her: "Are you satisfied?"

But Jacqueline's hand was already on the *portière* which separated the little room from Marien's bed-chamber.

"Oh! I beg pardon," she exclaimed, pausing on the threshold.

"One would think you would like to see me asleep," said Marien with some little embarrassment.

"I never should have thought your bedroom would

have been so pretty. Why, it is as elegant as a lady's chamber," said Jacqueline, slipping into it as she spoke, with an exciting consciousness of doing something she ought not to do.

"What an insult, when I thought all my tastes were simple and severe," he replied; but he had not followed her into the chamber, withheld by an impulse of modesty men sometimes feel, when innocence is led into audacity through ignorance.

"What lovely flowers you have!" said Jacqueline, from within. "Don't they make your head ache?"

"I take them out at night."

"I did not know that men liked, as we do, to be surrounded by flowers. Won't you give me one?"

"All, if you like."

"Oh! one pink will be enough for me."

"Then take it," said Marien; her curiosity alarmed him, and he was anxious to get her away.

"Would it not be nicer if you gave it me yourself?" she replied, with reproach in her tones.

"Here is one, Mademoiselle. And now I must tell you that I want to dress. I have to go out immediately."

She pinned the pink into her bodice so high that she could inhale its perfume.

"I beg your pardon. Thank you, and good-by," she said, extending her hand to him with a sigh.

"*Au revoir.*"

"Yes—*au revoir* at home—but that will not be like here."

As she stood there before him there came into her

eyes a strange expression, to which, without exactly knowing why, he replied by pressing his lips fervently on the little hand he was still holding in his own.

Very often since her infancy he had kissed her before witnesses, but this time she gave a little cry, and turned as white as the flower whose petals were touching her cheek.

Marien started back alarmed.

"Good-by," he said in a tone that he endeavored to make careless—but in vain.

Though she was much agitated herself she failed not to remark his emotion, and on the threshold of the *atelier*, she blew a kiss back to him from the tips of her gloved fingers, without speaking or smiling. Then she went back to Fraulein Schult, who was still sitting in the place where she had left her, and said: "Let us go."

The next time Madame de Nailles saw her stepdaughter she was dazzled by a radiant look in her young face.

"What has happened to you?" she asked, "you look triumphant."

"Yes—I have good reason to triumph," said Jacqueline. "I think that I have won a victory."

"How so? Over yourself?"

"No, indeed—victories over one's self give us the comfort of a good conscience, but they do not make us gay—as I am."

"Then tell me——"

"No—no! I can not tell you yet. I must be silent

two days more," said Jacqueline, throwing herself into her mother's arms.

Madame de Nailles asked no more questions, but she looked at her stepdaughter with an air of great surprise. For some weeks past she had had no pleasure in looking at Jacqueline. She began to be aware that near her, at her side, an exquisite butterfly was about for the first time to spread its wings—wings of a radiant loveliness, which, when they fluttered in the air, would turn all eyes away from other butterflies, which had lost some of their freshness during the summer.

A difficult task was before her. How could she keep this too precocious insect in its chrysalis state? How could she shut it up in its dark cocoon and retard its transformation?

"Jacqueline," she said, and the tones of her voice were less soft than those in which she usually addressed her, "it seems to me that you are wasting your time a great deal. You hardly practise at all; you do almost nothing at the *cours*. I don't know what can be distracting your attention from your lessons, but I have received complaints which should make a great girl like you ashamed of herself. Do you know what I am beginning to think?—That Madame de Monredon's system of education has done better than mine."

"Oh! mamma, you can't be thinking of sending me to a convent!" cried Jacqueline, in tones of comic despair.

"I did not say that—but I really think it might be good for you to make a retreat where your cousin

Giselle is, instead of plunging into follies which interrupt your progress."

"Do you call Madame d'Etaples's *bal blanc* a folly?"

"You certainly will not go to it—that is settled," said the young stepmother, dryly.

CHAPTER V

N all other ways Madame de Nailles did her best to assist in the success of the surprise. On the second of June, the eve of Ste.-Clotilde's day, she went out, leaving every opportunity for the grand plot to mature. Had she not absented herself in like manner the year before at the same date— thus enabling an upholsterer to drape artistically her little salon with beautiful thick silk tapestries which had just been imported from the East? Her idea was that this year she might find a certain lacquered screen which she coveted. The Baroness belonged to her period; she liked Japanese things. But, alas! the charming object that awaited her, with a curtain hung over it to prolong the suspense, had nothing Japanese about it whatever. Madame de Nailles received the good wishes of her family, responded to them with all proper cordiality, and then was dragged up joyously to a picture hanging on the wall of her room, but still concealed under the cloth that covered it.

"How good of you!" she said, with all confidence to her husband.

"It is a picture by Marien!—A portrait by Marien! A likeness of Jacqueline!"

JACQUELINE

And he uncovered the masterpiece of the great artist, expecting to be joyous in the joy with which she would receive it. But something strange occurred. Madame de Nailles sprang back a step or two, stretching out her arms as if repelling an apparition, her face was distorted, her head was turned away; then she dropped into the nearest seat and burst into tears.

"Mamma!—dear little mamma!—what is it?" cried Jacqueline, springing forward to kiss her.

Madame de Nailles disengaged herself angrily from her embrace.

"Let me alone!" she cried, "let me alone!—How dared you?——"

And impetuously, hardly restraining a gesture of horror and hate, she rushed into her own chamber. Thither her husband followed her, anxious and bewildered, and there he witnessed a nervous attack which ended in a torrent of reproaches.

Was it possible that he had not seen the impropriety of those sittings to Marien? Oh, yes! No doubt he was an old friend of the family, but that did not prevent all these deceptions, all these disguises, and all the other follies which he had sanctioned—he—Jacqueline's father!—from being very improper. Did he wish to take from her all authority over his child?—a girl who was already too much disposed to emancipate herself. Her own efforts had all been directed to curb this alarming propensity—yes, alarming—alarming for the future. And all in vain! There was no use in saying more. *Mon Dieu!* had he no trust in her devotion to his child, in her prudence and her foresight, that he

[73]

must thwart her thus? And she had always imagined that for ten years she had faithfully fulfilled a mother's duties! What ingratitude from every one! Mademoiselle Schult should be sent away at once. Jacqueline should go to a convent. They would break off all intercourse with Marien. They had conspired against her— every one.

And then she wept more bitterly than ever—tears of rage, salt tears which rubbed the powder off her cheeks and disfigured the face that had remained beautiful by her power of will and self-control. But now the disorder of her nerves got the better of precautions. The blonde angel, whose beauty was on the wane, was transformed into a fury. Her six-and-thirty years were fully apparent, her complexion appeared slightly blotched, all her defects were obtrusive in contrast with the precocious development of beauty in Jacqueline. She was firmly resolved that her stepdaughter's obtrusive womanhood should remain in obscurity a very much longer time, under pretence that Jacqueline was still a child. She was a child, at any rate! The portrait was a lie! an imposture! an affront! an outrage!

Meantime M. de Nailles, almost beside himself, fancied at first that his wife was going mad, but in the midst of her sobs and reproaches he managed to discover that he had somehow done her wrong, and when, with a broken voice, she cried, "You no longer love me!" he did not know what to do to prove how bitterly he repented having grieved her. He stammered, he made excuses, he owned that he had been to blame, that he had been very stupid, and he begged her pardon. As to the portrait, it should be taken from the salon, where, if seen, it might become a pretext for foolish compliments to Jacqueline. Why not send it at once to Grandchaux? In short, he would do anything she wished, provided she would leave off crying.

But Madame de Nailles continued to weep. Her husband was forced at last to leave her and to return to Jacqueline, who stood petrified in the salon.

"Yes," he said, "your mamma is right. We have made a deplorable mistake in what we have done. Besides, you must know that this unlucky picture is not in the least like you. Marien has made some use of your features to paint a fancy portrait—so we will let nobody see it. They might laugh at you."

In this way he hoped to repair the evil he had done in flattering his daughter's vanity, and promoting that dangerous spirit of independence, denounced to him a few minutes before, but of which, up to that time, he had never heard.

Jacqueline, in her turn, began to sob.

Mademoiselle Schult had cause, too, to wipe her eyes, pretending a more or less sincere repentance for her share in the deception. Vigorously cross-questioned by Madame de Nailles, who called upon her to tell all she knew, under pain of being dismissed immediately, she saw but one way of retaining her situation, which was to deliver up Jacqueline, bound hand and foot, to the anger of her stepmother, by telling all she knew of the childish romance of which she had been the confidante. As a reward she was permitted (as she had foreseen) to retain her place in the character of a spy.

It was a sad Ste.-Clotilde's day that year. Marien, who came in the evening, heard with surprise that the Baroness was indisposed and could see no one. For twelve days after this he continued in disgrace, being refused admittance when he called. Those twelve days were days of anguish for Jacqueline. To see Marien no longer, to be treated with coldness by her father, to see in the blue eyes of her stepmother—eyes so soft and tender when they looked upon her hitherto—only a harsh, mistrustful glare, almost a look of hatred, was a punishment greater than she could bear. What had she done to deserve punishment? Of what was she accused? She spoke of her wretchedness to Fraulein Schult, who, perfidiously, day after day, drew from her something to report to Madame de Nailles. That lady was somewhat consoled, while suffering tortures of jealousy, to know that the girl to whom these sufferings were due was paying dearly for her fault and was very unhappy.

On the twelfth day something occurred which, though it made no noise in the household, had very serious consequences. The effect it produced on Jacqueline was decisive and deplorable. The poor child, after going through all the states of mind endured by those who suffer under unmerited disgrace—revolt, indignation, sulkiness, silent obstinacy—felt unable to bear it longer. She resolved to humble herself, hoping that by so doing the wall of ice that had arisen between her stepmother and herself might be cast down. By this time she cared less to know of what fault she was supposed to be guilty than to be taken back into favor as before. What must she do to obtain forgiveness? Explanations are usually worthless; besides, none might be granted her. She remembered that when she was a small child she had obtained immediate oblivion of any fault by throwing herself impulsively into the arms of her little mamma, and asking her to forget whatever she had done to displease her, for she had not done it on purpose. She would do the same thing now. Putting aside all pride and obstinacy, she would go to this mamma, who, for some days, had seemed so different. She would smother her in kisses. She might possibly be repelled at first. She would not mind it. She was sure that in the end she would be forgiven.

No sooner was this resolution formed than she hastened to put it into execution. It was the time of day when Madame de Nailles was usually alone. Jacqueline went to her bedchamber, but she was not there, and a moment after she stood on the threshold of the little salon. There she stopped short, not quite certain how she should proceed, asking herself what would be her reception.

"How shall I do it?" she thought. "How had I better do it?"

"Bah!" she answered these doubts. "It will be very easy. I will go in on tiptoe, so that she can't hear me. I will slip behind her chair, and I will hug her suddenly, so tight, so tenderly, and kiss her till she tells me that all has been forgiven."

As she thought thus Jacqueline noiselessly opened the

door of the salon, over which, on the inner side, hung a thick plush *portière*. But as she was about to lift it, the sound of a voice within made her stand motionless. She recognized the tones of Marien. He was pleading, imploring, interrupted now and then by the sharp and still angry voice of her mamma. They were not speaking above their breath, but if she listened she could hear them, and, without any scruples of conscience, she *did* listen intently, anxious to see her way through the dark fog in which, for twelve days, she had wandered.

"I do not go quite so far as that," said Madame de Nailles, dryly. "It is enough for me that she produced an illusion of such beauty upon you. Now I know what to expect—"

"That is nonsense," replied Marien—"mere foolishness. *You* jealous! jealous of a baby whom I knew when she wore white pinafores, who has grown up under my very eyes? But, so far as I am concerned, she exists no longer. She is not, she never will be in my eyes, a woman. I shall think of her as playing with her doll, eating sugar-plums, and so on."

Jacqueline grew faint. She shivered and leaned against the door-post.

"One would not suppose so, to judge by the picture with which she has inspired you. You may say what you like, but I know that in all this there was a set purpose to insult me."

"Clotilde!"

"In the first place, on no pretext ought you to have been induced to paint her portrait."

"Do you think so? Consider, had I refused, the

danger of awakening suspicion? I accepted the commission most unwillingly, much put out by it, as you may suppose. But you are making too much of an imaginary fault. Consign the wretched picture to the barn, if you like. We will never say another word about so foolish a matter. You promise me to forget it, won't you? . . . Dear! you will promise me?" he added, after a pause.

Madame de Nailles sighed and replied: "If not she it will be some one else. I am very unhappy. . . . I am weak and contemptible. . . ."

"Clotilde!" replied Marien, in an accent that went to Jacqueline's heart like a knife.

She fancied that after this she heard the sound of a kiss, and, with her cheeks aflame and her head burning, she rushed away. She understood little of what she had overheard. She only realized that he had given her up, that he had turned her into ridicule, that he had said "Clotilde!" to her mother, that he had called her *dear*—she!—the woman she had so adored, so venerated, her best friend, her father's wife, her mother by adoption! Everything in this world seemed to be giving way under her feet. The world was full of falsehood and of treason, and life, so bad, so cruel, was no longer what she had supposed it to be. It had broken its promise to herself, it had made her bad—bad forever. She loved no one, she believed in no one. She wished she were dead.

How she reached her own room in this state Jacqueline never knew. She was aware at last of being on her knees beside her bed, with her face hidden in the bedclothes. She was biting them to stifle her desire to scream. Her hands were clenched convulsively.

"Mamma!" she cried, "mamma!"

Was this a reproach addressed to her she had so long called by that name? Or was it an appeal, vibrating with remorse, to her real mother, so long forgotten in favor of this false idol, her rival, her enemy?

Undoubtedly, Jacqueline was too innocent, too igno- rant to guess the real truth from what she had over- heard. But she had learned enough to be no longer the pure-minded young girl of a few hours before. It seemed to her as if a fetid swamp now lay before her, barring her entrance into life. Vague as her percep- tions were, this swamp before her seemed more deep, more dark, more dreadful from uncertainty, and Jacqueline felt that thenceforward she could make no step in life without risk of falling into it. To whom now could she open her heart in confidence—that heart bleeding and bruised as if it had been trampled on, as if some one had crushed it? The thing that she now knew was not like her own little personal secrets, such as she had imprudently confided to Fraulein Schult. The words that she had overheard she could repeat to no one. She must carry them in her heart, like the barb of an arrow in a secret wound, where they would fester and grow more painful day by day.

"But, above all," she said at length, rising from her knees, "let me show proper pride."

She bathed her fevered face in cold water, then she walked up to her mirror. As she gazed at herself with a strange interest, trying to see whether the entire change so suddenly accomplished in herself had left its visible traces on her features, she seemed to see something in her eyes that spoke of the clairvoyance of despair. She smiled at herself, to see whether the new Jacqueline could play the part, which—whether she would or not—was now assigned to her. What a sad smile it was!

"I have lost everything," she said, "I have lost everything!" And she remembered, as one remembers something in the far-off long ago, how that very morning, when she awoke, her first thought had been: "Shall I see him to-day?" Each day she passed without seeing him had seemed to her a lost day, and she had accustomed herself to go to sleep thinking of him, remembering all he had said to her, and how he had looked at her. Of course, sometimes she had been unhappy, but what a difference it seemed between such vague unhappiness and what she now experienced? And then, when she was sad, she could always find a refuge in that dear mamma—in that Clotilde whom she vowed she would never kiss again, except with such kisses as might be necessary to avoid suspicion. Kisses of that kind were worth nothing. Quite the contrary! Could she kiss her father now without a pang? Her father! He had gone wholly over to the side of *that other* in this affair. She had seen him in one moment turn against herself. No!—no one was left her! . . . If she could only lay her head in Modeste's lap and be soothed while she crooned her old songs as in the nursery! But, whatever Marien or any one else might choose to say, she was no longer a baby. The bitter sense of her isolation arose in her. She could hardly breathe. Suddenly she pressed her lips upon the glass which reflected her own image, so sad, so pale, so desolate. She put the pity for herself into a long, long, fervent kiss, which seemed to say: "Yes, I am all alone— alone forever." Then, in a spirit of revenge, she opened what seemed a safety-valve, preventing her from giving way to any other emotion.

She rushed for a little box which she had converted into a sort of reliquary. She took out of it the half-burned cigarette, the old glove, the withered violets, and a visiting-card with his name, on which three unimportant lines had been written. She insulted these keepsakes, she tore them with her nails, she trampled them underfoot, she reduced them to fragments; she left nothing whatever of them, except a pile of shreds, which at last she set fire to. She had a feeling as if she were employed in executing two great culprits, who deserved cruel tortures at her hands; and, with them, she slew now and forever the foolish fancy she had called her love. By a strange association of ideas, the famous composition, so praised by M. Regis, came back to her memory, and she cried:

"*Je ne veux me souvenir. . . . me souvenir de rien!* If I remember, I shall be more unhappy. All has been a dream. His look was a dream, his pressure of my hand, his kiss on the last day, all—all—were dreams. He was making a fool of me when he gave me that pink which is now in this pile of ashes. He was laughing when he told me I was more beautiful than was natural. Never have I been—never shall I be in his eyes—more than the baby he remembers playing with her doll."

And unconsciously, as Jacqueline said these words, she imitated the careless accent with which she had heard them fall from the lips of the artist. And she would have again to meet him! If she had had thunder and lightning at her command, as she had had the match with which she had set fire to the memorials of her juvenile folly, Marien would have been annihilated on the spot. She was at that moment a murderess at heart. But the dinner-bell rang. The young fury gave a last glance at the adornments of her pretty bedchamber, so elegant, so original—all blue and pink, with a couch covered with silk embroidered with flowers. She seemed to say to them all: "Keep my secret. It is a sad one. Be careful: keep it safely." The cupids on the clock, the little book-rest on a velvet stand, the picture of the Virgin that hung over her bed, with rosaries and palms entwined about it, the photographs of her girl-friends standing on her writing-table in pretty frames of old-fashioned silk—all seemed to see her depart with a look of sympathy.

She went down to the dining-room, resolved to prove that she would not submit to punishment. The best way to brave Madame de Nailles was, she thought, to affect great calmness and indifference, aye, even, if she could, some gayety. But the task before her was more difficult than she had expected. Apparently, as a proof of reconciliation, Marien had been kept to dinner. To see him so soon again after his words of outrage was more than she could bear. For one moment the earth

[83]

seemed to sink under her feet; she roused her pride by an heroic effort, and that sustained her. She exchanged with the artist, as she always did, a friendly "Good-evening!" and ate her dinner, though it nearly choked her.

Madame de Nailles had red eyes; and Jacqueline made the reflection that women who are thirty-five should never weep. She knew that her face had not been made ugly by her tears, and this gave her a perverse satisfaction in the midst of her misery. Of Marien she thought: "He sits there as if he had been put *en pénitence.*" No doubt he could not endure scenes, and the one he had just passed through must have given him the downcast look which Jacqueline noticed with contempt.

What she did not know was that his depression had more than one cause. He felt—and felt with shame and with discouragement—that the fetters of a connection which had long since ceased to charm had been fastened on his wrists tighter than ever; and he thought: "I shall lose all my energy, I shall lose even my talent! While I wear these chains I shall see ever before me— ah! tortures of Tantalus!—the vision of a new love, fresh as the dawn which beckons to me as it passes before my sight, which lays on me the light touch of a caress, while I am forced to see it glide away, to let it vanish, disappear forever! And alas! that is not all. If I have deceived an inexperienced heart by words spoken or deeds done in a moment of weakness or temptation, can I flatter myself that I have acted like an honest man?"

JACQUELINE

This is what Marien was really thinking, while Jacqueline looked at him with an expression she strove to make indifferent, but which he interpreted, though she knew it not: "You have done me all the harm you can."

M. de Nailles meantime went on talking, with little response from his wife or his guest, about some vehement discussion of a new law going on just then in the Chamber, and he became so interested in his own discourse that he did not remark the constraint of the others.

Marien at last, tired of responding in monosyllables to his remarks, said abruptly, a short time before dessert was placed upon the table, something about the probability of his soon going to Italy.

"A pilgrimage of art to Florence!" cried the Baron, turning at once from politics. "That's good. But wait a little—let it be after the rising of the Chamber. We will follow your steps. It has been the desire of my wife's life—a little jaunt to Italy. Has it not, Clotilde? So we will all go in September or October. What say you?"

"In September or October, whichever suits you," said Marien, with despair.

Not one month of liberty! Why couldn't they leave him to his *Savonarola!* Must he drag about a ball and chain like a galley-slave?

Clotilde rewarded M. de Nailles with a smile—the first smile she had given him since their quarrel about Jacqueline.

"My wife has got over her displeasure," he said to himself, delightedly.

[85]

Jacqueline, on her part, well remembered the day when Hubert had spoken to her for the first time of his intended journey, and how he had added, in a tone which she now knew to be badinage, but which then, alas! she had believed serious: "Suppose we go together!"

And her impulse to shed tears became so great, that when they left the dinner-table she escaped to her own room, under pretence of a headache.

"Yes—you are looking wretchedly," said her stepmother. And, turning to M. de Nailles, she added: "Don't you think, *mon ami*, she is as yellow as a quince!" Marien dared not press the hand which she, who had been his little friend for years, offered him as usual, but this time with repugnance.

"You are suffering, my poor Jacqueline!" he ventured to say.

"Oh! not much," she answered, with a glance at once haughty and defiant, "to-morrow I shall be quite well again."

And, saying this, she had the courage to laugh.

But she was not quite well the next day; and for many days after she was forced to stay in bed. The doctor who came to see her talked about "low fever," attributed it to too rapid growth, and prescribed sea-bathing for her that summer. The fever, which was not very severe, was of great service to Jacqueline. It enabled her to recover in quiet from the effects of a bitter deception.

Madame de Nailles was not sufficiently uneasy about her to be always at her bedside. Usually the sick girl stayed alone, with her window-curtains closed, lying there in the soft half-light that was soothing to her nerves. The silence was broken at intervals by the voice of Modeste, who would come and offer her her medicine. When Jacqueline had taken it, she would shut her eyes, and resume, half asleep, her sad reflections. These were always the same. What could be the tie between her stepmother and Marien?

She tried to recall all the proofs of friendship she had seen pass between them, but all had taken place openly. Nothing that she could remember seemed suspicious. So she thought at first, but as she thought more, lying, feverish, upon her bed, several things, little noticed at the time, were recalled to her remembrance. They might mean nothing, or they might mean much. In the latter case, Jacqueline could not understand them very well. But she knew he had called her "Clotilde," that he had even dared to say "thou" to her in private—these were things she knew of her own knowledge. Her pulse beat quicker as she thought of them; her head burned. In that studio, where she had passed so many happy hours, had Marien and her stepmother ever met as lovers?

Her stepmother and Marien! She could not understand what it meant. Must she apply to them a dreadful word that she had picked up in the history books, where it had been associated with such women as Margaret of Burgundy, Isabeau of Bavaria, Anne Boleyn, and other princesses of very evil reputation? She had looked it out in the dictionary, where the meaning given was: "To be unfaithful to conjugal vows." Even then she could not understand precisely the meaning of *adultery*, and she set herself to solve it during the long lonely days when she was convalescent. When she was able to walk from one room to another, she wandered in a loose dressing-gown, whose long, lank folds showed that she had grown taller and thinner during her illness, into the room that held the books, and went boldly up to the bookcase, the key of which had been left in the lock, for everybody had entire confidence in Jacqueline's scrupulous honesty. Never before had she broken a promise; she knew that a well-brought-up young girl ought to read only such books as were put into her hands. The idea of taking a volume from those shelves had no more occurred to her than the idea of taking money out of somebody's purse; that is, up to this moment it had not occurred to her to do so; but now that she had lost all respect for those in authority over her, Jacqueline considered herself released from any obligation to obey them. She therefore made use of the first opportunity that presented itself to take down a novel of George Sand, which she had heard spoken of as a very dangerous book, not doubting it would throw some light on the subject that absorbed her. But she shut up the volume in a rage when she found that it had nothing but excuses to offer for the fall of a married woman. After that, and guided only by chance, she read a number of other novels, most of which were of antediluvian date, thus accounting, she supposed, for their sentiments, which she found old-fashioned. We should be wrong, however, if we supposed that Jacqueline's crude judgment of these books

JACQUELINE

had nothing in common with true criticism. Her only object, however, in reading all this sentimental prose was to discover, as formerly she had found in poetry, something that applied to her own case; but she soon discovered that all the sentimental heroines in the so-called bad books were persons who had had bad husbands; besides, they were either widows or old women —at least thirty years old! It was astounding! There was nothing—absolutely nothing—about young girls, except instances in which they renounced their hopes of happiness. What an injustice! Among these victims the two that most attracted her sympathy were Madame de Camors and Renée Mauperin. But what horrors surrounded them! What a varied assortment of deceptions, treacheries, and mysteries, lay hidden under the outward decency and respectability of what men called "the world!" Her young head became a stage on which strange plays were acted. What one reads is good or bad for us, according to the frame of mind in which we read it—according as we discover in a volume healing for the sickness of our souls—or the contrary. In view of the circumstances in which she found herself, what Jacqueline absorbed from these books was poison.

When, after the physical and moral crisis through which she had passed, Jacqueline resumed the life of every day, she had in her sad eyes, around which for some time past had been dark circles, an expression of anxiety such as the first contact with a knowledge of evil might have put into Eve's eyes after she had plucked the apple. Her investigations had very im-

perfectly enlightened her. She was as much perplexed
as ever, with some false ideas besides. When she was
well again, however, she continued weak and languid;
she felt somehow as if she had come back to her old
surroundings from some place far away. Everything
about her now seemed sad and unfamiliar, though
outwardly nothing was altered. Her parents had apparently forgotten the unhappy episode of the picture.
It had been sent away to Grandchaux, which was tan-
tamount to its being buried. Hubert Marien had resumed his habits of intimacy in the family. From that
time forth he took less and less notice of Jacqueline—
whether it were that he owed her a grudge for all the
annoyance she had been the means of bringing upon
him, or whether he feared to burn himself in the flame
which had once scorched him more than he admitted
to himself, who can say? Perhaps he was only acting
in obedience to orders.

CHAPTER VI

A CONVENT FLOWER

NE of Jacqueline's first walks, after she had recovered, was to see her cousin Giselle at her convent. She did not seek this friend's society when she was happy and in a humor for amusement, for she thought her a little straightlaced, or, as she said, too like a nun; but nobody could condole or sympathize with a friend in trouble like Giselle. It seemed as if nature herself had intended her for a Sister of Charity—a Gray Sister, as Jacqueline would sometimes call her, making fun of her somewhat dull intellect, which had been benumbed, rather than stimulated, by the education she had received.

The Bénédictine Convent is situated in a dull street on the left bank of the Seine, all gardens and *hôtels*—that is, detached houses. Grass sprouted here and there among the cobblestones. There were no street-lamps and no policemen. Profound silence reigned there. The petals of an acacia, which peeped timidly over its high wall, dropped, like flakes of snow, on the few pedestrians who passed by it in the springtime. The enormous *porte-cochère* gave entrance into a square courtyard, on one side of which was the chapel, on the other, the door that led into the convent. Here Jacqueline presented herself, accompanied by her old nurse, Modeste. She had not yet resumed her German lessons, and was striving to put off as long as possible any intercourse with Fraulein Schult, who had known of her foolish fancy, and who might perhaps renew the odious subject. Walking with Modeste, on the contrary, seemed like going back to the days of her childhood, the remembrance of which soothed her like a recollection of happiness and peace, now very far away; it was a reminiscence of the far-off limbo in which her young soul, pure and white, had floated, without rapture, but without any great grief or pain.

The porteress showed them into the parlor. There they found several pupils who were talking to members of their families, from whom they were separated by a *grille*, whose black bars gave to those within the appearance of captives, and made rather a barrier to eager demonstrations of affection, though they did not hinder the reception of good things to eat.

"*Tiens!* I have brought you some chocolate," said Jacqueline to Giselle, as soon as her cousin appeared, looking far prettier in her black cloth frock than when she wore an ordinary walking-costume. Her fair hair was drawn back *à la Chinoise* from a white forehead resembling that of a German Madonna;—it was one of those foreheads, slightly and delicately curved, which phrenologists tell us indicate reflection and enthusiasm.

But Giselle, without thanking Jacqueline for the

chocolate, exclaimed at once: "*Mon Dieu!* What has been the matter with you?"

She spoke rather louder than usual, it being understood that conversations were to be carried on in a low tone, so as not to interfere with those of other persons. She added: "I find you so altered."

"Yes—I have been ill," said Jacqueline, carelessly, "sorrow has made me ill," she added, in a whisper, looking to see whether the nun, who was discreetly keeping watch, walking to and fro behind the *grille*, might chance to be listening. "Oh, ask me no questions! I must never tell you—but for me, you must know—the happiness of my life is at an end—is at an end——"

She felt herself to be very interesting while she was speaking thus; her sorrows were somewhat assuaged. There was undoubtedly a certain pleasure in letting some one look down into the unfathomable, mysterious depths of a suffering soul.

She had expected much curiosity on the part of Giselle, and had resolved beforehand to give her no answers; but Giselle only sighed, and said, softly:

"Ah—my poor darling! I, too, am very unhappy. If you only knew——"

"How? Good heavens! what can have happened to you here?"

"Here? oh! nothing, of course; but this year I am to leave the convent—and I think I can guess what will then be before me."

Here, seeing that the nun who was keeping guard was listening, Giselle, with great presence of mind, spoke louder on indifferent subjects till she had passed out of earshot, then she rapidly poured her secret into Jacqueline's ear.

From a few words that had passed between her grandmother and Madame d'Argy, she had found out that Madame de Monredon intended to marry her.

"But that need not make you unhappy," said Jacqueline, "unless he is really distasteful to you."

"That is what I am not sure about—perhaps he is not the one I think. But I hardly know why—I have a dread, a great dread, that it is one of our neighbors in the country. Grandmamma has several times spoken in my presence of the advantage of uniting our two estates—they touch each other—oh! I know her ideas! she wants a man well-born, one who has a position in the world—some one, as she says, who knows something of life—that is, I suppose, some one no longer young, and who has not much hair on his head—like Monsieur de Talbrun."

"Is he very ugly—this Monsieur de Talbrun?"

"He's not ugly—and not handsome. But, just think! he is thirty-four!"

Jacqueline blushed, seeing in this speech a reflection on her own taste in such matters.

"That's twice my age," sighed Giselle.

"Of course that would be dreadful if he were to stay always twice your age—for instance, if you were now thirty-five, he would be seventy, and a hundred and twenty when you reached your sixtieth year—but really to be twice your age now will only make him seventeen years older than yourself."

JACQUELINE

In the midst of this chatter, which was beginning to attract the notice of the nun, they broke off with a laugh, but it was only one of those laughs *au bout des lèvres*, uttered by persons who have made up their minds to be unhappy. Then Giselle went on:

"I know nothing about him, you understand—but he frightens me. I tremble to think of taking his arm, of talking to him, of being his wife. Just think even of saying *thou* to him!"

"But married people don't say *thou* to each other nowadays," said Jacqueline, "it is considered vulgar."

"But I shall have to call him by his Christian name!"

"What is Monsieur de Talbrun's Christian name?"

"Oscar."

"Humph! That is not a very pretty name, but you could get over the difficulty—you could say *mon ami*. After all, your sorrows are less than mine."

"Poor Jacqueline!" said Giselle, her soft hazel eyes moist with sympathy.

"I have lost at one blow all my illusions, and I have made a horrible discovery, that it would be wicked to tell to any one—you understand—not even to my confessor."

"Heavens! but you could tell your mother!"

"You forget, I have no mother," replied Jacqueline in a tone which frightened her friend: "I had a dear mamma once, but she would enter less than any one into my sorrows; and as to my father—it would make things worse to speak to him," she added, clasping her hands. "Have you ever read any novels, Giselle?"

THÉO BENTZON

"Hem!" said the discreet voice of the nun, by way of warning.

"Two or three by Walter Scott."

"Oh! then you can imagine nothing like what I could tell you—How horrid that nun is, she stops always as she comes near us! Why can't she do as Modeste does, and leave us to talk by ourselves?"

It seemed indeed as if the Argus in a black veil had overheard part of this conversation, not perhaps the griefs of Jacqueline, which were not very intelligible, but some of the words spoken by Giselle, for, drawing near her, she said, gently: "We, too, shall all grieve to lose you, my dearest child; but remember one can serve God anywhere, and save one's soul—in the world as well as in a convent." And she passed on, giving a kind smile to Jacqueline, whom she knew, having seen her several times in the convent parlor, and whom she thought a nice girl, notwithstanding what she called her "fly-away airs"—"the airs they acquire from modern education," she said to herself, with a sigh.

"Those poor ladies would have us think of nothing but a future life," said Jacqueline, shrugging her shoulders.

"We ought to think of it first of all," said Giselle, who had become serious. "Sometimes I think my place should have been among these ladies who have brought me up. They are so good, and they seem to be so happy. Besides, do you know, I stand less in awe of them than I do of my grandmother. When grandmamma orders me I never shall dare to object, even if—But you must think me very selfish, my poor

JACQUELINE

Jacqueline! I am talking only of myself. Do you know what you ought to do as you go away? You should go into the chapel, and pray with all your heart for me, that I may be brought in safety through my troubles about which I have told you, and I will do the same for yours, about which you have not told me. An exchange of prayers is the best foundation for a friendship," she added; for Giselle had many little convent maxims at her fingers' ends, to which, when she uttered them, her sincerity of look and tone gave a personal meaning.

"You are right," said Jacqueline, much moved. "It has done me good to see you. Take this chocolate."

"And you must take this," said Giselle, giving her a little illuminated card, with sacred words and symbols.

"Adieu, dearest—say, have you ever detested any one?"

"Never!" cried Giselle, with horror.

"Well! I do detest—detest—— You are right, I will go into the chapel. I need some exorcism."

And laughing at her use of this last word—the same little mirthless laugh that she had uttered before— Jacqueline went away, followed by the admiring glances of the other girls, who from behind the bars of their cage noted the brilliant plumage of this bird who was at liberty. She crossed the courtyard, and, followed by Modeste, entered the chapel, where she sank upon her knees. The mystic half-light of the place, tinged purple by its passage through the stained-windows, seemed to enlarge the little chancel, parted in two by a double *grille*, behind which the nuns could hear the service without being seen.

The silence was so deep that the low murmur of a prayer could now and then be heard. The worshipers might have fancied themselves a hundred leagues from all the noises of the world, which seemed to die out when they reached the convent walls.

Jacqueline read, and re-read mechanically, the words printed in letters of gold on the little card Giselle had given her. It was a symbolical picture, and very ugly; but the words were: "Oh! that I had wings like a dove, for then would I flee away and be at rest."

"Wings!" she repeated, with vague aspiration. The aspiration seemed to disengage her from herself, and from this earth, which had nothing more to offer her. Ah! how far away was now the time when she had entered churches, full of happiness and hope, to offer a candle that her prayer might be granted, which she felt sure it would be! All was vanity! As she gazed at the *grille*, behind which so many women, whose worldly lives had been cut short, now lived, safe from the sorrows and temptations of this world, Jacqueline seemed for the first time to understand why Giselle regretted that she might not share forever the blessed peace enjoyed in the convent. A torpor stole over her, caused by the dimness, the faint odor of the incense, and the solemn silence. She imagined herself in the act of giving up the world. She saw herself in a veil, with her eyes raised to Heaven, very pale, standing behind the *grille*. She would have to cut off her hair.

That seemed hard, but she would make the sacrifice. She would accept anything, provided the ungrateful pair, whom she would not name, could feel sorrow for her loss—maybe even remorse. Full of these ideas, which certainly had little in common with the feelings of those who seek to forgive those who trespass against them, Jacqueline continued to imagine herself a Bénédictine sister, under the soothing influence of her surroundings, just as she had mistaken the effects of physical weakness when she was ill for a desire to die. Such feelings were the result of a void which the whole universe, as she thought, never could fill, but it was really a temporary vacuum, like that caused by the loss of a first tooth. These teeth come out with the first jar, and nature intends them to be speedily replaced by others, much more permanent; but children cry when they are pulled out, and fancy they are in very tight. Perhaps they suffer, after all, nearly as much as they think they do.

"Mademoiselle!" said Modeste, touching her on the shoulder.

"I was content to be here," answered Jacqueline, with a sigh. "Do you know, Modeste," she went on, when they got out of doors, "that I have almost made up my mind to be a nun. What do you say to that?"

"Heaven forbid!" cried the old nurse, much startled.

"Life is so hard," replied her young mistress.

"Not for you, anyhow. It would be a sin to say so."

"Ah! Modeste, we so little know the real truth of things—we can see only appearances. Don't you think that a linen band over my forehead would be very becoming to me? I should look like Saint Theresa."

"And what would be the good of your looking like Saint Theresa, when there would be nobody to tell you so?" said Modeste, with the practical good-sense that never forsook her. "You would be beautiful for yourself alone. You would not even be allowed a looking-glass. Just talk about that fancy to Monsieur—we should soon see what he would say to such a notion."

M. de Nailles, having just left the Chamber, was crossing the Pont de la Concorde on foot at this moment. His daughter ran up to him, and caught him by the arm. They walked homeward talking of very different things from bolts and bars. The Baron, who was a weak man, thought in his heart that he had been too severe with his daughter for some time past. As he recalled what had taken place, the anger of Madame de Nailles in the matter of the picture seemed to him to have been extreme and unnecessary. Jacqueline was just at an age when young girls are apt to be nervous and impressionable; they had been wrong to be rough with one who was so sensitive. His wife was quite of his opinion, she acknowledged (not wishing him to think too much on the subject) that she had been too quick-tempered.

"Yes," she had said, frankly, "I am jealous; I want things to myself. I own I was angry when I thought that Jacqueline was about to throw off my authority, and hurt when I found she was capable of keeping up a concealment—when I believed she was so open

always with me. My behavior was foolish, I acknowledge. But what can we do? Neither of us can go
and ask her pardon?"

"Of course not," said the father, "all we can do is
to treat her with a little more consideration for the
future; and, with your permission, I shall use her
illness as an excuse for spoiling her a little."

"You have *carte blanche*, my dear, I agree to everything." So M. de Nailles, with his daughter's arm in
his, began to spoil her, as he had intended.

"You are still rather pale," he said, "but sea-bathing
will change all that. Would you like to go to the sea-
side next month?"

Jacqueline answered with a little incredulous smile:
"Oh, certainly, papa."

"You don't seem very sure about it. In the first
place, where shall we go? Your mamma seems to
fancy Houlgate?"

"Of course we must do what she wishes," replied
Jacqueline, rather bitterly.

"But, little daughter, what would you like? What
do you say to Tréport?"

"I should like Tréport very much, because there we
should be near Madame d'Argy."

Jacqueline had felt much drawn to Madame d'Argy
since her troubles, for she had been the nearest friend
of her own mother—her own dead mother, too long
forgotten. The château of Madame d'Argy, called
Lizerolles, was only two miles from Tréport, in a
charming situation on the road to St. Valéry.

"That's the very thing, then!" said M. de Nailles.

"Fred is going to spend a month at Lizerolles with his mother. You might ride on horseback with him. He is going to enjoy a holiday, poor fellow! before he has to be sent off on long and distant voyages."

"I don't know how to ride," said Jacqueline, still in the tone of a victim.

"The doctor thinks riding would be good for you, and you have time enough yet to take some lessons. Mademoiselle Schult could take you nine or ten times to the riding-school. And I will go with you the first time," added M. de Nailles, in despair at not having been able to please her. "To-day we will go to Blackfern's and order a habit—a riding-habit!—Can I do more?"

At this, as if by magic, whether she would or not, the lines of sadness and sullenness disappeared from Jacqueline's face; her eyes sparkled. She gave one more proof, that to every Parisienne worthy of the name, the two pleasures in riding are, first to have a perfectly fitting habit, secondly, to have the opportunity of showing how pretty she can be after a new fashion.

"Shall we go to Blackfern's now?"

"This very moment, if you wish it."

"You really mean Blackfern? Yvonne's habit came from Blackfern's!" Yvonne d'Etaples was the incarnation of *chic*—of fashionable elegance—in Jacqueline's eyes. Her heart beat with pleasure when she thought how Belle and Dolly would envy her when she told them: "I have a myrtle-green riding-habit, just like Yvonne's." She danced rather than walked as they went together to Blackfern's. A habit was much nicer than a long gown.

A quarter of an hour later they were in the waiting-room, where the last creations of the great ladies' tailor, were displayed upon lay figures, among sales-women and *essayeuses*, the very prettiest that could be found in England or the Batignolles, chosen because they showed off to perfection anything that could be put upon their shoulders, from the ugliest to the most extravagant. Deceived by the unusual elegance of these beautiful figures, ladies who are neither young nor well-shaped allow themselves to be beguiled and cajoled into buying things not suited to them. Very seldom does a hunchbacked dowager hesitate to put upon her shoulders the garment that draped so charm-ingly those of the living statue hired to parade be-fore her. Jacqueline could not help laughing as she watched this way of hunting larks; and thought the mirror might have warned them, like a scarecrow, rather than have tempted them into the snare.

The head tailor of the establishment made them wait long enough to allow the pretty showgirls to ac-complish their work of temptation. They fascinated Jacqueline's father by their graces and their glances, while at the same time they warbled into his daughter's ear, with a slightly foreign accent: "That would be so becoming to Mademoiselle."

For ladies going to the seaside there were things of the most exquisite simplicity: this white fur, trimmed with white velvet, for instance; that jacket like the uniform of a naval officer with a cap to match—"All

to please Fred," said Jacqueline, laughing. M. de
Nailles, while they waited for the tailor, chose two
costumes quite as original as those of Mademoiselle
d'Etaples, which delighted Jacqueline all the more,
because she thought it probable they would displease
her stepmother. At last the magnificent personage, his
face adorned with luxuriant whiskers, appeared with
the bow of a great artist or a diplomatist; took Jacqueline's measure as if he were fulfilling some important
function, said a few brief words to his secretary, and
then disappeared; the group of English beauties saying in chorus that Mademoiselle might come back that
day week and try it on.

Accordingly, a week later Jacqueline, seated on the
wooden horse used for this purpose, had the satisfaction of assuring herself that her habit, fitting marvel-
lously to her bust, showed not a wrinkle, any more
than a *gant de Suède* shows on the hand; it was closely
fitted to a figure not yet fully developed, but which the
creator of the *chef-d'œuvre* deigned to declare was
faultless. Usually, he said, he recommended his customers to wear a certain corset of a special cut, with
elastic material over the hips covered by satin that
matched the riding-habit, but at Mademoiselle's age,
and so supple as she was, the corset was not necessary.
In short, the habit was fashioned to perfection, and
fitted like her skin to her little flexible figure. In her
close-fitting petticoat, her riding-trousers and nothing
else, Jacqueline felt herself half naked, though she was
buttoned up to her throat. She had taken an attitude
on her wooden horse such as might have been envied

JACQUELINE

by an accomplished *équestrienne*, her elbows held well back, her shoulders down, her chest expanded, her right leg over the pommel, her left foot in the stirrup, and never after did any real gallop give her the same delight as this imaginary ride on an imaginary horse, she looking at herself with entire satisfaction all the time in an enormous cheval-glass.

CHAPTER VII

THE BLUE BAND

LOVE, like any other human malady, should be treated according to the age and temperament of the sufferer. Madame de Nailles, who was a very keen observer, especially where her own interests were concerned, lent herself with the best possible grace to everything that might amuse and distract Jacqueline, of whom she had by this time grown afraid. Not that she now dreaded her as a rival. The attitude of coldness and reserve that the young girl had adopted in her intercourse with Marien, her stepmother could see, was no evidence of coquetry. She showed, in her behavior to the friend of the family, a freedom from embarrassment which was new to her, and a frigidity which could not possibly have been assumed so persistently. No! what struck Madame de Nailles was the suddenness of this transformation. Jacqueline evidently took no further interest in Marien; she had apparently no longer any affection for herself —she, who had been once her dear little mamma, whom she had loved so tenderly, now felt herself to be considered only as a stepmother. Fraulein Schult, too, received no more confidences. What did it all mean?

JACQUELINE

Had Jacqueline, through any means, discovered a secret, which, in her hands, might be turned into a most dangerous weapon? She had a way of saying before the guilty pair: "Poor papa!" with an air of pity, as she kissed him, which made Madame de Nailles's flesh creep, and sometimes she would amuse herself by making ambiguous remarks which shot arrows of suspicion into a heart already afraid. "I feel sure," thought the Baroness, "that she has found out everything. But, no! it seems impossible. How can I discover what she knows?"

Jacqueline's revenge consisted in leaving her step-mother in doubt. She more than suspected, not without cause, that Fraulein Schult was false to her, and had the wit to baffle all the clever questions of her *promeneuse*.

"My worship of a man of genius—a great artist? Oh! that has all come to an end since I have found out that his devotion belongs to an elderly lady with a fair complexion and light hair. I am only sorry for him."

Jacqueline had great hopes that these cruel words would be reported—as they were—to her stepmother, and, of course, they did not mitigate the Baroness's uneasiness. Madame de Nailles revenged herself for this insult by dismissing the innocent echo of the impertinence—of course, under some plausible pretext. She felt it necessary also to be very cautious how she treated the enemy whom she was forced to shelter under her own roof. Her policy—a policy imposed on her by force of circumstances—was one of great indulgence and consideration, so that Jacqueline, soon feeling that she was for the present under no control, took the bit between her teeth. No other impression can adequately convey an idea of the sort of fury with which she plunged into pleasure and excitement, a state of mind which apparently, without any transition, succeeded her late melancholy. She had done with sentiment, she thought, forever. She meant to be practical and positive, a little Parisienne, and "in the swim." There were plenty of examples among those she knew that she could follow. Berthe, Hélène, and Claire Wermant were excellent leaders in that sort of thing. Those three daughters of the *agent de change* were at this time at Tréport, in charge of a governess, who let them do whatever they pleased, subject only to be scolded by their father, who came down every Saturday to Tréport, on that train that was called the *train des maris*. They had made friends with two or three American girls, who were called "fast," and Jacqueline was soon enrolled in the ranks of that gay company.

The cure that was begun on the wooden horse at Blackfern's was completed on the sea-shore.

The girls with whom she now associated were nine or ten little imps of Satan, who, with their hair flying in the wind and their caps over one ear, made the quiet beach ring with their boy-like gayety. They were called "the Blue Band," because of a sort of uniform that they adopted. We speak of them intentionally as masculine, and not feminine, because what is masculine best suited their appearance and behavior, for, though all could flirt like coquettes of experience, they were more like boys than girls, if judged by their age and their costume.

These Blues lived close to one another on that avenue that is edged with *châlets*, cottages, and villas, whose lower floors are abundantly provided with great glass windows, which seem to let the ocean into their very rooms, as well as to lay bare everything that passes in them to the public eye, as frankly as if their inmates bivouacked in the open street. Nothing was private; neither the meals, nor the coming and going of visitors. It must be said, however, that the inhabitants of these glass houses were very seldom at home. Bathing, and croquet, or tennis, at low water, on the sands, searching for shells, fishing with nets, dances at the Casino, little family dances alternating with concerts, to which even children went till nine o'clock, would seem enough to fill up the days of these young people, but they had also to make boating excursions to Cayeux, Crotoy, and Hourdel, besides riding parties in the beautiful country that surrounded the Château of Lizerolles, where they usually dismounted on their return.

At Lizerolles they were received by Madame d'Argy, who was delighted that they provided safe amusement for her son, who appeared in the midst of this group of half-grown girls like a young cock among the hens of his harem. Frédéric d'Argy, the young naval officer, who was enjoying his holiday, as M. de Nailles had said, was enjoying it exceedingly. How often, long after, on board the ship *Flore*, as he paced the silent quarter-deck, far from any opportunity of flirting, did he recall the forms and faces of these young girls, some dark, some fair, some rosy—half-women and half-children, who made much of him, and scolded him, and teased him, and contended for his attentions, while no better could be had, on purpose to tease one another. Oh! what a delightful time he had had! They did not leave him to himself one moment. He had to lift them into their saddles, to assist them as they clambered over the rocks, to superintend their attempts at swimming, to dance with them all by turns, and to look after them in the difficult character of Mentor, for he was older than they, and were they not entrusted to his care? What a serious responsibility! Had not Mentor even found himself too often timid and excited when one little firm foot was placed in his hand, when his arm was round one little waist, when he could render her as a cavalier a thousand little services, or accept with gladness the *rôle* of her consoler. He did everything he could think of to please them, finding all of them charming, though Jacqueline never ceased to be the one he preferred, a preference which she might easily have inferred from the poor lad's unusual timidity and awkwardness when he was brought into contact with her. But she paid no attention to his devotion, accepting himself and all he did for her as, in some sort, her personal property.

He was of no consequence, he did not count; what was he but her comrade and former playfellow?

Happily for Fred, he took pleasure in the familiarity with which she treated him—a familiarity which, had he known it, was not flattering. He was in the seventh heaven for a whole fortnight, during which he was tne recipient of more dried flowers and bows of ribbon than he ever got in all the rest of his life—the American girls were very fond of giving keepsakes—but then his star waned. He was no longer the *only one*. The grown-up brother of the Wermants came to Tréport— Raoul, with his air of a young man about town—a *boulevardier*, with his jacket cut in the latest fashion, with his cockle-shell of a boat, which he managed as well on salt water as on fresh, sculling with his arms bare, a cigarette in his mouth, a monocle in his eye, and a pith-helmet, such as is worn in India. The young ladies used to gather on the sands to watch him as he struck the water with the broad blade of his scull, near enough for them to see and to admire his nautical ability. They thought all his jokes amusing, and they delighted in his way of seizing his partner for a waltz and bearing her off as if she were a prize, hardly allowing her to touch the floor.

Fred thought him, with his stock of old jokes, very ill-mannered. He laughed at his sculling, and had a great mind to strike him after he saw him waltzing with Jacqueline. But he had to acknowledge the general appreciation felt for the fellow whom he called vulgar.

Raoul Wermant did not stay long at Tréport. He had only come to see his sisters on his way to Dieppe, where he expected to meet a certain Leah Skip, an actress from the *Nouveautés*. If he kept her waiting, however, for some days, it was because he was loath to leave the handsome Madame de Villegry, who was

THÉO BENTZON

living near her friend Madame de Nailles, recruiting herself after the fatigues of the winter season. Such being the situation, the young girls of the Blue Band might have tried in vain to make any impression upon him. But the hatred with which he inspired Fred found some relief in the composition of fragments of melancholy verse, which the young midshipman hid under his mattresses. It is not an uncommon thing for naval men to combine a love of the sea with a love of poetry. Fred's verses were not good, but they were full of dejection. The poor fellow compared Raoul Wermant to Faust, and himself to Siebel. He spoke of

> The youth whose eyes were brimming with salt tears,
> Whose heart was troubled by a thousand fears,
> Poor slighted lover!—since in his heavy heart
> All his illusions perish and depart.

Again, he wrote of Siebel:

> O Siebel!—thine is but the common fate!
> They told thee Fortune upon youth would wait;
> 'Tis false when love's in question—and you may——

Here he enumerated all the proofs of tenderness possible for a woman to give her lover, and then he added:

> You may know all, poor Siebel!—all, some day,
> When weary of this life and all its dreams,
> You learn to know it is not what it seems;
> When there is nothing that can cheer you more,
> All that remains is fondly to adore!

JACQUELINE

And after trying in vain to find a rhyme for lover, he cried:

Oh! tell me—if one grief exceeds another—
Is not this worst, to feel mere friendship moves
To cruel kindness the dear girl he loves?

Fred's mother surprised him one night while he was watering with his tears the ink he was putting to so sorry a use. She had been aware that he sat up late at night—his sleeplessness was not the insomnia of genius—for she had seen the glare of light from his little lamp burning later than the usual bedtime of the *château*, in one of the turret chambers at Lizerolles.

In vain Fred denied that he was doing anything, in vain he tried to put his papers out of sight; his mother was so persuasive that at last he owned everything to her, and in addition to the comfort he derived from his confession, he gained a certain satisfaction to his *amour-propre*, for Madame d'Argy thought the verses beautiful. A mother's geese are always swans. But it was only when she said, "I don't see why you should not marry your Jacqueline—such a thing is not by any means impossible," and promised to do all in her power to insure his happiness, that Fred felt how dearly he loved his mother. Oh, a thousand times more than he had ever supposed he loved her! However, he had not yet done with the agonies that lie in wait for lovers.

Madame de Monredon arrived one day at the Hôtel de la Plage, accompanied by her granddaughter, whom she had taken away from the convent before the beginning of the holidays. Since she had fully arranged the marriage with M. de Talbrun, it seemed important that Giselle should acquire some liveliness, and recruit her health, before the fatal wedding-day arrived. M. de Talbrun liked ladies to be always well and always lively, and it was her duty to see that Giselle accommodated herself to his taste; sea-bathing, life in the open air, and merry companions, were the things she needed to make her a little less thin, to give her tone, and to take some of her convent stiffness out of her. Besides, she could have free intercourse with her intended husband, thanks to the greater freedom of manners permitted at the sea-side. Such were the ideas of Madame de Monredon.

Poor Giselle! In vain they dressed her in fine clothes, in vain they talked to her and scolded her from morning till night, she continued to be the little convent-bred schoolgirl she had always been; with downcast eyes, pale as a flower that has known no sunlight, and timid to a point of suffering. M. de Talbrun frightened her as much as ever, and she had looked forward to the comfort of weeping in the arms of Jacqueline, who, the last time she had seen her, had been herself so unhappy. But what was her astonishment to find the young girl, who, a few weeks before, had made her such tragic confidences through the *grille* in the convent parlor, transformed into a creature bent on excitement and amusement. When she attempted to allude to the subject on which Jacqueline had spoken to her at the convent, and to ask her what it was that had then made her so unhappy, Jacqueline cried: "Oh! my dear, I have forgotten all about it!" But there was exaggeration in this profession of forgetfulness, and she hurriedly drew Giselle back to the game of croquet, where they were joined by M. de Talbrun.

The future husband of Giselle was a stout young fellow, short and thick-set, with broad shoulders, a large flat face, and strong jaws, ornamented with an enormous pair of whiskers, which partly compensated him for a loss of hair. He had never done anything but shoot and hunt over his property nine months in the year, and spend the other three months in Paris, where the Jockey Club and ballet-dancers sufficed for his amusement. He did not pretend to be a man whose bachelor life had been altogether blameless, but he considered himself to be a "correct" man, according to what he understood by that expression, which implied neither talents, virtues, nor good manners; nevertheless, all the Blue Band agreed that he was a finished type of gentlemanhood. Even Raoul's sisters had to confess, with a certain disgust, that, whatever people may say, in our own day the aristocracy of wealth has to lower its flag before the authentic quarterings of the old *noblesse*. They secretly envied Giselle because she was going to be a *grande dame*, while all the while they asserted that old-fashioned distinctions had no longer any meaning. Nevertheless, they looked forward to the day when they, too, might take their places in the Faubourg St. Germain. One may purchase that luxury with a fortune of eight hundred thousand francs.

The croquet-ground, which was under water at high

tide, was a long stretch of sand that fringed the shingle. Two parties were formed, in which care was taken to make both sides as nearly equal as possible, after which the game began, with screams, with laughter, a little cheating and some disputes, as is the usual custom. All this appeared to amuse Oscar de Talbrun exceedingly. For the first time during his wooing he was not bored. The Misses Sparks—Kate and Nora—by their "high spirits" agreeably reminded him of one or two excursions he had made in past days into Bohemian society.

He formed the highest opinion of Jacqueline when he saw how her still short skirts showed pretty striped silk stockings, and how her well-shaped foot was planted firmly on a blue ball, when she was preparing to *roquer* the red one. The way in which he fixed his eyes upon her gave great offense to Fred, and did it not alarm and shock Giselle? No! Giselle looked on calmly at the fun and talk around her, as unmoved as the stump of a tree, spoiling the game sometimes by her ignorance or her awkwardness, well satisfied that M. de Talbrun should leave her alone. Talking with him was very distasteful to her.

"You have been more stupid than usual," had been what her grandmother had never failed to say to her in Paris after one of his visits, which he alternated with bouquets. But at Tréport no one seemed to mind her being stupid, and indeed M. de Talbrun hardly thought of her existence, up to the moment when they were all nearly caught by the first wave that came rolling in over the croquet-ground, when all the girls took flight, flushed, animated, and with lively gesticulation, while the gentlemen followed with the box into which had been hastily flung hoops, balls, and mallets.

On their way Count Oscar condescendingly explained to Fred, as to a novice, that the only good thing about croquet was that it brought men and girls together. He was himself very good at games, he said, having remarkably firm muscles and exceptionally sharp sight; but he went on to add that he had not been able to show what he could do that day. The wet sand did not make so good a croquet-ground as the one he had had made in his park! It is a good thing to know one's ground in all circumstances, but especially in playing croquet. Then, dexterously passing from the game to the players, he went on to say, under cover of giving Fred a warning, that a man need not fear going too far with those girls from America— they had known how to flirt from the time they were born. They could look out for themselves, they had talons and beaks; but up to a certain point they were very easy to get on with. Those other players were queer little things; the three sisters Wermant were not wanting in *chic*, but, hang it!—the sweetest flower of them all, to his mind, was the tall one, the dark one— unripe fruit in perfection! "And a year or two hence," added M. de Talbrun, with all the self-confidence of an expert, "every one will be talking about her in the world of society."

Poor Fred kept silent, trying to curb his wrath. But the blood mounted to his temples as he listened to these remarks, poured into his ear by a man of thirty-five, between puffs of his cigar, because there was nobody else to whom he could make them. But they seemed to Fred very ill-mannered and ill-timed. If he had not dreaded making himself absurd, he would gladly have stood forth as the champion of the Sparks, the Wermants, and all the other members of the Blue Band, so that he might give vent to the anger raging in his heart on hearing that odious compliment to Jacqueline. Why was he not old enough to marry her? What right had that detestable Talbrun to take notice of any girl but his *fiancée?* If he himself could marry now, *his* choice would soon be made! No doubt, later—as his mother had said to him. But would Jacqueline wait? Everybody was beginning to admire her. Somebody would carry her off—somebody would cut him out while he was away at sea. Oh, horrible thought for a young lover!

That night, at the Casino, while dancing a quadrille with Giselle, he could not refrain from saying to her, "Don't you object to Monsieur de Talbrun's dancing so much with Jacqueline?"

"Who?—I?" she cried, astonished, "I don't see why he should not." And then, with a faint laugh, she added: "Oh, if she would only take him—and keep him!"

But Madame de Monredon kept a sharp eye upon M. de Talbrun. "It seems to me," she said, looking fixedly into the face of her future grandson-in-law, "that you really take pleasure in making children skip about with you."

JACQUELINE

"So I do," he replied, frankly and good-humoredly. "It makes me feel young again."

And Madame de Monredon was satisfied. She was ready to admit that most men marry women who have not particularly enchanted them, and she had brought up Giselle with all those passive qualities, which, together with a large fortune, usually suit best with a *mariage de convenance*.

Meantime Jacqueline piqued herself upon her worldly wisdom, which she looked upon as equal to Madame de Monredon's, since the terrible event which had filled her mind with doubts. She thought M. de Talbrun would do well enough for a husband, and she took care to say so to Giselle.

"It is a fact," she told her, with all the self-confidence of large experience, "that men who are very fascinating always remain bachelors. That is probably why Monsieur de Cymier, Madame de Villegry's handsome cousin, does not think of marrying."

She was mistaken. The Comte de Cymier, a satellite who revolved around that star of beauty, Madame de Villegry, had been by degrees brought round by that lady herself to thoughts of matrimony.

Madame de Villegry, notwithstanding her profuse use of henna and many cosmetics, which was always the first thing to strike those who saw her, prided herself on being uncompromised as to her moral character. There are some women who, because they stop short of actual vice, consider themselves irreproachable. They are willing, so to speak, to hang out the bush, but keep no tavern. In former times an appearance of evil was avoided in order to cover evil deeds, but at present there are those who, under the cover of being only "fast," risk the appearance of evil.

Madame de Villegry was what is sometimes called a "professional beauty." She devoted many hours daily to her toilette, she liked to have a crowd of admirers around her. But when one of them became too troublesome, she got rid of him by persuading him to marry. She had before this proposed several young girls to Gérard de Cymier, each one plainer and more insignificant than the others. It was to tell his dear friend that the one she had last suggested was positively too ugly for him, that the young attaché to an embassy had come down to the sea-side to visit her.

The day after his arrival he was sitting on the shingle at Madame de Villegry's feet, both much amused by the grotesque spectacle presented by the bathers, who exhibited themselves in all degrees of ugliness and deformity. Of course Madame de Villegry did not bathe, being, as she said, too nervous. She was sitting under a large parasol and enjoying her own superiority over those wretched, amphibious creatures who waddled on the sands before her, comparing Madame X—— to a seal and Mademoiselle Z—— to the skeleton of a cuttle-fish.

"Well! it was that kind of thing you wished me to marry," said M. de Cymier, in a tone of resentment.

"But, my poor friend, what would you have? All young girls are like that. They improve when they are married."

"If one could only be sure."

JACQUELINE

"One is never sure of anything, especially anything relating to young girls. One can not say that they do more than exist till they are married. A husband has to make whatever he chooses out of them. You are quite capable of making what you choose of your wife. Take the risk, then."

"I could educate her as to morals—though, I must say, I am not much used to that kind of instruction; but you will permit me to think that, as to person, I should at least wish to see a rough sketch of what I may expect in my wife before my marriage."

At that moment, a girl who had been bathing came out of the water a few yards from them; the elegant outline of her slender figure, clad in a bathing-suit of white flannel, which clung to her closely, was thrown into strong relief by the clear blue background of a summer sky.

"*Tiens!*—but she is pretty!" cried Gérard, breaking off what he was saying: "And she is the first pretty one I have seen!"

Madame de Villegry took up her tortoiseshell opera-glasses, which were fastened to her waist, but already the young girl, over whose shoulders an attentive servant had flung a wrapper—a *peignoir-éponge*—had run along the board-walk and stopped before her, with a gay "Good-morning!"

"Jacqueline!" said Madame de Villegry. "Well, my dear child, did you find the water pleasant?"

"Delightful!" said the young girl, giving a rapid glance at M. de Cymier, who had risen.

He was looking at her with evident admiration, an

admiration at which she felt much flattered. She was closely wrapped in her soft, snow-white *peignoir*, bordered with red, above which rose her lovely neck and head. She was trying to catch, on the point of one little foot, one of her bathing shoes, which had slipped from her. The foot which, when well shod, M. de Talbrun, through his eyeglass, had so much admired, was still prettier without shoe or stocking. It was so perfectly formed, so white, with a little pink tinge here and there, and it was set upon so delicate an ankle! M. de Cymier looked first at the foot, and then his glance passed upward over all the rest of the young figure, which could be seen clearly under the clinging folds of the wet drapery. Her form could be discerned from head to foot, though nothing was uncovered but the pretty little arm which held together with a careless grace the folds of her raiment. The eye of the experienced observer ran rapidly over the outline of her figure, till it reached the dark head and the brown hair, which rippled in little curls over her forehead. Her complexion, slightly golden, was not protected by one of those absurd hats which many bathers place on top of oiled silk caps which fit them closely. Neither was the precaution of oiled silk wanted to protect the thick and curling hair, now sprinkled with great drops that shone like pearls and diamonds. The water, instead of plastering her hair upon her temples, had made it more curly and more fleecy, as it hung over her dark eyebrows, which, very near together at the nose, gave to her eyes a peculiar, slightly oblique expression. Her teeth were dazzling, and were displayed by the smile which parted her lips—lips which were, if anything, too red for her pale complexion. She closed her eyelids now and then to shade her eyes from the too blinding sunlight. Those eyes were not black, but that hazel which has golden streaks. Though only half open, they had quickly taken in the fact that the young man sitting beside Madame de Villegry was very handsome.

As she went on with a swift step to her bathing-house, she drew out two long pins from her back hair, shaking it and letting it fall down her back with a slightly impatient and imperious gesture; she wished, probably, that it might dry more quickly.

"The devil!" said M. de Cymier, watching her till she disappeared into the bathing-house. "I never should have thought that it was all her own! There is nothing wanting in her. That is a young creature it is pleasant to see."

"Yes," said Madame de Villegry, quietly, "she will be very good-looking when she is eighteen."

"Is she nearly eighteen?"

"She is and she is not, for time passes so quickly. A girl goes to sleep a child, and wakes up old enough to be married. Would you like to be informed, without loss of time, as to her fortune?"

"Oh! I should not care much about her *dot*. I look out first for other things."

"I know, of course; but Jacqueline de Nailles comes of a very good family."

"Is she the daughter of the deputy?"

"Yes, his only daughter. He has a pretty house in

the Parc Monceau and a château of some importance in the Haute-Vienne."

"Very good; but, I repeat, I am not mercenary. Of course, if I should marry, I should like, for my wife's sake, to live as well as a married man as I have lived as a bachelor."

"Which means that you would be satisfied with a fortune equal to your own. I should have thought you might have asked more. It is true that if you have been suddenly thunderstruck that may alter your calculations—for it was very sudden, was it not? Venus rising from the sea!"

"Please don't exaggerate! But you are not so cruel, seeing you are always urging me to marry, as to wish me to take a wife who looks like a fright or a horror."

"Heaven preserve me from any such wish! I should be very glad if my little friend Jacqueline were destined to work your reformation."

"I defy the most careful parent to find anything against me at this moment, unless it be a platonic devotion. The youth of Mademoiselle de Nailles is an advantage, for I might indulge myself in that till we were married, and then I should settle down and leave Paris, where nothing keeps me but——"

"But a foolish fancy," laughed Madame de Villegry. "However, in return for your madrigal, accept the advice of a friend. The Nailles seem to me to be prosperous, but everybody in society appears so, and one never knows what may happen any day. You would not do amiss if, before you go on, you were to talk with Wermant, the *agent de change*, who has a considerable knowledge of the business affairs of Jacqueline's father. He could tell you about them better than I can."

"Wermant is at Tréport, is he not? I thought I saw him——"

"Yes, he is here till Monday. You have twenty-four hours."

"Do you really think I am in such a hurry?"

"Will you take a bet that by this time to-morrow you will not know exactly the amount of her *dot* and the extent of her expectations?"

"You would lose. I have something else to think of —now and always."

"What?" she said, carelessly.

"You have forbidden me ever to mention it."

Silence ensued. Then Madame de Villegry said, smiling:

"I suppose you would like me to present you this evening to my friends the De Nailles?"

And in fact they all met that evening at the Casino, and Jacqueline, in a gown of scarlet foulard, which would have been too trying for any other girl, seemed to M. de Cymier as pretty as she had been in her bathing-costume. Her hair was not dressed high, but it was gathered loosely together and confined by a ribbon of the same color as her gown, and she wore a little sailor hat besides. In this costume she had been called by M. de Talbrun the "Fra Diavolo of the Seas," and she never better supported that part, by liveliness and audacity, than she did that evening, when she made a conquest that was envied—wildly envied—by the three Demoiselles Wermant and the two Misses Sparks, for the handsome Gérard, after his first waltz with Madame de Villegry, asked no one to be his partner but Mademoiselle de Nailles.

The girls whom he neglected had not even Fred to fall back upon, for Fred, the night before, had received orders to join his ship. He had taken leave of Jacqueline with a pang in his heart which he could hardly hide, but to which no keen emotion on her part seemed to respond. However, at least, he was spared the unhappiness of seeing the star of De Cymier rising above the horizon.

"If he could only see me," thought Jacqueline, waltzing in triumph with M. de Cymier. "If he could only see me I should be avenged."

But *he* was not Fred. She was not giving him a thought. It was the last flash of resentment and hatred that came to her in that moment of triumph, adding to it a touch of exquisite enjoyment.

Thus she performed the obsequies of her first love!

Not long after this M. de Nailles said to his wife:

"Do you know, my dear, that our little Jacqueline is very much admired? Her success has been extraordinary. It is not likely she will die an old maid."

The Baronne assented rather reluctantly.

"Wermant was speaking to me the other day," went on M. de Nailles. "It seems that that young Count de Cymier, who is always hanging around you, by the way, has been making inquiries of him, in a manner that looks as if it had some meaning, as to what is our fortune, our position. But really, such a match seems too good to be true."

JACQUELINE

"Why so?" said the Baronne. "I know more about it than you do, from Blanche de Villegry. She gave me to understand that her cousin was much struck by Jacqueline at first sight, and ever since she does nothing but talk to me of M. de Cymier—of his birth, his fortune, his abilities—the charming young fellow seems gifted with everything. He could be Secretary of Legation, if he liked to quit Paris. In the meantime *attaché* to an Embassy looks very well on a card. *Attaché* to the Ministry of the Foreign Affairs does not seem so good. Jacqueline would be a countess, possibly an ambassadress. What would you think of that!"

Madame de Nailles, who understood policy much better than her husband, had suddenly become a convert to opportunism, and had made a change of base. Not being able to devise a plan by which to suppress her young rival, she had begun to think that her best way to get rid of her would be by promoting her marriage. The little girl was fast developing into a woman —a woman who would certainly not consent quietly to be set aside. Well, then, it would be best to dispose of her in so natural a way. When Jacqueline's slender and graceful figure and the freshness of her bloom were no longer brought into close comparison with her own charms, she felt she should appear much younger, and should recover some of her *prestige;* people would be less likely to remark her increasing stoutness, or the red spots on her face, increased by the salt air which was so favorable to young girls' complexions. Yes, Jacqueline must be married; that was the resolution to which Madame de Nailles had come after several nights of sleeplessness. It was her fixed idea, replacing in her brain that other fixed idea which, willingly or unwillingly, she saw she must give up—the idea of keeping her stepdaughter in the shade.

"Countess! Ambassadress!" repeated M. de Nailles, with rather a melancholy smile. "You are going too fast, my dear Clotilde. I don't doubt that Wermant gave the best possible account of our situation; but when it comes to saying what I could give her as a *dot*, I am very much afraid. We should have, in that case, to fall back on Fred, for I have not told you everything. This morning Madame d'Argy, who has done nothing but weep since her boy went away, and who, she says, never will get accustomed to the life of misery and anxiety she will lead as a sailor's mother, exclaimed, as she was talking to me: "Ah! there is but one way of keeping him at Lizerolles, of having him live there as the D'Argys have lived before him, quietly, like a good landlord, and that would be to give him your daughter; with her he would be entirely satisfied."

"Ah! so that is the reason why she asked whether Jacqueline might not stay with her when we go to Italy! She wishes to court her by proxy. But I don't think she will succeed. Monsieur de Cymier has the best chance."

"Do you suppose the child suspects——"

"That he admires her? My dear friend, we have to do with a very sharp-sighted young person. Nothing escapes the observation of Mademoiselle *votre fille*."

And Madame de Nailles, in her turn, smiled somewhat bitterly.

"Well," said Jacqueline's father, after a few moments' reflection, "it may be as well that she should weigh for and against a match before deciding. She may spend several years that are difficult and dangerous trying to find out what she wants and to make up her mind."

"Several years?"

"Hang it! You would not marry off Jacqueline at once?"

"Bah! many a girl, practically not as old as she, is married at sixteen or seventeen."

"Why! I fancied you thought so differently!"

"Our ways of thinking are sometimes altered by events, especially when they are founded upon sincere and disinterested affection."

"Like that of good parents, such as we are," added M. de Nailles, ending her sentence with an expression of grateful emotion.

For one moment the Baronne paled under this compliment.

"What did you say to Madame d'Argy?" she hastened to ask.

"I said we must give the young fellow's beard time to grow."

"Yes, that was right. I prefer Monsieur de Cymier a hundred times over. Still, if nothing better offers— a bird in the hand, you know——"

Madame de Nailles finished her sentence by a wave of her fan.

9   [129]

"Oh! our bird in the hand is not to be despised. A very handsome estate——"

"Where Jacqueline would be bored to death. I should rather see her radiant at some foreign court. Let me manage it. Let me bring her out. Give me *carte blanche* and let me have some society this winter."

Madame de Nailles, whether she knew it or not—probably she did, for she had great skill in reading the thoughts of others—was acting precisely in accordance with the wishes or the will of Jacqueline, who, having found much enjoyment in the dances at the Casino, had made up her mind that she meant to come out into society before any of her young companions.

"I shall not have to beg and implore her," she said to herself, anticipating the objections of her stepmother. "I shall only have politely to let her suspect that such a thing may have occurred as having had a listener at a door. I paid dearly enough for this hold over her. I have no scruple in using it."

Madame de Nailles was not mistaken in her stepdaughter; she was very far advanced beyond her age, thanks to the cruel wrong that had been done her by the loss of her trust in her elders and her respect for them. Her heart had had its past, though she was still hardly more than a child—a sad past, though its pain was being rapidly effaced. She now thought about it only at intervals. Time and circumstances were operating on her as they act upon us generally; only in her case more quickly than usual, which pro-

JACQUELINE

duced in her character and feelings phenomena that might have seemed curious to an observer. She was something of a woman, something of a child, something of a philosopher. At night, when she was dancing with Wermant, or Cymier, or even Talbrun, or on horseback, an exercise which all the Blues were wild about, she was an audacious flirt, a girl up to anything; and in the morning, at low tide, she might be seen, with her legs and feet bare, among the children, of whom there were many on the sands, digging ditches, making ramparts, constructing towers and fortifications in wet sand, herself as much amused as if she had been one of the babies themselves. There was screaming and jumping, and rushing out of reach of the waves which came up ready to overthrow the most complicated labors of the little architects, rough romping of all kinds, enough to amaze and disconcert a lover. But no one could have guessed at the thoughts which, in the midst of all this fun and frolic, were passing through the too early ripened mind of Jacqueline. She was thinking that many things to which we attach great value and importance in this world are as easily swept away as the sand barriers raised against the sea by childish hands; that everywhere there must be flux and reflux, that the beach the children had so dug up would soon become smooth as a mirror, ready for other little ones to dig it over again, tempting them to work, and yet discouraging their industry. Her heart, she thought, was like the sand, ready for new impressions. The elegant form of M. de Cymier slightly overshadowed it, distinct among other shadows more confused.

[131]

And Jacqueline said to herself with a smile, exactly what her father and Madame de Nailles had said to each other:

"Countess!—who knows? Ambassadress! Perhaps —some day——"

CHAPTER VIII

"BUT I can not see any reason why we should not take Jacqueline with us to Italy. She is just of an age to profit by it."

These words were spoken by M. de Nailles after a long silence at the breakfast-table. They startled his hearers like a bomb.

Jacqueline waited to hear what would come next, fixing a keen look upon her stepmother. Their eyes met like the flash of two swords.

The eyes of the one said: "Now, let us hear what you will answer!" while the other strove to maintain that calmness which comes to some people in a moment of danger. The Baroness grew a little pale, and then said, in her softest tones:

"You are quite right, *mon ami*, but Jacqueline, I think, prefers to stay."

"I decidedly prefer to stay," said Jacqueline.

Her adversary, much relieved by this response, could not repress a sigh.

"It seems singular," said M. de Nailles.

"What! that I prefer to pass a month or six weeks with Madame d'Argy? Besides, Giselle is going to be married during that time."

[133]

THÉO BENTZON

"They might put it off until we come back, I should suppose."

"Oh! I don't think they would," cried the Baroness. "Madame de Monredon is so selfish. She was offended to think we should talk of going away on the eve of an event she considers so important. Besides, she has so little regard for me that I should think her more likely to hasten the wedding-day rather than retard it, if it were only for the pleasure of giving us a lesson."

"I am sorry. I should have been glad to be, as she wished, one of Giselle's witnesses, but people don't take my position into consideration. If I do not take advantage of the recess——"

"Besides," interrupted Jacqueline, carelessly, "your journey must coincide with that of Monsieur Marien."

She had the pleasure of seeing her stepmother again slightly change color. Madame de Nailles was pouring out for herself a cup of tea with singular care and attention.

"Of course," said M. de Nailles. His daughter pitied him, and cried, with an increasing wish to annoy her stepmother: "Mamma, don't you see that your teapot has no tea in it? Yes," she went on, "it must be delightful to travel in Italy in company with a great artist who would explain everything; but then one would be expected to visit all the picture-galleries, and I hate pictures, since——"

She paused and again looked meaningly at her stepmother, whose soft blue eyes showed anguish of spirit, and seemed to say: "Oh, what a cruel hold she has upon me!" Jacqueline continued, carelessly:

JACQUELINE

"Picture-galleries I don't care for—I like nature a hundred times better. Some day I should like to take a journey to suit myself, my own journey! Oh, papa, may I? A journey on foot with you in the Tyrol?"

Madame de Nailles was no great walker.

"Both of us, just you and I alone, with our alpen-stocks in our hands—it would be lovely! But Italy and painters——"

Here, with a boyish flourish of her hands, she seemed to send that classic land to Jericho!

"Do promise me, papa!"

"Before asking a reward, you must deserve it," said her father, severely, who saw something was wrong.

During her stay at Lizerolles, which her perverseness, her resentment, and a repugnance founded on instincts of delicacy, had made her prefer to a journey to Italy, Jacqueline, having nothing better to do, took it into her head to write to her friend Fred. The young man received three letters at three different ports in the Mediterranean and in the West Indies, whose names were long associated in his mind with delightful and cruel recollections. When the first was handed to him with one from his mother, whose letters always awaited him at every stopping-place, the blood flew to his face, his heart beat violently, he could have cried aloud but for the necessity of self-command in the presence of his comrades, who had already remarked in whispers to each other, and with envy, on the pink envelope, which exhaled *l'odor di femina*. He hid his treasure quickly, and carried it to a spot where he could be alone; then he kissed the bold, pointed handwriting that he recog-

[135]

nized at once, though never before had it written his
address. He kissed, too, more than once, the pink
seal with a J on it, whose slender elegance reminded
him of its owner. Hardly did he dare to break the seal;
then forgetting altogether, as we might be sure, his
mother's letter, which he knew beforehand was full of
good advice and expressions of affection, he eagerly
read this, which he had not expected to receive:

"LIZEROLLES, October, 5, 188—

"MY DEAR FRED:

"Your mother thinks you would be pleased to receive a letter
from me, and I hope you will be. You need not answer this if
you do not care to do so. You will notice, *par parenthèse*, that
I take this opportunity of saying *you* and not *thou* to you. It is
easier to change the familiar mode of address in writing than in
speaking, and when we meet again the habit will have become
confirmed. But, as I write, it will require great attention, and
I can not promise to keep to it to the end. Half an hour's chat
with an old friend will also help me to pass the time, which I own
seems rather long, as it is passed by your sweet, dear mother and
myself at Lizerolles. Oh, if you were only here it would be different! In the first place, we should talk less of a certain Fred,
which would be one great advantage. You must know that you
are the subject of our discourse from morning to night; we talk
only of the dangers of the seas, the future prospects of a seaman,
and all the rest of it. If the wind is a little higher than usual,
your mother begins to cry; she is sure you are battling with a
tempest. If any fishing-boat is wrecked, we talk of nothing but
shipwrecks; and I am asked to join in another *novena*, in addition to those with which we must have already wearied Nôtre
Dame de Tréport. Every evening we spread out the map: 'See,
Jacqueline, he must be here now—no, he is almost there,' and
lines of red ink are traced from one port to another, and little
crosses are made to show the places where we hope you will get

[136]

JACQUELINE

your letters—'Poor boy, poor, dear boy!' In short, notwithstanding all the affectionate interest I take in you, this is sometimes too much for me. In fact, I think I must be very fond of thee not to have grown positively to hate thee for all this fuss. There! In this last sentence, instead of saying *you*, I have said *thee!* That ought to gild the pill for you!

We do not go very frequently to visit Tréport, except to invoke for you the protection of Heaven, and I like it just as well, for since the last fortnight in September, which was very rainy, the beach is dismal—so different from what it was in the summer. The town looks gloomy under a cloudy sky with its blackened old brick houses! We are better off at Lizerolles, whose autumnal beauties you know so well that I will say nothing about them. Oh, Fred, how often I regret that I am not a boy! I could take your gun and go shooting in the swamps, where there are clouds of ducks now. I feel sure that if you were in my place, you could kill time without killing game; but I am at the end of my small resources when I have played a little on the piano to amuse your mother and have read her the *Gazette de France.* In the evening we read a translation of some English novel. There are neighbors, of course, old fogies who stay all the year round in Picardy—but, tell me, don't you find them sometimes a little too respectable? My greatest comfort is in your dog, who loves me as much as if I were his master, though I can not take him out shooting. While I write he is lying on the hem of my gown and makes a little noise, as much as to tell me that I recall you to his remembrance. Yet you are not to suppose that I am suffering from *ennui*, or am ungrateful, nor above all must you imagine that I have ceased to love your excellent mother with all my heart. I love her, on the contrary, more than ever since I passed this winter through a great, great sorrow—a sorrow which is now only a sad remembrance, but which has changed for me the face of everything in this world. Yes, since I have suffered myself, I understand your mother. I admire her, I love her more than ever.

How happy you are, my dear Fred, to have such a sweet mother,

[137]

—a real mother who never thinks about her face, or her figure, or her age, but only of the success of her son; a dear little mother in a plain black gown, and with pretty gray hair, who has the manners and the toilette that just suit her, who somehow always seems to say: 'I care for nothing but that which affects my son.' Such mothers are rare, believe me. Those that I know, the mothers of my friends, are for the most part trying to appear as young as their daughters—nay, prettier, and of course more elegant. When they have sons they make them wear jackets *a l'anglaise* and turn-down collars, up to the age when I wore short skirts. Have you noticed that nowadays in Paris there are only ladies who are young, or who are trying to make themselves appear so? Up to the last moment they powder and paint, and try to make themselves different from what age has made them. If their hair was black it grows blacker—if red, it is more red. But there is no longer any gray hair in Paris—it is out of fashion. That is the reason why I think your mother's pretty silver curls so lovely and *distingués*. I kiss them every night for you, after I have kissed them for myself.

"Have a good voyage, come back soon, and take care of yourself, dear Fred."

The young sailor read this letter over and over again. The more he read it the more it puzzled him. Most certainly he felt that Jacqueline gave him a great proof of confidence when she spoke to him of some mysterious unhappiness, an unhappiness of which it was evident her stepmother was the cause. He could see that much; but he was infinitely far from suspecting the nature of the woes to which she alluded. Poor Jacqueline! He pitied her without knowing what for, with a great outburst of sympathy, and an honest desire to do anything in the world to make her happy. Was it really possible that she could have been enduring any grief that summer when she had seemed so madly gay, so ready for a little flirtation? Young girls must be very skilful in concealing their inmost feelings! When he was unhappy he had it out by himself, he took refuge in solitude, he wanted to be done with existence. Everybody knew when anything went wrong with him. Why could not Jacqueline have let him know more plainly what it was that troubled her, and why could she not have shown a little tenderness toward him, instead of assuming, even when she said the kindest things to him, her air of mockery? And then, though she might pretend not to find Lizerolles stupid, he could see that she was bored there. Yet why had she chosen to stay at Lizerolles rather than go to Italy?

Alas! how that little pink letter made him reflect and guess, and turn things over in his mind, and wish himself at the devil—that little pink letter which he carried day and night on his breast and made it crackle as it lay there, when he laid his hand on the satin folds so near his heart! It had an odor of sweet violets which seemed to him to overpower the smell of pitch and of salt water, to fill the air, to perfume everything.

"That young fellow has the instincts of a sailor," said his superior officers when they saw him standing in attitudes which they thought denoted observation, though with him it was only reverie. He would stand with his eyes fixed upon some distant point, whence he fancied he could see emerging from the waves a small, brown, shining head, with long hair streaming behind, the head of a girl swimming, a girl he knew so well.

"One can see that he takes an interest in nautical

phenomena, that he is heart and soul in his profession, that he cares for nothing else. Oh, he'll make a sailor! We may be sure of that!"

Fred sent his young friend and cousin, by way of reply, a big packet of manuscript, the leaves of which were of all sizes, over which he had poured forth torrents of poetry, amorous and descriptive, under the title: *At Sea*.

Never would he have dared to show her this if the ocean had not lain between them. He was frightened when his packet had been sent. His only comfort was in the thought that he had hypocritically asked Jacqueline for her literary opinion of his verses; but she could not fail, he thought, to understand.

Long before an answer could have been expected, he got another letter, sky-blue this time, much longer than the first, giving him an account of Giselle's wedding.

"Your mother and I went together to Normandy, where the marriage was to take place after the manner of old times, 'in the fashion of the Middle Ages,' as our friends the Wermants said to me, who might perhaps not have laughed at it had they been invited. Madame de Monredon is all for old customs, and she had made it a great point that the wedding should not take place in Paris. Had I been Giselle, I should not have liked it. I know nothing more elegant or more solemn than the entrance of a bridal party into the Madeleine, but we shall have to be content with Saint-Augustin. Still, the toilettes, as they pass up the aisle, even there, are very effective, and the decoration of the tall, high altar is magnificent. Toc! Toc! First come the beadles with their halberds, then the loud notes of the organ, then the wide doors are thrown open, making a noise as they turn on their great hinges, letting the noise of carriages outside be heard in the church;

JACQUELINE

and then comes the bride in a ray of sunshine. I could wish for
nothing more. A grand wedding in the country is much more
quiet, but it is old-fashioned. In the little village church the
guests were very much crowded, and outside there was a great
mob of country folk. Carpets had been laid down over the dilapi-
dated pavement, composed principally of tombstones. The rough
walls were hung with scarlet. All the clergy of the neighborhood
were present. A Monsignor—related to the Talbruns—pronounced the nuptial benediction; his address was a panegyric on
the two families. He gave us to understand that if he did not go
back quite as far as the Crusades, it was only because time was
wanting.

Madame de Monredon was all-glorious, of course. She certainly
looked like an old vulture, in a pelisse of gray velvet, with a chin-
chilla boa round her long, bare neck, and her big beak, with mar-
abouts overshadowing it, of the same color. Monsieur de Talbrun
—well! Monsieur de Talbrun was very bald, as bald as he could
be. To make up for the want of hair on his head, he has plenty of
it on his hands. It is horrid, and it makes him look like an animal.
You have no idea how queer he looked when he sat down, with his
big, pink head just peeping over the back of the crimson velvet
chair, which was, however, almost as tall as he is. He is short,
you may remember. As to our poor Giselle, the prettiest persons
sometimes look badly as brides, and those who are not pretty look
ugly. Do you recollect that picture—by Velasquez, is it not?—
of a fair little Infanta stiffly swathed in cloth of gold, as becomes
her dignity, and looking crushed by it? Giselle's gown was of
point d'Alençon, old family lace as yellow as ancient parchment,
but of inestimable value. Her long *corsage*, made in the fashion
of Anne of Austria, looked on her like a cuirass, and she dragged
after her, somewhat awkwardly, a very long train, which impeded
her movement as she walked. A lace veil, as hereditary and
time-worn as the gown, but which had been worn by all the Monredons at their weddings, the present dowager's included, hid the
pretty, light hair of our dear little friend, and was supported by a
sort of heraldic comb and some orange-flowers; in short, you can

not imagine anything more heavy or more ugly. Poor Giselle, loaded down with it, had red eyes, a face of misery, and the air of a martyr. For all this her grandmother scolded her sharply, which of course did not mend matters. *Du reste*, she seemed absorbed in prayer or thought during the ceremony, in which I took up the offerings, by the way, with a young lieutenant of dragoons just out of the military school at Saint Cyr: a uniform always looks well on such occasions. Nor was Monsieur de Talbrun one of those lukewarm Christians who hear mass with their arms crossed and their noses in the air. He pulled a jewelled prayer-book out of his pocket, which Giselle had given him. Speaking of presents, those he gave her were superb: pearls as big as hazel-nuts, a ruby heart that was a marvel, a diamond crescent that I am afraid she will never wear with such an air as it deserves, and two strings of diamonds *en rivière*, which I should suppose she would have reset, for *rivières* are no longer in fashion. The stones are enormous.

"But, poor dear! she could care little for such things. All she wanted was to get back as quickly as she could into her usual clothes. She said to me, again and again: 'Pray God for me that I may be a good wife. I am so afraid I may not be. To belong to Monsieur de Talbrun in this world, and in the next; to give up everything for him, seems so extraordinary. Indeed, I think I hardly knew what I was promising.' I felt sorry for her; I kissed her. I was ready to cry myself, and poor Giselle went on: 'If you knew, dear, how I love you! how I love all my friends! really to love, people must have been brought up together—must have always known each other.' I don't think she was right, but everybody has his or her ideas about such things. I tried, by way of consoling her, to draw her attention to the quantities of presents she had received. They were displayed on several tables in the smaller drawing-room, but her grandmother would not let them put the name of the giver upon each, as is the present custom. She said that it humiliated those who had not been able to make gifts as expensive as others. She is right, when one comes to think of it. Nor would she let the trousseau be displayed; she did not think

JACQUELINE

it proper, but I saw enough to know that there were marvels in linen, muslin, silks, and surahs, covered all over with lace. One could see that the great mantuamaker had not consulted the grandmother, who says that women of distinction in her day did not wear paltry trimmings.

"Dinner was served under a tent for all the village people during the two mortal hours we had to spend over a repast, in which Madame de Monredon's cook excelled himself. Then came complimentary addresses in the old-fashioned style, composed by the village schoolmaster who, for a wonder, knew what he was about; groups of village children, boys and girls, came bringing their offerings, followed by pet lambs decked with ribbons; it was all in the style of the days of Madame de Genlis. While we danced in the salons there was dancing in the barn, which had been decorated for the occasion. In short, lords and ladies and laborers all seemed to enjoy themselves, or made believe they did. The Parisian gentlemen who danced were not very numerous. There were a few friends of Monsieur de Talbrun's, however—among them, a Monsieur de Cymier, whom possibly you remember having seen last summer at Tréport; he led the cotillon divinely. The bride and bridegroom drove away during the evening, as they do in England, to their own house, which is not far off. Monsieur de Talbrun's horses—a magnificent pair, harnessed to a new *calèche*—carried off Psyche, as an old gentleman in gold spectacles said near me. He was a pretentious old personage, who made a speech at table, very inappropriate and much applauded. Poor Giselle! I have not seen her since, but she has written me one of those little notes which, when she was in the convent, she used to sign *Enfant de Marie*. It begged me again to pray earnestly for her that she might not fail in the fulfilment of her new duties. It seems hard, does it not? Let us hope that Monsieur de Talbrun, on his part, may not find that his new life rather wearies him! Do you know what should have been Giselle's fate—since she has a mania about people being thoroughly acquainted before marriage? What would two or three years more or less have mattered? She would have made an admirable wife for a sailor; she would have spent the months of your absence kneeling before the altar; she would have multiplied the lamentations and the tendernesses of your excellent mother. I have been thinking this ever since the wedding-day—a very sad day, after all.

"But how I have let my pen run on. I shall have to put on two stamps, notwithstanding my thin paper. But then you have plenty of time to read on board-ship, and this account may amuse you. Make haste and thank me for it.

"Your old friend,   "JACQUELINE."

Amuse him! How could he be amused by so great an insult? What! thank her for giving him over even in thought to Giselle or to anybody? Oh, how wicked, how ungrateful, how unworthy!

The six pages of foreign-post paper were crumpled up by his angry fingers. Fred tore them with his teeth, and finally made them into a ball which he flung into the sea, hating himself for having been so foolish as to let himself be caught by the first lines, as a foolish fish snaps at the bait, when, *àpropos* to the church in which she would like to be married, she had added: "But *we* should have to be content with Saint-Augustin."

Those words had delighted him as if they had really been meant for himself and Jacqueline. This promise for the future, that seemed to escape involuntarily from her pen, had made him find all the rest of her letter piquant and amusing. As he read, his mind had reverted to that little phrase which he now found he had interpreted wrongly. What a fall! How his hopes now crumbled under his feet! She must have done it on purpose—but no, he need not blacken her! She had

JACQUELINE

written without thought, without purpose, in high spirits; she wanted to be witty, to be droll, to write gossip without any reference to him to whom her letter was addressed. That *we* who some day would make a triumphal entry into St. Augustin would be herself and some other man—some man with whom her acquaintance had been short, since she did not seem to feel in that matter like Giselle. Some one she did not yet know? Was that sure? She might know her future husband already, even now she might have made her choice—Marcel d'Etaples, perhaps, who looked so well in uniform, or that M. de Cymier, who led the cotillon so divinely. Yes! No doubt it was he—the last-comer. And once more Fred suffered all the pangs of jealousy. It seemed to him that in his loneliness, between sky and sea, those pangs were more acute than he had ever known them. His comrades teased him about his melancholy looks, and made him the butt of all their jokes in the cockpit. He resolved, however, to get over it, and at the next port they put into, Jacqueline's letter was the cause of his entering for the first time some discreditable scenes of dissipation.

At Bermuda he received another letter, dated from Paris, where Jacqueline had rejoined her parents, who had returned from Italy. She sent him a commission. Would he buy her a riding-whip? Bermuda was renowned for its horsewhips, and her father had decided that she must go regularly to the riding-school. They seemed anxious now to give her, as preliminary to her introduction into society, not only such pleasures as

10   [145]

horseback exercise, but intellectual enjoyment also. She had been taken to the Institute to hear M. Legouvé, and what was better still, in December her stepmother would give a little party every fortnight and would let her sit up till eleven o'clock. She was also to be taken to make some calls. In short, she felt herself rising in importance, but the first thing that had made her feel so was Fred's choice of her to be his literary confidant. She was greatly obliged to him, and did not know how she could better prove to him that she was worthy of so great an honor than by telling him quite frankly just what she thought of his verses. They were very, very pretty. He had talent—great talent. Only, as in attending the classes of M. Regis she had acquired some little knowledge of the laws of versification, she would like to warn him against impairing a thought for the benefit of a rhyme, and she pointed out several such places in his compositions, ending thus:

"Bravo! for sunsets, for twilights, for moonshine, for deep silence, for starry nights, and silvery seas—in such things you excel; one feels as if one were there, and one envies you the fairy scenes of ocean. But, I implore you, be not sentimental. That is the feeble part of your poetry, to my thinking, and spoils the rest. By the way, I should like to ask you whose are those soft eyes, that silky hair, that radiant smile, and all that assortment of amber, jet, and coral occurring so often in your visions? Is she— or rather, are they—black, yellow, green, or tattooed, for, of course, you have met everywhere beauties of all colors? Several times when it appeared as if the lady of your dreams were white, I fancied you were drawing a portrait of Isabelle Ray. All the girls, your old friends, to whom I have shown At Sea, send you their compliments, to which I join my own. Each of them will beg you to write her a sonnet; but first of all, in virtue of our ancient friendship, I want one myself.

"JACQUELINE."

So! she had shown to others what was meant for her alone; what profanation! And what was more abominable, she had not recognized that he was speaking of herself. Ah! there was nothing to be done now but to forget her. Fred tried to do so conscientiously during all his cruise in the Atlantic, but the moment he got ashore and had seen Jacqueline, he fell again a victim to her charms.

CHAPTER IX

BEAUTY AT THE FAIR

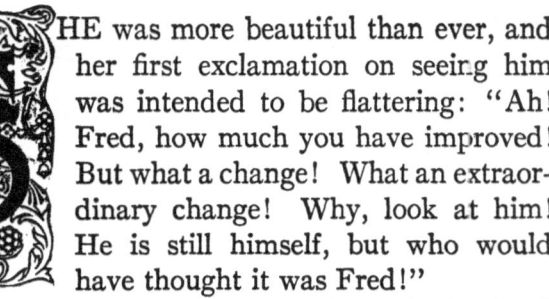HE was more beautiful than ever, and her first exclamation on seeing him was intended to be flattering: "Ah! Fred, how much you have improved! But what a change! What an extraordinary change! Why, look at him! He is still himself, but who would have thought it was Fred!"

He was not disconcerted, for he had acquired *aplomb* in his journeys round the globe, but he gave her a glance of sad reproach, while Madame de Nailles said, quietly:

"Yes, really—How are you, Fred? The tan on your face is very becoming to you. You have broadened at the shoulders, and are now a man—something more than a man, an experienced sailor, almost an old sea-dog."

And she laughed, but only softly, because a frank laugh would have shown little wrinkles under her eyes and above her cheeks, which were getting too large.

Her toilette, which was youthful, yet very carefully adapted to her person, showed that she was by no means as yet "laid on the shelf," as Raoul Wermant elegantly said of her. She stood up, leaning over a table covered with toys, which it was her duty to sell at the highest price possible, for the place of a meeting so full of emotions for Fred was a charity bazaar.

The moment he arrived in Paris the young officer had been, so to speak, seized by the collar. He had found a great glazed card, bidding him to attend this fair, in a fashionable quarter, and forthwith he had forgotten his resolution of not going near the Nailles for a long time.

"This is not the same thing," he said to himself. "One must not let one's self be supposed to be stingy." So with these thoughts he went to the bazaar, very glad in his secret heart to have an excuse for breaking his resolution.

The fair was for the benefit of sufferers from a fire— somewhere or other. In our day multitudes of people fall victims to all kinds of dreadful disasters, explosions of boilers, explosions of fire-damp, of everything that *can* explode, for the agents of destruction seem to be in a state of unnatural excitement as well as human beings. Never before, perhaps, have inanimate things seemed so much in accordance with the spirit of the times. Fred found a superb placard, the work of Chéret, a pathetic scene in a mine, banners streaming in the air, with the words *Bazar de Charité* in gold letters on a red ground, and the courtyard of the mansion where the fair was held filled with more carriages than one sees at a fashionable wedding. In the vestibule many footmen were in attendance, the *chasseurs* of an Austrian ambassador, the great hulking fellows of the English embassy, the gray-liveried servants of old Rozenkranz, with their powdered heads, the negro man belonging to Madame Azucazillo, etc., etc. At each arrival there was a *frou-frou* of satin and lace, and inside the sales-room was a hubbub like the noise in an aviary. Fred, finding himself at once in the full stream of Parisian life, but for the moment not yet part of it, indulged in some of those philosophic reflections to which he had been addicted on shipboard.

Each of the tables showed something of the tastes, the character, the peculiarities of the lady who had it in charge. Madame Sterny, who had the most beautiful hands in the world, had undertaken to sell gloves, being sure that the gentlemen would be eager to buy if she would only consent to try them on; Madame de Louis-grif, the *chanoiness*, whose extreme emaciation was not perceived under a sort of ecclesiastical cape, had an assortment of embroideries and objects of devotion, in-tended only for ladies—and indeed for only the most serious among them; for the table that held umbrellas, parasols and canes suited to all ages and both sexes, a good, upright little lady had been chosen. Her only thought was how much money she could make by her sales. Madame Strahlberg, the oldest of the Odin-skas, obviously expected to sell only to gentlemen; her table held pyramids of cigars and cigarettes, but noth-ing else was in the corner where she presided, *souple* and frail, not handsome, but far more dangerous than if she had beên, with her unfathomable way of looking at you with her light eyes set deep under her eyebrows, eyes that she kept half closed, but which were yet so keen, and the cruel smile that showed her little sharp

JACQUELINE

teeth. Her dress was of black grenadine embroidered with silver. She wore half mourning as a sort of announcement that she was a widow, in hopes that this might put a stop to any wicked gossip which should assert that Count Strahlberg was still living, having got a divorce and been very glad to get it. Yet people talked about her, but hardly knew what to bring against her, because, though anything might be suspected, nothing was known. She was received and even sought after in the best society, on account of her wonderful talents, which she employed in a manner as perverse as everything else about her, but which led some people to call her the *Judic des salons*. Wanda Strahlberg was now holding between her lips, which were artificially red, in contrast to the greenish paleness of her face, which caused others to call her a vampire, one of the cigarettes she had for sale. With one hand, she was playing, graceful as a cat, with her last package of regalias, tied with green ribbon, which, when offered to the highest bidder, brought an enormous sum. Her sister Colette was selling flowers, like several other young girls, but while for the most part these waited on their customers in silence, she was full of lively talk, and as unblushing in her eagerness to sell as a *bouquetière* by profession. She had grown dangerously pretty. Fred was dazzled when she wanted to fasten a rose into his buttonhole, and then, as he paid for it, gave him another, saying: "And here is another thrown in for old acquaintance' sake."

"Charity seems to cover many things," thought the young man as he withdrew from her smiles and her

[151]

glances, but yet he had seen nothing so attractive among the black, yellow, green or tattooed ladies about whom Jacqueline had been pleased to tease him.

"Fred!"

It was Jacqueline's voice that arrested him. It was sharp and almost angry. She, too, was selling flowers, while at the same time she was helping Madame de Nailles with her toys; but she was selling with that decorum and graceful reserve which custom prescribes for young girls. "Fred, I do hope you will wear no roses but mine. Those you have are frightful. They make you look like a village bridegroom. Take out those things; come! Here is a pretty *boutonnière*, and I will fasten it much better in your buttonhole—let me."

In vain did he try to seem cold to her; his heart thawed in spite of himself. She held him so charmingly by the lapel of his coat, touching his cheek with the tip end of an *aigrette* which set so charmingly on the top of the most becoming of fur caps which she wore. Her hair was turned up now, showing her beautiful neck, and he could see little rebellious hairs curling at their own will over her pure, soft skin, while she, bending forward, was engaged in his service. He admired, too, her slender waist, only recently subjected to the restraint of a corset. He forgave her on the spot. At this moment a man with brown hair, tall, elegant, and with his moustache turned up at the ends, after the old fashion of the Valois, revived recently, came hurriedly up to the table of Madame de Nailles. Fred felt that that inimitable moustache reduced his not yet abundant beard to nothing.

JACQUELINE

"Mademoiselle Jacqueline," said the newcomer, "Madame de Villegry has sent me to beg you to help her at the buffet. She can not keep pace with her customers, and is asking for volunteers."

All this was uttered with a familiar assurance which greatly shocked the young naval man.

"You permit me, Madame?"

The Baroness bowed with a smile, which said, had he chosen to interpret it, "I give you permission to carry her off now—and forever, if you wish it."

At that moment she was placing in the half-unwilling arms of Hubert Marien an enormous rubber balloon and a jumping-jack, in return for five *louis* which he had laid humbly on her table. But Jacqueline had not waited for her stepmother's permission; she let herself be borne off radiant on the arm of the important personage who had come for her, while Colette, who perhaps had remarked the substitution for her two roses, whispered in Fred's ear, in a tone of great significance: "Monsieur de Cymier."

The poor fellow started, like a man suddenly awakened from a happy dream to face the most unwelcome of realities. Impelled by that natural longing, that we all have, to know the worst, he went toward the buffet, affecting a calmness which it cost him a great effort to maintain. As he went along he mechanically gave money to each of the ladies whom he knew, moving off without waiting for their thanks or stopping to choose anything from their tables. He seemed to feel the floor rock under his feet, as if he had been walking the deck of a vessel. At last he reached a recess decorated with palms, where, in a robe worthy of *Peau d'Ane* in the story, and absolutely a novelty in the world of fashion— a robe all embroidered with gold and rubies, which glittered with every movement made by the wearer— Madame de Villegry was pouring out Russian tea and Spanish chocolate and Turkish coffee, while all kinds of deceitful promises of favor shone in her eyes, which wore a certain tenderness expressive of her interest in charity. A party of young nymphs formed the court of this fair goddess, doing their best to lend her their aid. Jacqueline was one of them, and, at the moment Fred approached, she was offering, with the tips of her fingers, a glass of champagne to M. de Cymier, who at the same time was eagerly trying to persuade her to believe something, about which she was gayly laughing, while she shook her head. Poor Fred, that he might hear, and suffer, drank two mouthfuls of sherry which he could hardly swallow.

"One who was really charitable would not hesitate," said M. de Cymier, "especially when every separate hair would be paid for if you chose. Just one little curl—for the sake of the poor. It is very often done: anything is allowable for the sake of the poor."

"Maybe it is because, as you say, that it is very often done that I shall not do it," said Jacqueline, still laughing. "I have made up my mind never to do what others have done before me."

"Well, we shall see," said M. de Cymier, pretending to threaten her.

And her young head was thrown back in a burst of inextinguishable laughter.

JACQUELINE

Fred fled, that he might not be tempted to make a disturbance.

When he found himself again in the street, he asked himself where he should go. His anger choked him; he felt he could not keep his resentment to himself, and yet, however angry he might be with Jacqueline, he would have been unwilling to hear his mother give utterance to the very sentiments that he was feeling, or to harsh judgments, of which he preferred to keep the monopoly. It came into his mind that he would pay a little visit to Giselle, who, of all the people he knew, was the least likely to provoke a quarrel. He had heard that Madame de Talbrun did not go out, being confined to her sofa by much suffering, which, it might be hoped, would soon come to an end; and the certainty that he should find her if he called at once decided him. Since he had been in Paris he had done nothing but leave cards. This time, however, he was sure that the lady upon whom he called would be at home.

He was taken at once into the young wife's boudoir, where he found her very feeble, lying back upon her cushions, alone, and working at some little bits of baby-clothes. He was not slow to perceive that she was very glad to see him. She flushed with pleasure as he came into the room, and, dropping her sewing, held out to him two little, thin hands, white as wax.

"Take that footstool—sit down there—what a great, great pleasure it is to see you back again!" She was more expansive than she had been formerly; she had gained a certain ease which comes from intercourse with the world, but how delicate she seemed! Fred for a moment looked at her in silence, she seemed so changed as she lay there in a loose robe of pale blue cashmere, whose train drawn over her feet made her look tall as it stretched to the end of the gilded couch, round which Giselle had collected all the little things required by an invalid—bottles, boxes, work-bag, dressing-case, and writing materials.

"You see," she said, with her soft smile, "I have plenty to occupy me, and I venture to be proud of my work and to think I am creating marvels."

As she spoke she turned round on her closed hand a cap that seemed microscopic to Fred.

"What!" he cried, "do you expect him to be small enough to wear that!"

"*Him!* you said *him;* and I am sure you will be right. I know it will be a boy," replied Giselle, eagerly, her fair face brightened by these words. "I have some that are still smaller. Look!" and she lifted up a pile of things trimmed with ribbons and embroidery. "See, these are the first! Ah! I lie here and fancy how he will look when he has them on. He will be sweet enough to eat. Only his papa wants us to give him a name that I think is too long for him, because it has always been in the family—Enguerrand."

"His name will be longer than himself, I should say, judging by the dimensions of this cap," said Fred, trying to laugh.

"Bah!" replied Giselle, gayly, "but we can get over it by calling him Gué-gué or Ra-ra. What do you think? The difficulty is that names of that kind are apt to stick to a boy for fifty years, and then they seem ridiculous. Now a pretty abbreviation like Fred is another matter. But I forget they have brought up my chocolate. Please ring, and let them bring you a cup. We will take our luncheon together, as we used to do."

"Thank you, I have no appetite. I have just come from a certain buffet where I lost it all."

"Oh! I suppose you have been to the Bazaar—the famous Charity Fair! You must have made a sensation there on your return, for I am told that the gentlemen who are expected to spend the most are likely to send their money, and not to show themselves. There are many complaints of it."

"There were plenty of men round certain persons," replied Fred, dryly. "Madame de Villegry's table was literally besieged."

"Really! What, hers! You surprise me! So it was the good things she gave you that make you despise my poor chocolate," said Giselle, rising on her elbow, to receive the smoking cup that a servant brought her on a little silver salver.

"I didn't take much at her table," said Fred, ready to enter on his grievances. "If you wish to know the reason why, I was too indignant to eat or drink."

"Indignant?"

"Yes, the word is not at all too strong. When one has passed whole months away from what is unwholesome and artificial, such things as make up life in Paris, one becomes a little like Alceste, Molière's misanthrope, when one gets back to them. It is ridiculous at my age, and yet if I were to tell you——"

"What?—you puzzle me. What can there be that is unwholesome in selling things for the poor?"

"The poor! A pretty pretext! Was it to benefit the poor that that odious Countess Strahlberg made all those disreputable grimaces? I have seen *kermesses* got up by actresses, and, upon my word, they were good form in comparison."

"Oh! Countess Strahlberg! People have heard about her doings until they are tired of them," said Giselle, with that air of knowing everything assumed by a young wife whose husband has told her all the current scandals, as a sort of initiation.

"And her sister seems likely to be as bad as herself before long."

"Poor Colette! She has been so badly brought up. It is not her fault."

"But there's Jacqueline," cried Fred, in a sudden outburst, and already feeling better because he could mention her name.

· "*Allons, donc!* You don't mean to say anything against Jacqueline?" cried Giselle, clasping her hands with an air of astonishment. "What can she have done to scandalize you—poor little dear?"

Fred paused for half a minute, then he drew the stool in the form of an X, on which he was sitting, a little nearer to Giselle's sofa, and, lowering his voice, told her how Jacqueline had acted under his very eyes. As he went on, watching as he spoke the effect his words produced upon Giselle, who listened as if slightly amused by his indignation, the case seemed not nearly so bad as he had supposed, and a delicious sense of

relief crept over him when she to whom he told his
wrongs, after hearing him quietly to the end, said,
smiling:

"And what then? There is no great harm in all that.
Would you have had her refuse to go with the gentleman
Madame de Villegry had sent to fetch her? And why,
may I ask, should she not have done her best to help
by pouring out champagne? An air put on to please
is indispensable to a woman, if she wishes to sell anything. Good Heavens! I don't approve any more
than you do of all these worldly forms of charity, but
this kind of thing is considered right; it has come into
fashion. Jacqueline had the permission of her parents,
and I really can't see any good reason why you should
complain of her. Unless—why not tell me the whole
truth, Fred? I know it—don't we always know what
concerns the people that we care for? And I might
possibly some day be of use to you. Say! don't you
think you are—a little bit jealous?"

Less encouragement than this would have sufficed to
make him open his heart to Giselle. He was delighted
that some woman was willing he should confide in her.
And what was more, he was glad to have it proved that
he had been all wrong. A quarter of an hour later
Giselle had comforted him, happy herself that it had
been in her power to undertake a task of consolation,
a work in which, with sweet humility, she felt herself
at ease. On the great stage of life she knew now she
should never play any important part, any that would
bring her greatly into view. But she felt that she was
made to be a confidant, one of those perfect confidants

who never attempt to interfere rashly with the course
of events, but who wait upon the ways of Providence,
removing stones, and briers and thorns, and making
everything turn out for the best in the end. Jacqueline, she said, was so young! A little wild, perhaps, but
what a treasure! She was all heart! She would need
a husband worthy of her, such a man as Fred. Madame d'Argy, she knew, had already said something on
the subject to her father. But it would have to be the
Baroness that Fred must bring over to their views; the
Baroness was acquiring more and more influence over
her husband, who seemed to be growing older every
day. M. de Nailles had evidently much, very much
upon his mind. It was said in business circles that he
had for some time past been given to speculation.
Oscar said so. If that were the case, many of Jacqueline's suitors might withdraw. Not all men were so
disinterested as Fred.

"Oh! As to her *dot*—what do I care for her *dot?*"
cried the young man. "I have enough for two, if she
would only be satisfied to live quietly at Lizerolles!"

"Yes," said the judicious little matron, nodding her
head, "but who would like to marry a midshipman?
Make haste and be a lieutenant, or an ensign."

She smiled at herself for having made the reward
depend upon exertion, with a sort of maternal instinct.
It was the same instinct that would lead her in the
future to promise Enguerrand a sugar-plum if he said
his lesson. "Nobody will steal your Jacqueline till you
are ready to carry her off. Besides, if there were any
danger I could give you timely warning."

JACQUELINE

"Ah! Giselle, if she only had your kind heart—your good sense."

"Do you think I am better and more reasonable than other people? In what way? I have done as so many other girls do; I have married without knowing well what I was doing."

She stopped short, fearing she might have said too much, and indeed Fred looked at her anxiously.

"You don't regret it, do you?"

"You must ask Monsieur de Talbrun if he regrets it," she said, with a laugh. "It must be hard on him to have a sick wife, who knows little of what is passing outside of her own chamber, who is living on her reserve fund of resources—a very poor little reserve fund it is, too!"

Then, as if she thought that Fred had been with her long enough, she said: "I would ask you to stay and see Monsieur de Talbrun, but he won't be in, he dines at his club. He is going to see a new play to-night which they say promises to be very good."

"What! Will he leave you alone all the evening?"

"Oh! I am very glad he should find amusement. Just think how long it is that I have been pinned down here! Poor Oscar!"

CHAPTER X

THE arrival of the expected Enguerrand hindered Giselle from pleading Fred's cause as soon as she could have wished. Her life for twenty-four hours was in great danger, and when the crisis was past, which M. de Talbrun treated very indifferently, as a matter of course, her first cry was "My baby!" uttered in a tone of tender eagerness such as had never been heard from her lips before.

The nurse brought him. He lay asleep swathed in his swaddling clothes like a mummy in its wrappings, a motionless, mysterious being, but he seemed to his mother beautiful—more beautiful than anything she had seen in those vague visions of happiness she had indulged in at the convent, which were never to be realized. She kissed his little purple face, his closed eyelids, his puckered mouth, with a sort of respectful awe. She was forbidden to fatigue herself. The wet-nurse, who had been brought from Picardy, drew near with her peasant cap trimmed with long blue streamers; her big, experienced hands took the baby from his mother, she turned him over on her lap, she patted him, she laughed at him. And the mother-happiness that had lighted up Giselle's pale face died away.

JACQUELINE

"What right," she thought, "has that woman to my child?" She envied the horrid creature, coarse and stout, with her tanned face, her bovine features, her shapeless figure, who seemed as if Nature had predestined her to give milk and nothing more. Giselle would so gladly have been in her place! Why wouldn't they permit her to nurse her baby?

M. de Talbrun said in answer to this question:

"It is never done among people in our position. You have no idea of all it would entail on you—what slavery, what fatigue! And most probably you would not have had milk enough."

"Oh! who can tell? I am his mother! And when this woman goes he will have to have English nurses, and when he is older he will have to go to school. When shall I have him to myself?"

And she began to cry.

"Come, come!" said M. de Talbrun, much astonished, "all this fuss about that frightful little monkey!"

Giselle looked at him almost as much astonished as he had been at her. Love, with its jealousy, its transports, its anguish, its delights had for the first time come to her—the love that she could not feel for her husband awoke in her for her son. She was ennobled —she was transfigured by a sense of her maternity; it did for her what marriage does for some women—it seemed as if a sudden radiance surrounded her.

When she raised her infant in her arms, to show him to those who came to see her, she always seemed like a most chaste and touching representation of the Virgin Mother. She would say, as she exhibited him: "Is he

[163]

not superb?" Every one said: "Yes, indeed!" out of politeness, but, on leaving the mother's presence, would generally remark: "He is Monsieur de Talbrun in baby-clothes: the likeness is perfectly horrible!"

The only visitor who made no secret of this impression was Jacqueline, who came to see her cousin as soon as she was permitted—that is, as soon as her friend was able to sit up and be prettily dressed, as became the mother of such a little gentleman as the heir of all the Talbruns. When Jacqueline saw the little creature half-smothered in the lace that trimmed his pillows, she burst out laughing, though it was in the presence of his mother.

"Oh, *mon Dieu!*" she cried, "how ugly! I never should have supposed we could have been as ugly as that! Why, his face is all the colors of the rainbow; who would have imagined it? And he crumples up his little face like those things in gutta-percha. My poor Giselle, how can you bear to show him! I never, never could covet a baby!"

Giselle, in consternation, asked herself whether this strange girl, who did not care for children, could be a proper wife for Fred; but her habitual indulgence came to her aid, and she thought:

"She is but a child herself, she does not know what she is saying," and profiting by her first *tête-à-tête* with Jacqueline's stepmother, she spoke as she had promised to Madame de Nailles.

"A matchmaker already!" said the Baroness, with a smile. "And so soon after you have found out what it costs to be a mother! How good of you, my dear

JACQUELINE

Giselle! So you support Fred as a candidate? But I can't say I think he has much chance; Monsieur de Nailles has his own ideas."

She spoke as if she really thought that M. de Nailles could have any ideas but her own. When the adroit Clotilde was at a loss, she was likely to evoke this chimerical notion of her husband's having an opinion of his own.

"Oh! Madame, you can do anything you like with him!"

The clever woman sighed:

"So you fancy that when people have been long married a wife retains as much influence over her husband as you have kept over Monsieur de Talbrun? You will learn to know better, my dear."

"But I have no influence," murmured Giselle, who knew herself to be her husband's slave.

"Oh! I know better. You are making believe!"

"Well, but we were not talking about me, but——"

"Oh! yes. I understood. I will think about it. I will try to bring over Monsieur de Nailles."

She was not at all disposed to drop the meat for the sake of the shadow, but she was not sure of M. de Cymier, notwithstanding all that Madame de Villegry was at pains to tell her about his serious intentions. On the other hand, she would have been far from willing to break with a man so brilliant, who made himself so agreeable at her Tuesday receptions.

"Meantime, it would be well if you, dear, were to try to find out what Jacqueline thinks. You may not find it very easy."

THÉO BENTZON

"Will you authorize me to tell her how well he loves her? Oh, then, I am quite satisfied!" cried Giselle.

But she was under a mistake. Jacqueline, as soon as she began to speak to her of Fred's suit, stopped her:

"Poor fellow! Why can't he amuse himself for some time longer and let me do the same? Men seem to me so strange! Now, Fred is one who, just because he is good and serious by nature, fancies that everybody else should be the same; he wishes me to be tethered in the flowery meads of Lizerolles, and browse where he would place me. Such a life would be an end of everything—an end to my life, and I should not like it at all. I should prefer to grow old in Paris, or some other capital, if my husband happened to be engaged in diplomacy. Even supposing I marry—which I do not think an absolute necessity, unless I can not get rid otherwise of an inconvenient chaperon—and to do my stepmother justice, she knows well enough that I will not submit to too much of her dictation!"

"Jacqueline, they say you see too much of the Odinskas."

"There! that's another fault you find in me. I go there because Madame Strahlberg is so kind as to give me some singing-lessons. If you only knew how much progress I am making, thanks to her. Music is a thousand times more interesting, I can tell you, than all that you can do as mistress of a household. You don't think so? Oh! I know—Enguerrand's first tooth, his first steps, his first gleams of intelligence, and all that. Such things are not in my line, you know. Of course I think your boy very funny, very cunning, very—anything you like to fancy him, but forgive me if I am glad he does not belong to me. There, don't you see now that marriage is not my vocation, so please give up speaking to me about matrimony."

"As you will," said Giselle, sadly, "but you will give great pain to a good man whose heart is wholly yours."

"I did not ask for his heart. Such gifts are exasperating. One does not know what to do with them. Can't he—poor Fred—love me as I love him, and leave me my liberty?"

"Your liberty!" exclaimed Giselle; "liberty to ruin your life, that's what it will be."

"Really, one would suppose there was only one kind of existence in your eyes—this life of your own, Giselle. To leave one cage to be shut up in another—that is the fate of many birds, I know, but there are others who like to use their wings to soar into the air. I like that expression. Come, little mother, tell me right out, plainly, that your lot is the only one in this world that ought to be envied by a woman."

Giselle answered with a strange smile:

"You seem astonished that I adore my baby; but since he came great things seem to have been revealed to me. When I hold him to my breast I seem to understand, as I never did before, duty and marriage, family ties and sorrows, life itself, in short, its griefs and joys. You can not understand that now, but you will some day. You, too, will gaze upon the horizon as I do. I am ready to suffer; I am ready for self-sacrifice. I know now whither my life leads me. I am led, as it were, by this little being, who seemed to me at first only

[167]

a doll, for whom I was embroidering caps and dresses.
You ask whether I am satisfied with my lot in life.
Yes, I am, thanks to this guide, this guardian angel,
thanks to my precious Enguerrand."

Jacqueline listened, stupefied, to this unexpected outburst, so unlike her cousin's usual language; but the
charm was broken by its ending with the tremendous-
ly long name of Enguerrand, which always made her
laugh, it was in such perfect harmony with the feudal
pretensions of the Monredons and the Talbruns.

"How solemn and eloquent and obscure you are, my
dear," she answered. "You speak like a sibyl. But
one thing I see, and that is that you are not so perfectly
happy as you would have us believe, seeing that you
feel the need of consolations. Then, why do you wish
me to follow your example?"

"Fred is not Monsieur de Talbrun," said the young
wife, for the moment forgetting herself.

"Do you mean to say——"

"I meant nothing, except that if you married Fred
you would have had the advantage of first knowing
him."

"Ah! that's your fixed idea. But I am getting to
know Monsieur de Cymier pretty well."

"You have betrayed yourself," cried Giselle, with indignation. "Monsieur de Cymier!"

"Monsieur de Cymier is coming to our house on
Saturday evening, and I must get up a Spanish song
that Madame Strahlberg has taught me, to charm his
ears and those of other people. Oh! I can do it very
well. Won't you come and hear me play the castanets,

if Monsieur Enguerrand can spare you? There is a
young Polish pianist who is to play our accompaniment.
Ah, there is nothing like a Polish pianist to play Chopin!
He is charming, poor young man! an exile, and in poverty; but he is cared for by those ladies, who take him
everywhere. That is the sort of life I should like—the
life of Madame Strahlberg—to be a young widow,
free to do what I pleased."

"She may be a widow—but some say she is divorced."

"Oh! is it you who repeat such naughty scandals,
Giselle? Where shall charity take refuge in this world
if not in your heart? I am going—your seriousness
may be catching. Kiss me before I go."

"No," said Madame de Talbrun, turning her head
away.

After this she asked herself whether she ought not
to discourage Fred. She could not resolve on doing
so, yet she could not tell him what was false; but by
eluding the truth with that ability which kind-hearted
women can always show when they try to avoid inflict-
ing pain, she succeeded in leaving the young man hope
enough to stimulate his ambition.

CHAPTER XI

IME, whatever may be said of it by the calendars, is not to be measured by days, weeks, and months in all cases; expectation, hope, happiness and grief have very different ways of counting hours, and we know from our own experience that some are as short as a minute, and others as long as a century. The love or the suffering of those who can tell just how long they have suffered, or just how long they have been in love, is only moderate and reasonable.

Madame d'Argy found the two lonely years she passed awaiting the return of her son, who was winning his promotion to the rank of ensign, so long, that it seemed to her as if they never would come to an end. She had given a reluctant consent to his notion of adopting the navy as a profession, thinking that perhaps, after all, there might be no harm in allowing her dear boy to pass the most dangerous period of his youth under strict discipline, but she could not be patient forever! She idolized her son too much to be resigned to living without him; she felt that he was hers no longer. Either he was at sea or at Toulon, where she could very rarely join him, being detained at Lizerolles by the necessity of looking after their property. With what eagerness she awaited his promotion, which she did not doubt was all the Nailles waited for to give their consent to the marriage; of their happy half-consent she hastened to remind them in a note which announced the new grade to which he had been promoted. Her indignation was great on finding that her formal request received no decided answer; but, as her first object was Fred's happiness, she placed the reply she had received in its most favorable light when she forwarded it to the person whom it most concerned. She did this in all honesty. She was not willing to admit that she was being put off with excuses; still less could she believe in a refusal.

She accepted the excuse that M. de Nailles gave for returning no decided answer, viz.: that "Jacqueline was too young," though she answered him with some vehemence: "Fred was born when I was eighteen." But she had to accept it. Her ensign would have to pass a few more months on the coast of Senegal, a few more months which were made shorter by the encouragement forwarded to him by his mother, who was careful to send him everything she could find out that seemed to be, or that she imagined might be, in his favor; she underlined such things and commented upon them, so as to make the faintest hypothesis seem a certainty. Sometimes she did not even wait for the post. Fred would find, on putting in at some post, a cablegram: "Good news," or "All goes well," and he would be beside himself with joy and excitement until, on receiving his poor, dear mother's next letter, he found out on how slight a foundation her assurance had been founded.

Sometimes, she wrote him disagreeable things about Jacqueline, as if she would like to disenchant him, and then he said to himself: "By this, I am to understand that my affairs are not going on well; I still count for little, notwithstanding my promotion." Ah! if he could only have had, so near the beginning of his career, any opportunity of distinguishing himself! No brilliant deed would have been too hard for him. He would have scaled the very skies. Alas! he had had no chance to win distinction, he had only had to follow in the beaten track of ordinary duty; he had encountered no glorious perils, though at St. Louis he had come very near leaving his bones, but it was only a case of typhoid fever. This fever, however, brought about a scene between M. de Nailles and his mother.

"When," she cried, with all the fury of a lioness, "do you expect to come to the conclusion that my son is a suitable match for Jacqueline? Do you imagine that I shall let him wait till he is a post-captain to satisfy the requirements of Mademoiselle your daughter —provided he does not die in a hospital? Do you think that I shall be willing to go on living—if you can call it living!—all alone and in continual apprehension? Why do you let him keep on in uncertainty? You know his worth, and you know that with him Jacqueline would be happy. Instead of that—instead of saying once for all to this young man, who is more in love with her than any other man will ever be: 'There,

take her, I give her to you,' which would be the straight-
forward, sensible way, you go on encouraging the caprices of a child who will end by wasting, in the life
you are permitting her to lead, all the good qualities
she has and keeping nothing but the bad ones."

"*Mon Dieu!* I can't see that Jacqueline leads a life
like that!" said M. de Nailles, who felt that he must
say something.

"You don't see, you don't see! How can any one
see who won't open his eyes? My poor friend, just
look for once at what is going on around you, under
your own roof——"

"Jacqueline is devoted to music," said her father,
good-humoredly. Madame d'Argy in her heart thought
he was losing his mind.

And in truth he was growing older day by day, becoming more and more anxious, more and more absorbed in the great struggle—not for life; that might
exhaust a man, but at least it was energetic and noble
—but for superfluous wealth, for vanity, for luxury,
which, for his own part, he cared nothing for, and
which he purchased dearly, spurred on to exertion by
those near to him, who insisted on extravagances.

"Oh! yes, Jacqueline, I know, is devoted to music,"
went on Madame d'Argy, with an air of extreme disapproval, "too much so! And when she is able to
sing like Madame Strahlberg, what good will it do
her? Even now I see more than one little thing about
her that needs to be reformed. How can she escape
spoiling in that crowd of Slavs and Yankees, people of
no position probably in their own countries, with whom

you permit her to associate? People nowadays are so
imprudent about acquaintances! To be a foreigner is
a passport into society. Just think what her poor
mother would have said to the bad manners she is
adopting from all parts of the globe? My poor, dear
Adelaide! She was a genuine Frenchwoman of the
old type; there are not many such left now. Ah!"
continued Madame d'Argy, without any apparent connection with her subject, "Monsieur de Talbrun's
mother, if he had one, would be truly happy to see him
married to Giselle!"

"But," faltered M. de Nailles, struck by the truth
of some of these remarks, "I make no opposition—
quite the contrary—I have spoken several times about
your son, but I was not listened to!"

"What can she say against Fred?"

"Nothing. She is very fond of him, that you know
as well as I do. But those childish attachments do
not necessarily lead to love and marriage."

"Friendship on her side might be enough," said
Madame d'Argy, in the tone of a woman who had
never known more than that in marriage. "My poor
Fred has enthusiasm and all that, enough for two.
And in time she will be madly in love with him—she
must! It is impossible it should be otherwise."

"Very good, persuade her yourself if you can; but
Jacqueline has a pretty strong will of her own."

Jacqueline's will was a reality, though the ideas of
M. de Nailles may have been illusion.

"And my wife, too!" resumed the Baron, after a
long sigh. "I don't know how it is, but Jacqueline,

JACQUELINE

as she has grown up, has become like an unbroken colt, and those two, who were once all in all to each other, are now seldom of one mind. How am I to act when their two wills cross mine, as they often do? I have so many things on my mind. There are times when——"

"Yes, one can see that. You don't seem to know where you are. And do you think that the disposition she shows to act, as you say, like an unbroken colt, is nothing to me? Do you think I am quite satisfied with my son's choice? I could have wished that he had chosen for his wife—but what is the use of saying what I wished? The important thing is that he should be happy in his own way. Besides, I dare say the young thing will calm down of her own accord. Her mother's daughter must be good at heart. All will come right when she is removed from a circle which is doing her no good; it is injuring her in people's opinion already, you must know. And how will it be by-and-bye? I hear people saying everywhere: 'How can the Nailles let that young girl associate so much with foreigners?' You say they are old school-fellows, they went to the *cours* together. But see if Madame d'Etaples and Madame Ray, under the same pretext, let Isabelle and Yvonne associate with the Odinskas! As to that foolish woman, Madame d'Avrigny, she goes to their house to look up recruits for her operettas, and Madame Strahlberg has one advantage over regular artists, there is no call to pay her. That is the reason why she invites her. Besides which, she won't find it so easy to marry Dolly."

[175]

THÉO BENTZON

"Oh! there are several reasons for that," said the Baron, who could see the mote in his neighbor's eye, "Mademoiselle d'Avrigny has led a life so very worldly ever since she was a child, so madly fast and lively, that suitors are afraid of her. Jacqueline, thank heaven, has never yet been in what is called the world. She only visits those with whom she is on terms of intimacy."

"An intimacy which includes all Paris," said Madame d'Argy, raising her eyes to heaven. "If she does not go to great balls, it is only because her stepmother is bored by them. But with that exception it seems to me she is allowed to do anything. I don't see the difference. But, to be sure, if Jacqueline is not for us, you have a right to say that I am interfering in what does not concern me."

"Not at all," said the unfortunate father, "I feel how much I ought to value your advice, and an alliance with your family would please me more than anything."

He said the truth, for he was disturbed by seeing M. de Cymier so slow in making his proposals, and he was also aware that young girls in our day are less sought for in marriage than they used to be. His friend Wermant, rich as he was, had had some trouble in capturing for Berthe a fellow of no account in the Faubourg St. Germain, and the prize was not much to be envied. He was a young man without brains and without a sou, who enjoyed so little consideration among his own people that his wife had not been received as she expected, and no one spoke of Madame

JACQUELINE

de Belvan without adding: "You know, that little
Wermant, daughter of the *agent de change*."

Of course, Jacqueline had the advantage of good
birth over Berthe, but how great was her inferiority
in point of fortune! M. de Nailles sometimes confided
these perplexities to his wife, without, however, receiving much comfort from her. Nor did the Baroness
confess to her husband all her own fears. In secret
she often asked herself, with the keen insight of a woman
of the world well trained in artifice and who possessed
a thorough knowledge of mankind, whether there
might not be women capable of using a young girl
so as to put the world on a wrong scent; whether, in
other words, Madame de Villegry did not talk everywhere about M. de Cymier's attentions to Mademoiselle
de Nailles in order to conceal his relations to herself?
Madame de Villegry indeed cared little about standing
well in public opinion, but rather the contrary; she
would not, however, for the world have been willing,
by too openly favoring one man among her admirers,
to run the risk of putting the rest to flight. No doubt
M. de Cymier was most assiduous in his attendance
on the receptions and dances at Madame de Nailles's,
but he was there always at the same time as Madame
de Villegry herself. They would hold whispered con-
ferences in corners, which might possibly have been
about Jacqueline, but there was no proof that they
were so, except what Madame de Villegry herself
said. "At any rate," thought Madame de Nailles,
"if Fred comes forward as a suitor it may stimulate
Monsieur de Cymier. There are men who put off

12   [177]

taking a decisive step till the last moment, and are only to be spurred up by competition."

So every opportunity was given to Fred to talk freely with Jacqueline when he returned to Paris. By this time he wore two gold-lace stripes upon his sleeve. But Jacqueline avoided any *tête-à-tête* with him as if she understood the danger that awaited her. She gave him no chance of speaking alone with her. She was friendly—nay, sometimes affectionate when other people were near them, but more commonly she teased him, bewildered him, excited him. After an hour or two spent in her society he would go home sometimes savage, sometimes desponding, to ponder in his own room, and in his own heart, what interpretation he ought to put upon the things that she had said to him.

The more he thought, the less he understood. He would not have confided in his mother for the world; she might have cast blame on Jacqueline. Besides her, he had no one who could receive his confidences, who would bear with his perplexities, who could assist in delivering him from the network of hopes and fears in which, after every interview with Jacqueline, he seemed to himself to become more and more entangled.

At last, however, at one of the *soirées* given every fortnight by Madame de Nailles, he succeeded in gaining her attention.

"Give me this quadrille," he said to her.

And, as she could not well refuse, he added, as soon as she had taken his arm: "We will not dance, and I defy you to escape me."

JACQUELINE

"This is treason!" she cried, somewhat angrily. "We are not here to talk; I can almost guess beforehand what you have to say, and——"

But he had made her sit down in the recess of that bow-window which had been called the young girls' corner years ago. He stood before her, preventing her escape, and half-laughing, though he was deeply moved.

"Since you have guessed what I wanted to say, answer me quickly."

"Must I? Must I, really? Why didn't you ask my father to do your commission? It is so horribly disagreeable to do these things for one's self."

"That depends upon what the things may be that have to be said. I should think it ought to be very agreeable to pronounce the word on which the happiness of a whole life is to depend."

"Oh! what a grand phrase! As if I could be essential to anybody's happiness? You can't make me believe that!"

"You are mistaken. You are indispensable to mine."

"There! my declaration has been made," thought Fred, much relieved that it was over, for he had been afraid to pronounce the decisive words.

"Well, if I thought that were true, I should be very sorry," said Jacqueline, no longer smiling, but looking down fixedly at the pointed toe of her little slipper; "because——"

She stopped suddenly. Her face flushed red.

"I don't know how to explain to you," she said.

"Explain nothing," pleaded Fred; "all I ask is *Yes,* nothing more. There is nothing else I care for."

She raised her head coldly and haughtily, yet her voice trembled as she said:

"You *will* force me to say it? Then, no! No!" she repeated, as if to reaffirm her refusal.

Then, alarmed by Fred's silence, and above all by his looks, he who had seemed so gay shortly before and whose face now showed an anguish such as she had never yet seen on the face of man, she added:

"Oh, forgive me!—Forgive me," she repeated in a lower voice, holding out her hand. He did not take it.

"You love some one else?" he asked, through his clenched teeth.

She opened her fan and affected to examine attentively the pink landscape painted on it to match her dress.

"Why should you think so? I wish to be free."

"Free? Are you free? Is a woman ever free?"

Jacqueline shook her head, as if expressing vague dissent.

"Free at least to see a little of the world," she said, "to choose, to use my wings, in short——"

And she moved her slender arms with an audacious gesture which had nothing in common with the flight of that mystic dove upon which she had meditated when holding the card given her by Giselle.

"Free to prefer some other man," said Fred, who held fast to his idea with the tenacity of jealousy.

"Ah! that is different. Supposing there were any

one whom I liked—not more, but differently from the way I like you—it is possible. But you spoke of loving!"

"Your distinctions are too subtle," said Fred.

"Because, much as it seems to astonish you, I am quite capable of seeing the difference," said Jacqueline, with the look and the accent of a person who has had large experience. "I have loved once—a long time ago, a very long time ago, a thousand years and more. Yes, I loved some one, as perhaps you love me, and I suffered more than you will ever suffer. It is ended; it is over—I think it is over forever."

"How foolish! At your age!"

"Yes, that kind of love is ended for me. Others may please me, others *do* please me, as you said, but it is not the same thing. Would you like to see the man I once loved?" asked Jacqueline, impelled by a juvenile desire to exhibit her experience, and also aware instinctively that to cast a scrap of past history to the curious sometimes turns off their attention on another track. "He is near us now," she added.

And while Fred's angry eyes, under his frowning brows, were wandering all round the salon, she pointed to Hubert Marien with a movement of her fan.

Marien was looking on at the dancing, with his old smile, not so brilliant now as it had been. He now only smiled at beauty collectively, which was well represented that evening in Madame de Nailles's salon. Young girls *en masse* continued to delight him, but his admiration as an artist became less and less personal.

He had grown stout, his hair and beard were getting gray; he was interested no longer in *Savonarola*, having obtained, thanks to his picture, the medal of honor, and the Institute some months since had opened its doors to him.

"Marien? You are laughing at me!" cried Fred.

"It is simply the truth."

Some magnetic influence at that moment caused the painter to turn his eyes toward the spot where they were talking.

"We were speaking of you," said Jacqueline.

And her tone was so singular that he dared not ask what they were saying. With humility which had in it a certain touch of bitterness he said, still smiling:

"You might find something better to do than to talk good or evil of a poor fellow who counts now for nothing."

"Counts for nothing! A fellow to be pitied!" cried Fred, "a man who has just been elected to the Institute—you are hard to satisfy!"

Jacqueline sat looking at him like a young sorceress engaged in sticking pins into the heart of a waxen figure of her enemy. She never missed an opportunity of showing her implacable dislike of him.

She turned to Fred: "What I was telling you," she said, "I am quite willing to repeat in his presence. The thing has lost its importance now that he has become more indifferent to me than any other man in the world."

She stopped, hoping that Marien had understood what she was saying and that he resented the humiliating avowal from her own lips that her childish love was now only a memory.

"If that is the only confession you have to make to me," said Fred, who had almost recovered his composure, "I can put up with my former rival, and I pass a sponge over all that has happened in your long past of seventeen years and a half, Jacqueline. Tell me only that at present you like no one better than me."

She smiled a half-smile, but he did not see it. She made no answer.

"Is he here, too—like the other!" he asked, sternly.

And she saw his restless eyes turn for an instant to the conservatory, where Madame de Villegry, leaning back in her armchair, and Gérard de Cymier, on a low seat almost at her feet, were carrying on their platonic flirtation.

"Oh! you must not think of quarrelling with him," cried Jacqueline, frightened at the look Fred fastened on De Cymier.

"No, it would be of no use. I shall go out to Tonquin, that's all."

"Fred! You are not serious."

"You will see whether I am not serious. At this very moment I know a man who will be glad to exchange with me."

"What! go and get yourself killed at Tonquin for a foolish little girl like me, who is very, very fond of you, but hardly knows her own mind. It would be absurd!"

"People are not always killed at Tonquin, but I

must have new interests, something to divert my mind from——"

"Fred! my dear Fred"—Jacqueline had suddenly become almost tender, almost suppliant. "Your mother! Think of your mother! What would she say? Oh, my God!"

"My mother must be allowed to think that I love my profession better than all else. But, Jacqueline," continued the poor fellow, clinging in despair to the very smallest hope, as a drowning man catches at a straw, "if you do not, as you said, know exactly your own mind—if you would like to question your own heart—I would wait——"

Jacqueline was biting the end of her fan—a conflict was taking place within her breast. But to certain temperaments there is pleasure in breaking a chain or in leaping a barrier; she said:

"Fred, I am too much your friend to deceive you."

At that moment M. de Cymier came toward them with his air of assurance: "Mademoiselle, you forget that you promised me this waltz," he said.

"No, I never forget anything," she answered, rising.

Fred detained her an instant, saying, in a low voice:

"Forgive me. This moment, Jacqueline, is decisive. I must have an answer. I never shall speak to you again of my sorrow. But decide now—on the spot. Is all ended between us?"

"Not our old friendship, Fred," said Jacqueline, tears rising in her eyes.

"So be it, then, if you so will it. But our friendship

never will show itself unless you are in need of friendship, and then only with the discretion that your present attitude toward me has imposed."

"Are you ready, Mademoiselle," said Gérard, who, to allow them to end their conversation, had obligingly turned his attention to some madrigals that Colette Odinska was laughing over.

Jacqueline shook her head resolutely, though at that moment her heart felt as if it were in a vise, and the moisture in her eyes looked like anything but a refusal. Then, without giving herself time for further thought, she whirled away into the dance with M. de Cymier. It was over, she had flung to the winds her chance for happiness, and wounded a heart more cruelly than Hubert Marien had ever wounded hers. The most horrible thing in this unending warfare we call love is that we too often repay to those who love us the harm that has been done us by those whom we have loved. The seeds of mistrust and perversity sown by one man or by one woman bear fruit to be gathered by some one else.

CHAPTER XII

A COMEDY AND A TRAGEDY

HE departure of Frédéric d'Argy for
Tonquin occasioned a break in the
intercourse between his mother and
the family of De Nailles. The wails
of Hecuba were nothing to the lamentations of poor Madame d'Argy;
the unreasonableness of her wrath
and the exaggeration in her re-
proaches hindered even Jacqueline from feeling all
the remorse she might otherwise have felt for her
share in Fred's departure. She told her father, who
the first time in her life addressed her with some
severity, that she could not be expected to love all the
young men who might threaten to go to the wars, or
to fling themselves from fourth-story windows, for her
sake.

"It was very indelicate and inconsiderate of Fred
to tell any one that it was my fault that he was doing
anything so foolish," she said, with true feminine de-
ceit, "but he has taken the very worst possible means
to make me care for him. Everybody has too much
to say about this matter which concerns only him and
me. Even Giselle thought proper to write me a ser-
mon!"

JACQUELINE

And she gave vent to her feelings in an exclamation of three syllables that she had learned from the Odinskas, which meant: "I don't care!" (*je m'en moque*).

But this was not true. She cared very much for Giselle's good opinion, and for Madame d'Argy's friendship. She suffered much in her secret heart at the thought of having given so much pain to Fred. She guessed how deep it was by the step to which it had driven him. But there was in her secret soul something more than all the rest, it was a puerile, but delicious satisfaction in feeling her own importance, in having been able to exercise an influence over one heart which might possibly extend to that of M. de Cymier. She thought he might be gratified by knowing that she had driven a young man to despair, if he guessed for whose sake she had been so cruel. He knew it, of course. Madame de Nailles took care that he should not be ignorant of it, and the pleasure he took in such a proof of his power over a young heart was not unlike that pleasure Jacqueline experienced in her coquetry—which crushed her better feelings. He felt proud of the sacrifice this beautiful girl had made for his sake, though he did not consider himself thereby committed to any decision, only he felt more attached to her than ever. Ever since the day when Madame de Villegry had first introduced him at the house of Madame de Nailles, he had had great pleasure in going there. The daughter of the house was more and more to his taste, but his liking for her was not such as to carry him beyond prudence. "If I chose," he would say to himself after every time he met her, "if

I chose I could own that jewel. I have only to stretch out my hand and have it given me." And the next morning, after going to sleep full of that pleasant thought, he would awake glad to find that he was still as free as ever, and able to carry on a flirtation with a woman of the world, which imposed no obligations upon him, and yet at the same time make love to a young girl whom he would gladly have married but for certain reports which were beginning to circulate among men of business concerning the financial position of M. de Nailles.

They said that he was withdrawing money from secure investments to repair (or to increase) considerable losses made by speculation, and that he operated recklessly on the Bourse. These rumors had already withdrawn Marcel d'Etaples from the list of his daughter's suitors. The young fellow was a captain of Hussars, who had no scruple in declaring the reason of his giving up his interest in the young lady. Gérard de Cymier, more prudent, waited and watched, thinking it would be quite time enough to go to the bottom of things when he found himself called upon to make a decision, and greatly interested meantime in the daily increase of Jacqueline's beauty. It was evident she cared for him. After all, it was doing the little thing no harm to let her live on in the intoxication of vanity and hope, and to give her something to dwell upon in her innocent dreams. Never did Gérard allow himself to overstep the line he had marked out for himself; a glance, a slight pressure of the hand, which might have been intentional, or have meant nothing, a few ambiguous words in which an active imagination might find something to dream about, a certain way of passing his arm round her slight waist which would have meant much had it not been done in public to the sound of music, were all the proofs the young diplomatist had ever given of an attraction that was real so far as consisted with his complete selfishness, joined to his professional prudence, and that systematic habit of taking up fancies at any time for anything, which prevents each fancy as it occurs from ripening into passion.

He alluded indirectly to Fred's departure in a way that turned it into ridicule. While playing a game of *boston* he whispered into Jacqueline's ear something about the old-fashionedness and stupidity of Paul and Virginia, and his opinion of "calf-love," as the English call an early attachment, and something about the right of every girl to know a suitor long before she consents to marry him. He said he thought that the days of courtship must be the most delightful in the life of a woman, and that a man who wished to cut them short was a fellow without delicacy or discretion!

From this Jacqueline drew the conclusion that he was not willing to resemble such a fellow, and was more and more persuaded that there was tenderness in the way he pressed her waist, and that his voice had the softness of a caress when he spoke to her. He made many inquiries as to what she liked and what she wished for in the future, as if his great object in all things was to anticipate her wishes. As for his intimacy with Madame de Villegry, Jacqueline thought

[189]

nothing of it, notwithstanding her habitual mistrust of those she called *old women*. In the first place, Madame de Villegry was her own mistress, nothing hindered them from having been married long ago had they wished it; besides, had not Madame de Villegry brought the young man to their house and let every one see, even Jacqueline herself, what was her object in doing so? In this matter she was their ally, a most zealous and kind ally, for she was continually advising her young friend as to what was most becoming to her and how she might make herself most attractive to men in general, with little covert allusions to the particular tastes of Gérard, which she said she knew as well as if he had been her brother.

All this was lightly insinuated, but never insisted upon, with the tact which stood Madame de Villegry in stead of talent, and which had enabled her to perform some marvellous feats upon the tight-rope without losing her balance completely. She, too, made fun of the tragic determination of Fred, which all those who composed the society of the De Nailles had been made aware of by the indiscreet lamentations of Madame d'Argy.

"Is not Jacqueline fortunate?" cried Colette Odinska, who, herself always on a high horse, looked on love in its tragic aspect, and would have liked to resemble Marie Stuart as much as she could, "is she not fortunate? She has had a man who has gone abroad to get himself killed—and all for her!"

Colette imagined herself under the same circumstances, making the most of a slain lover, with a crape veil covering her fair hair, her mourning copied from that of her divorced sister, who wore her weeds so charmingly, but who was getting rather tired of a single life.

As for Miss Kate Sparks and Miss Nora, they could not understand why the breaking of half-a-dozen hearts should not be the prelude to every marriage. That, they said with much conviction, was always the case in America, and a girl was thought all the more of who had done so.

Jacqueline, however, thought more than was reasonable about the dangers that the friend of her childhood was going to encounter through her fault. Fred's departure would have lent him a certain prestige, had not a powerful new interest stepped in to divert her thoughts. Madame d'Avrigny was getting up her annual private theatricals, and wanted Jacqueline to take the principal part in the play, saying that she ought to put her lessons in elocution to some use. The piece chosen was to illustrate a proverb, and was entirely new. It was as unexceptionable as it was amusing; the most severe critic could have found no fault with its morality or with its moral, which turned on the eagerness displayed by young girls nowadays to obtain diplomas. *Scylla and Charybdis* was its name. Its story was that of a young bride, who, thinking to please a husband, a stupid and ignorant man, was trying to obtain in secret a high place in the examination at the Sorbonne—*un brevet supérieur*. The husband, disquieted by the mystery, is at first suspicious, then jealous, and then is overwhelmed with humiliation when he discovers that his wife knows more of everything than himself. He ends by imploring her to give up her higher education if she wishes to please him. The little play had all the modern loveliness and grace which Octave Feuillet alone can give, and it contained a lesson from which any one might profit; which was by no means always the case with Madame d'Avrigny's plays, which too often were full of risky allusions, of critical situations, and the like; likely, in short, to "sail too close to the wind," as Fred had once described them. But Madame d'Avrigny's prime object was the amusement of society, and society finds pleasure in things which, if innocence understood them, would put her to the blush. This play, however, was an exception. There had been very little to cut out this time. Madame de Nailles had been asked to take the mother's part, but she declined, not caring to act such a character in a house where years before in all her glory she had made a sensation as a young coquette. So Madame d'Avrigny had to take the part herself, not sorry to be able to superintend everything on the stage, and to prompt Dolly, if necessary—Dolly, who had but four words to say, which she always forgot, but who looked lovely in a little cap as a *femme de chambre*.

People had been surprised that M. de Cymier should have asked for the part of the husband, a local magistrate, stiff and self-important, whom everybody laughed at. Jacqueline alone knew why he had chosen it: it would give him the opportunity of giving her two kisses. Of course those kisses were to be reserved for the representation, but whether intentionally or otherwise, the young husband ventured upon them at every rehearsal, in spite of the general outcry—not, however, very much in earnest, for it is well understood that in private theatricals certain liberties may be allowed, and M. de Cymier had never been remarkable for reserve when he acted at the clubs, where the female parts were taken by ladies from the smaller theatres. In this school he had acquired some reputation as an amateur actor. "Besides," as he remarked on making his apology, "we shall do it very awkwardly upon the stage if we are not allowed to practise it beforehand." Jacqueline burst out laughing, and did not make much show of opposition. To play the part of his wife, to hear him say *tu* to her, to respond with the affectionate and familiar *toi*, was so amusing! It was droll to see her cut out her husband in chemistry, history, and grammar, and make him confound La Fontaine with Corneille. She had such a little air while doing it! And at the close, when he said to her: "If I give you a pony to-morrow, and a good hearty kiss this very minute, shall you be willing to give up getting that degree?" she responded, with such gusto: "Indeed, I shall!" and her manner was so eager, so boyish, so full of fun, that she was wildly applauded, while Gérard embraced her as heartily as he liked, to make up to himself for her having had, as his wife, the upper hand.

All this kissing threw him rather off his balance, and he might soon have sealed his fate, had not a very sad event occurred, which restored his self-possession.

THÉO BENTZON

The dress rehearsal was to take place one bright spring day at about four o'clock in the afternoon. A large number of guests was assembled at the house of Madame d'Avrigny. The performance had been much talked about beforehand in society. The beauty, the singing, and the histrionic powers of the principal actress had been everywhere extolled. Fully conscious of what was expected of her, and eager to do herself credit in every way, Jacqueline took advantage of Madame Strahlberg's presence to run over a little song, which she was to sing between the acts and in which she could see no meaning whatever. This little song, which, to most of the ladies present, seemed simply idiotic, made the men in the audience cry "Oh!" as if half-shocked, and then *"Encore! Encore!"* in a sort of frenzy. It was a so-called pastoral effusion, in which Colinette rhymed with *herbette*, and in which the false innocence of the eighteenth century was a cloak for much indelicate allusion.

"I never," said Jacqueline in self-defense, before she began the song, "sang anything so stupid. And that is saying much when one thinks of all the nonsensical words that people set to music! It's a marvel how any one can like this stuff. Do tell me what there is in it?" she added, turning to Gérard, who was charmed by her ignorance.

Standing beside the grand piano, with her arms waving as she sang, repeating, by the expression of her eyes, the question she had asked and to which she had received no answer, she was singing the verses she considered nonsense with as much point as if she had understood them, thanks to the hints given her by Madame Strahlberg, who was playing her accompaniment, when the entrance of a servant, who pronounced her name aloud, made a sudden interruption. "Mademoiselle de Nailles is wanted at home at once. Modeste has come for her."

Madame d'Avrigny went out to say to the old servant: "She can not possibly go home with you! It is only half an hour since she came. The rehearsal is just beginning."

But something Modeste said in answer made her give a little cry, full of consternation. She came quickly back, and going up to Jacqueline:

"My dear," she said, "you must go home at once—there is bad news, your father is ill."

"Ill?"

The solemnity of Madame d'Avrigny's voice, the pity in her expression, the affection with which she spoke and above all her total indifference to the fate of her rehearsal, frightened Jacqueline. She rushed away, not waiting to say good-by, leaving behind her a general murmur of "Poor thing!" while Madame d'Avrigny, recovering from her first shock, was already beginning to wonder—her instincts as an *impresario* coming once more to the front—whether the leading part might not be taken by Isabelle Ray. She would have to send out two hundred cards, at least, and put off her play for another fortnight. What a pity! It seemed as if misfortunes always happened just so as to interfere with pleasures.

The *fiacre* which had brought Modeste was at

the door. The old nurse helped her young lady into it.

"What has happened to papa?" cried Jacqueline, impetuously.

There was something horrible in this sudden transition from gay excitement to the sharpest anxiety.

"Nothing—that is to say—he is very sick. Don't tremble like that, my darling—courage!" stammered Modeste, who was frightened by her agitation.

"He was taken sick, you say. Where? How happened it?"

"In his study. Pierre had just brought him his letters. We thought we heard a noise as if a chair had been thrown down, and a sort of cry. I ran in to see. He was lying at full length on the floor."

"And now? How is he now?"

"We did what we could for him. Madame came back. He is lying on his bed."

Modeste covered her face with her hands.

"You have not told me all. What else?"

"*Mon Dieu!* you knew your poor father had heart disease. The last time the doctor saw him he thought his legs had swelled——"

"Had!" Jacqueline heard only that one word. It meant that the life of her father was a thing of the past. Hardly waiting till the *fiacre* could be stopped, she sprang out, rushed into the house, opened the door of her father's chamber, pushing aside a servant who tried to stop her, and fell upon her knees beside the bed where lay the body of her father, white and rigid.

"Papa! My poor dear—dear papa!"

JACQUELINE

The hand she pressed to her lips was as cold as ice.
She raised her frightened eyes to the face over which
the great change from life to death had passed. "What
does it mean?" Jacqueline had never looked on
death before, but she knew this was not sleep.

"Oh, speak to me, papa! It is I—it is Jacqueline!"

Her stepmother tried to raise her—tried to fold her
in her arms.

"Let me alone!" she cried with horror.

It seemed to her as if her father, where he was now,
so far from her, so far from everything, might have
the power to look into human hearts, and know the
perfidy he had known nothing of when he was living.
He might see in her own heart, too, her great despair.
All else seemed small and of no consequence when
death was present.

Oh! why had she not been a better daughter, more
loving, more devoted? why had she ever cared for
anything but to make him happy?

She sobbed aloud, while Madame de Nailles, pressing her handkerchief to her eyes, stood at the foot of
the bed, and the doctor, too, was near, whispering to
some one whom Jacqueline at first had not perceived
—the friend of the family, Hubert Marien.

Marien there? Was it not natural that, so intimate
as he had always been with the dead man, he should
have hastened to offer his services to the widow?

Jacqueline flung herself upon her father's corpse, as
if to protect it from profanation. She had an impulse
to bear it away with her to some desert spot where she
alone could have wept over it.

THÉO BENTZON

She lay thus a long time, beside herself with grief.

The flowers which covered the bed and lay scattered on the floor, gave a festal appearance to the death-chamber. They had been purchased for a *fête*, but circumstances had changed their destination. That evening there was to have been a reception in the house of M. de Nailles, but the unexpected guest that comes without an invitation had arrived before the music and the dancers.

CHAPTER XIII

MONSIEUR DE NAILLES was dead, struck down suddenly by what is called indefinitely heart-failure. The trouble in that organ from which he had long suffered had brought on what might have been long foreseen, and yet every one seemed stupefied by the event. It came upon them like a thunderbolt. It often happens so when people who are really ill persist in doing all that may be done with safety by other persons. They persuaded themselves, and those about them are easily persuaded, that small remedies will prolong indefinitely a state of things which is precarious to the last degree. Friends are ready to believe, when the sufferer complains that his work is too hard for him, that he thinks too much of his ailments and that he exaggerates trifles to which they are well accustomed, but which are best known to him alone. When M. de Nailles, several weeks before his death, had asked to be excused and to stay at home instead of attending some large gathering, his wife, and even Jacqueline, would try to convince him that a little amusement would be good for him; they were unwilling to leave him to the repose he needed, prescribed for him by the doctors, who had been unanimous that he must "put down the brakes," give less attention to business, avoid late hours and over-exertion of all kinds. "And, above all," said one of the lights of science whom he had consulted recently about certain feelings of faintness which were a bad symptom, "above all, you must keep yourself from mental anxiety."

How could he, when his fortune, already much impaired, hung on chances as uncertain as those in a game of *roulette?* What nonsense! The failure of a great financial company had brought about a crisis on the Bourse. The news of the inability of Wermant, the *agent de change*, to meet his engagements, had completed the downfall of M. de Nailles. Not only death, but ruin, had entered that house, where, a few hours before, luxury and opulence had seemed to reign.

"We don't know whether there will be anything left for us to live upon," cried Madame de Nailles, with anguish, even while her husband's body lay in the chamber of death, and Jacqueline, kneeling beside it, wept, unwilling to receive comfort or consolation.

She turned angrily upon her stepmother and cried:

"What matter? I have no father—there is nothing else I care for."

But from that moment a dreadful thought, a thought she was ashamed of, which made her feel a monster of selfishness, rose in her mind, do what she would to hinder it. Jacqueline was sensible that she cared for something else; great as was her sense of loss, a sort of reckless curiosity seemed haunting her, while all the time she felt that her great grief ought not to give place to anything besides. "How would Gérard de Cymier behave in these circumstances?" She thought about it all one dreadful night as she and Modeste, who was telling her beads softly, sat in the faint light of the death-chamber. She thought of it at dawn, when, after one of those brief sleeps which come to the young under all conditions, she resumed with a sigh a sense of surrounding realities. Almost in the same instant she thought: "My dear father will never wake again," and "Does he love me?—does he now wish me to be his wife?—will he take me away?" The devil, which put this thought into her heart, made her eager to know the answer to these questions. He suggested how dreadful life with her stepmother would be if no means of escape were offered her. He made her foresee that her stepmother would marry again—would marry Marien. "But I shall not be there!" she cried, "I will not countenance such an infamy!" Oh, how she hoped Gérard de Cymier loved her! The hypocritical tears of Madame de Nailles disgusted her. She could not bear to have such false grief associated with her own.

Men in black, with solemn faces, came and bore away the body, no longer like the form of the father she had loved. He had gone from her forever. Pompous funeral rites, little in accordance with the crash that soon succeeded them, were superintended by Marien, who, in the absence of near relatives, took charge of everything. He seemed to be deeply affected, and behaved with all possible kindness and consideration to Jacqueline, who could not, however, bring herself to thank him, or even to look at him. She hated him with an increase of resentment, as if the soul of her dead father, who now knew the truth, had passed into her own.

Meantime, M. de Cymier took care to inform himself of the state of things. It was easy enough to do so. All Paris was talking of the shipwreck in which life and fortune had been lost by a man whose kindliness as a host at his wife's parties every one had appreciated. That was what came, people said, of striving after big dividends! The house was to be sold, with the horses, the pictures, and the furniture. What a change for his poor wife and daughter! There were others who suffered by the Wermant crash, but those were less interesting than the De Nailles. M. de Belvan found himself left by his father-in-law's failure with a wife on his hands who not only had not a *sou*, but who was the daughter of an *agent de change* who had behaved dishonorably.

This was a text for dissertations on the disgrace of marrying for money; those who had done the same thing, minus the same consequences, being loudest in reprobating alliances of that kind. M. de Cymier listened attentively to such talk, looking and saying the right things, and as he heard more and more about the deplorable condition of M. de Nailles's affairs, he congratulated himself that a prudent presentiment had kept him from asking the hand of Jacqueline. He had had vague doubts as to the firm foundation of the opulence which made so charming a frame for her young beauty; it seemed to him as if she were now less beautiful than he had imagined her; the enchantment she had exercised upon him was thrown off by simple considerations of good sense. And yet he gave a long sigh of regret when he thought she was unattainable except by marriage. He, however, thanked heaven that he had not gone far enough to have compromised himself with her. The most his conscience could reproach him with was an occasional imprudence in moments of forgetfulness; no court of honor could hold him bound to declare himself her suitor. The evening that he made up his mind to this he wrote two letters, very nearly alike; one was to Madame d'Avrigny, the other to Madame de Nailles, announcing that, having received orders to join the Embassy to which he was attached at Vienna, he was about to depart at once, with great regret that he should not be able to take leave of any one. To Madame d'Avrigny he made apologies for having to give up his part in her theatricals; he entreated Madame de Nailles to accept both for herself and for Mademoiselle Jacqueline his deepest condolences and the assurance of his sympathy. The manner in which this was said was all it ought to have been, except that it might have been rather more brief. M. de Cymier said more than was necessary about his participation in their grief, because he was conscious of a total lack of sympathy. He begged the ladies would forgive him if, from feelings of delicacy and a sense of the respect due to a great sorrow, he did not, before leaving Paris, which he was about do to probably for a long time, personally present to them *ses hommages attristés*. Then followed a few lines in which he spoke of the pleasant recollections he should always retain of the hospitality he had enjoyed under M. de Nailles's roof, in a way that gave them clearly to understand that he had no expectation of ever entering their family on a more intimate footing.

Madame de Nailles received this letter just as she had had a conversation with a man of business, who had shown her how complete was the ruin for which in a great measure she herself was responsible. She had no longer any illusions as to her position. When the estate had been settled there would be nothing left but poverty, not only for herself, who, having brought her husband no *dot*, had no right to consider herself wronged by the bankruptcy, but for Jacqueline, whose fortune, derived from her mother, had suffered under her father's management (there are such men — unfaithful guardians of a child's property, but yet good fathers) in every way in which it was possible to evade the provisions of the Code intended to protect the rights of minor children. In the little salon so charmingly furnished, where never before had sorrow or sadness been discussed, Madame de Nailles poured out her complaints to her stepdaughter and insisted upon plans of strict economy, when M. de Cymier's letter was brought in.

"Read!" said the Baroness, handing the strange document to Jacqueline, after she had read it through.

Then she leaned back in her chair with a gesture which signified: "This is the last straw!" and remained motionless, apparently overwhelmed, with her face covered by one hand, but furtively watching the face of the girl so cruelly forsaken.

That face told nothing, for pride supplies some sufferers with necessary courage. Jacqueline sat for some time with her eyes fixed on the decisive adieu which swept away what might have been her secret hope. The paper did not tremble in her hand, a half-smile of contempt passed over her mouth. The answer to the restless question that had intruded itself upon her in the first moments of her grief was now before her. Its promptness, its polished brutality, had given her a shock, but not the pain she had expected. Perhaps her great grief—the real, the true, the grief death brings—recovered its place in her heart, and prevented her from feeling keenly any secondary emotion. Perhaps this man, who could pay court to her in her days of happiness and disappear when the first trouble came, seemed to her not worth caring for.

She silently handed back the letter to her stepmother.

"No more than I expected," said the Baroness.

"Indeed?" replied Jacqueline with complete indifference. She wished to give no opening to any expressions of sympathy on the part of Madame de Nailles.

"Poor Madame d'Avrigny," she added, "has bad luck; all her actors seem to be leaving her."

This speech was the vain bravado of a young soldier going into action. The poor child betrayed herself to the experienced woman, trained either to detect or to practise artifice, and who found bitter amusement in watching the girl's assumed *sang-froid*. But the mask fell off at the first touch of genuine sympathy. When Giselle, forgetful of a certain coolness between them ever since Fred's departure, came to clasp her in her arms, she showed only her true self, a girl suffering all the bitterness of a cruel, humiliating desertion. Long talks ensued between the friends, in which Jacqueline poured into Giselle's ear her sad discoveries in the past, her sorrows and anxieties in the present, and her vague plans for the future. "I must go away," she said; "I must escape somewhere; I can not go on living with Madame de Nailles—I should go mad, I should be tempted every day to upbraid her with her conduct."

Giselle made no attempt to curb an excitement which she knew would resist all she could say to calm it. She feigned agreement, hoping thereby to increase her future influence, and advised her friend to seek in a convent the refuge that she needed. But she must do nothing rashly; she should only consider it a temporary retreat whose motive was a wish to remain for a while within reach of religious consolation. In that way she would give people nothing to talk about, and her stepmother could not be offended. It was never of any use to get out of a difficulty by breaking all the glass windows with a great noise, and good resolutions are made firmer by being matured in quietness. Such were the lessons Giselle herself had been taught by the Bénédictine nuns, who, however deficient they might be in the higher education of women, knew at least how to bring up young girls with a view to making them good wives. Giselle illustrated this day by day in her relations to a husband as disagreeable as a husband well could be, a man of small intelligence, who was not even faithful to her. But she did not cite herself as an example. She never talked about herself, or her own difficulties.

"You are an angel of sense and goodness," sobbed Jacqueline. "I will do whatever you wish me to do."

"Count upon me—count upon all your friends," said Madame de Talbrun, tenderly.

And then, enumerating the oldest and the truest of these friends, she unluckily named Madame d'Argy. Jacqueline drew herself back at once:

"Oh, for pity's sake!" she cried, "don't mention them to me!"

Already a comparison between Fred's faithful affection and Gérard de Cymier's desertion had come into her mind, but she had refused to entertain it, declaring resolutely to herself that she never should repent her refusal. She was sore, she was angry with all men, she wished all were like Cymier or like Marien, that she might hate every one of them; she came to the conclusion in her heart of hearts that all of them, even the best, if put to the proof, would turn out selfish. She liked to think so—to believe in none of them. Thus it happened that an unexpected visit from Fred's mother, among those that she received in her first days of orphanhood, was particularly agreeable to her.

Madame d'Argy, on hearing of the death and of the ruin of M. de Nailles, was divided by two contradictory feelings. She clearly saw the hand of Providence in what had happened: her son was in the squadron on its way to attack Formosa; he was in peril from the climate, in peril from Chinese bullets, and assuredly those who had brought him into peril could not be punished too severely; on the other hand, the last mail from Tonquin had brought her one of those great joys which always incline us to be merciful. Fred had so greatly distinguished himself in a series of fights upon the river Min that he had been offered his choice between the Cross of the Legion of Honor or promotion. He told his mother now that he had quite recovered from a wound he had received which had brought him some glory, but which he assured her had done him no bodily harm, and he repeated to her what he would not tell her at first, some words of praise from Admiral Courbet of more value in his eyes than any reward.

Triumphant herself, and much moved by pity for Jacqueline, Madame d'Argy felt as if she must put an end to a rupture which could not be kept up when a great sorrow had fallen on her old friends, besides which she longed to tell every one, those who had been blind and ungrateful in particular, that Fred had proved himself a hero. So Jacqueline and her stepmother saw her arrive as if nothing had ever come between them. There were kisses and tears, and a torrent of kindly meant questions, affectionate explanations, and offers of service. But Fred's mother could not help showing her own pride and happiness to those in sorrow. They congratulated her with sadness. Madame d'Argy would have liked to think that the value of what she had lost was now made plain to Jacqueline. And if it caused her one more pang—what did it matter? He and his mother had suffered too. It was the turn of others. God was just. Resentment, and kindness, and a strange mixed feeling of forgiveness and revenge contended together in the really generous heart of Madame d'Argy, but that heart was still sore within her. Pity, however, carried the day, and had it not been for the irritating coldness of "that little hard-hearted thing," as she called Jacqueline, she would have entirely forgiven her. She never suspected that the exaggerated reserve of manner that offended her was owing to Jacqueline's dread (commendable in itself) of appearing to wish in her days of misfortune for the return of one she had rejected in the time of prosperity.

In spite of the received opinion that society abandons those who are overtaken by misfortune, all the friends of the De Nailles flocked to offer their condolences to the widow and the orphan with warm demonstrations of interest. Curiosity, a liking to witness, or to experience, emotion, the pleasure of being able to tell what has been seen and heard, to find out new facts and repeat them again to others, joined to a sort of vague, commonplace, almost intrusive pity, are sentiments, which sometimes in hours of great disaster, produce what appears to wear the look of sympathy. A fortnight after M. de Nailles's death, between the acts of *Scylla and Charybdis*, the principal parts in which were taken by young d'Etaples and Isabelle Ray, the company, as it ate ices, was glibly discussing the real drama which had produced in their own elegant circle much of the effect a blow has upon an ant-hill —fear, agitation, and a tumultuous rush to the scene of the disaster.

Great indignation was expressed against the man

14   [209]

who had risked the fortune of his family in speculation. Oh! the thing had been going on for a long while. His fortune had been gradually melting away; Grand-chaux was loaded down with mortgages and would bring almost nothing at a forced sale.

Everybody forgot that had M. de Nailles's speculations been successful they would have been called matters of business, conducted with great ability on a large scale. When a performer falls from the tight-rope, who remembers all the times he has not failed? It is simply said that he fell from his own carelessness.

"The poor Baroness is touchingly resigned," said Madame de Villegry, with a deep sigh; "and heaven knows how many other cares she has besides the loss of money! I don't mean only the death of her husband —and you know how much they were attached to each other—I am speaking of that unaccountable resolution of Jacqueline's."

Madame d'Avrigny here came forward with her usual equanimity which nothing disturbed, unless it were something which interfered with the success of her salon.

She was of course very sorry for her friends in trouble, but the vicissitudes that had happened to her theatricals she had more at heart.

"After all," she said, "the first act did not go off badly, did it? The musical part made up for the rest. That divine Strahlberg is ready for any emergency. How well she sang that air of *La Petite Mariée!* It was exquisite, but I regretted Jacqueline. She was so charming in that lively little part. What a catastrophe!

JACQUELINE

What a terrible catastrophe! Were you speaking of the retreat she wishes to make in a convent? Well, I quite understand how she feels about it! I should feel the same myself. In the bewilderment of a first grief one does not care to see anything of the world. *Mon Dieu!* youth always has these exaggerated notions. She will come back to us. Poor little thing! Of course it was no fault of hers, and I should not think of blaming Monsieur de Cymier. The exigencies of his career— but you all must own that unexpected things happen so suddenly in this life that it is enough to discourage any one who likes to open her house and provide amusement for her friends."

Every one present pitied her for the *contretemps* over which she had triumphed so successfully. Then she resumed, serenely:

"Don't you think that Isabelle played the part almost as well as Jacqueline? Up to the last moment I was afraid that something would go wrong. When one gets into a streak of ill-luck—but all went off to perfection, thank heaven!"

Meantime Madame Odinska was whispering to one of those who sat near her her belief that Jacqueline would never get over her father's loss. "It would not astonish me," she said, "to hear that the child, who has a noble nature, would remain in the convent and take the veil."

Any kind of heroic deed seemed natural to this foolish enthusiast, who, as a matter of fact, in her own life, had never shown any tendency to heroic virtues; her mission in life had seemed to be to spoil her daughters in every possible way, and to fling away more money than belonged to her.

"Really? Was she so very fond of her father!" asked Madame Ray, incredulously. "When he was alive, they did not seem to make much of him in his own house. Maybe this retreat is a good way of getting over a little wound to her *amour-propre*."

"The proper thing, I think," said Madame d'Etaples, "would be for the mother and daughter to keep together, to bear the troubles before them hand in hand. Jacqueline does not seem to think much of the last wishes of the father she pretends to be so fond of. The Baroness showed me, with many tears, a letter he left joined to his will, which was written some years ago, and which now, of course, is of no value. He told mother and daughter to take care of each other and hoped they would always remain friends, loving each other for love of him. Jacqueline's conduct amazes me; it looks like ingratitude."

"Oh! she is a hard-hearted little thing! I always thought so!" said Madame de Villegry, carelessly.

Here the rising of the curtain stopped short these discussions, which displayed so much good-nature and perspicacity. But some laid the blame on the influence of that little bigot of a Talbrun, who had secretly blown up the fire of religious enthusiasm in Jacqueline, when Madame d'Avrigny's energetic "Hush!" put an end to the discussion. It was time to come back to more immediate interests, to the play which went on in spite of wind and tide.

CHAPTER XIV

SOME people in this world who turn round and round in a daily circle of small things, like squirrels in a cage, have no idea of the pleasure a young creature, conscious of courage, has in trying its strength; this struggle with fortune loses its charm as it grows longer and longer and more and more difficult, but at the beginning it is an almost certain remedy for sorrow.

To her resolve to make head against misfortune Jacqueline owed the fact that she did not fall into those morbid reveries which might have converted her passing fancy for a man who was simply a male flirt into the importance of a lost love. Is there any human being conscious of energy, and with faith in his or her own powers, who has not wished to know something of adversity in order to rise to the occasion and confront it? To say nothing of the pleasure there is in eating brown bread, when one has been fed only on cake, or of the satisfaction that a child feels when, after strict discipline, he is left to do as he likes, to say nothing of the pleasure ladies boarding in nunneries are sure to feel on reëntering the world, at recovering their liberty, Jacqueline by nature loved independence, and she was attracted by the novelty of her situation as larks are attracted by a mirror. She was curious to know what life held for her in reserve, and she was extremely anxious to repair the error she had committed in giving way to a feeling of which she was now ashamed. What could do this better than hard work? To owe everything to herself, to her talents, to her efforts, to her industry, such was Jacqueline's ideal of her future life.

She had, before this, crowned her brilliant reputation in the *cours* of M. Regis by passing her preliminary examination at the Sorbonne; she was confident of attaining the highest degree—the *brevet supérieur*, and while pursuing her own studies she hoped to give lessons in music and in foreign languages, etc. Thus assured of making her own living, she could afford to despise the discreditable happiness of Madame de Nailles, who, she had no doubt, would shortly become Madame Marien; also the crooked ways in which M. de Cymier might pursue his fortune-hunting. She said to herself that she should never marry; that she had other objects of interest; that marriage was for those who had nothing better before them; and the world appeared to her under a new aspect, a sphere of useful activity full of possibilities, of infinite variety, and abounding in interests. Marriage might be all very well for rich girls, who unhappily were objects of value to be bought and sold; her semi-poverty gave her the right to break the chains that hampered the career of other well-born women— she would make her own way in the world like a man.

JACQUELINE

Thus, at eighteen, youth is ready to set sail in a light skiff on a rough sea, having laid in a good store of imagination and of courage, of childlike ignorance and self-esteem.

No doubt she would meet with some difficulties; that thought did but excite her ardor. No doubt Madame de Nailles would try to keep her with her, and Jacqueline had provided herself beforehand with some double-edged remarks by way of weapons, which she intended to use according to circumstances. But all these preparations for defense or attack proved unnecessary. When she told the Baroness of her plans she met with no opposition. She had expected that her project of separation would highly displease her stepmother; on the contrary, Madame de Nailles discussed her projects quietly, affecting to consider them merely temporary, but with no indication of dissatisfaction or resistance. In truth she was not sorry that Jacqueline, whose companionship became more and more embarrassing every day, had cut the knot of a difficult position by a piece of wilfulness and perversity which seemed to put her in the wrong. The necessity she would have been under of crushing such a girl, who was now eighteen, would have been distasteful and unprofitable; she was very glad to get rid of her stepdaughter, always provided it could be done decently and without scandal. Those two, who had once so loved each other and who were now sharers in the same sorrows, became enemies—two hostile parties, which only skilful strategy could ever again bring together. They tacitly agreed to certain conditions: they would save appearances; they would remain on outwardly good terms with each other whatever happened, and above all they would avoid any explanation. This programme was faithfully carried out, thanks to the great tact of Madame de Nailles.

No one could have been more watchful to appear ignorant of everything which, if once brought to light, would have led to difficulties; for instance, she feigned not to know that her stepdaughter was in possession of a secret which, if the world knew, would forever make them strangers to each other; nor would she seem aware that Hubert Marien, weary to death of the tie that bound him to her, was restrained from breaking it only by a scruple of honor. Thanks to this seeming ignorance, she parted from Jacqueline without any open breach, as she had long hoped to do, and she retained as a friend who supplied her wants a man who was only too happy to be allowed at this price to escape the act of reparation which Jacqueline, in her simplicity, had dreaded.

All those who, having for years dined and danced under the roof of the Nailles, were accounted their friends by society, formed themselves into two parties, one of which lauded to the skies the dignity and resignation of the Baroness, while the other admired the force of character in Jacqueline.

Visitors flocked to the convent which the young girl, by the advice of Giselle, had chosen for her retreat because it was situated in a quiet quarter. She who looked so beautiful in her crape garments, who showed herself so satisfied in her little cell with hardly any furniture, who was grateful for the services rendered her by the lay sisters, content with having no salon but the convent parlor, who was passing examinations to become a teacher, and who seemed to consider it a favor to be sometimes allowed to hear the children in the convent school say their lessons—was surely like a heroine in a novel. And indeed Jacqueline had the agreeable sensation of considering herself one. Public admiration was a great help to her, after she had passed through that crisis in her grief during which she could feel nothing but the horror of knowing she should never see her father again, when she had ceased to weep for him incessantly, to pray for him, and to turn, like a wounded lioness, on those who blamed his reckless conduct, though she herself had been its chief victim.

For three months she hardly left the convent, walking only in the grounds and gardens, which were of considerable extent. From time to time Giselle came for her and took her to drive in the Bois at that hour of the day when few people were there.

Enguerrand, who, thanks to his mother's care, was beginning to be an intelligent and interesting child, though he was still painfully like M. de Talbrun, was always with them in the *coupé*, kindhearted Giselle thinking that nothing could be so likely to assuage grief as the prattle of a child. She was astonished— she was touched to the heart, by what she called naïvely the conversion of Jacqueline. It was true that the young girl had no longer any whims or caprices. All the nuns seemed to her amiable, her lodging was all she needed, her food was excellent; her lessons gave her amusement. Possibly the excitement of the entire change had much to do at first with this philosophy, and in fact at the end of six months Jacqueline owned that she was growing tired of dining at the *table d'hôte*.

There was a little knot of crooked old ladies who were righteous overmuch, and several sour old maids whose only occupation seemed to be to make remarks on any person who had anything different in dress, manners, or appearance from what they considered the type of the becoming. If it is not good that man should live alone, it is equally true that women should not live together. Jacqueline found this out as soon as her powers of observation came back to her. And about the same time she discovered that she was not so free as she had flattered herself she should be. The appearance of a lady, fair and with light hair, very pretty and about her own age, gave her for the first time an inclination to talk at table. She and this young woman met twice a day at their meals, in the morning and in the evening; their rooms were next each other, and at night Jacqueline could hear her through the thin partition giving utterance to sighs, which showed that she was unhappy. Several times, too, she came upon her in the garden looking earnestly at a place where the wall had been broken, a spot whence it was said a Spanish countess had been carried off by a bold adventurer. Jacqueline thought there must be something romantic in the history of this newcomer, and would have liked exceedingly to know what it might be. As a prelude to acquaintance, she offered the young stranger some holy water when they met in the chapel, a bow and a smile were interchanged, their fingers touched. They seemed almost friends. After this, Jacqueline contrived to change her seat at table to one next to this unknown person, so prettily dressed, with her hair so nicely arranged, and, though her expression was very sad, with a smile so very winning. She alone represented the world, the world of Paris, among all those ladies, some of whom were looking for places as companions, some having come up from the provinces, and some being old ladies who had seen better days. Her change of place was observed by the nun who presided at the table, and a shade of displeasure passed over her face. It was slight, but it portended trouble. And, indeed, when grace had been said, Mademoiselle de Nailles was sent for by the Mother Superior, who gave her to understand that, being so young, it was especially incumbent on her to be circumspect in her choice of associates. Her place thenceforward was to be between Madame de X——, an old, deaf lady, and Mademoiselle J——, a former governess, as cold as ice and exceedingly respectable. As to Madame Saville, she had been received in the convent for especial reasons, arising out of circumstances which did not make her a fit companion for inexperienced girls. The Superior hesitated a moment and then said: "Her husband requested us to take charge of her," in a tone by which Jacqueline quite understood that "take charge" was a synonym for "keep a strict watch upon her." She was spied upon, she was persecuted—unjustly, no doubt.

All this increased the interest that Jacqueline already felt in the lady with the light hair. But she made a low curtsey to the Mother Superior and returned no answer. Her intercourse with her neighbor was thenceforward, however, sly and secret, which only made it more interesting and exciting. They would exchange a few words when they met upon the stairs, in the garden, or in the cloisters, when there was no curious eye to spy them out; and the first time Jacqueline went out alone Madame Saville was on the watch, and, without speaking, slipped a letter into her hand.

This first time Jacqueline went out was an epoch in her life, as small events are sometimes in the annals of nations; it was the date of her emancipation, it coincided with what she called her choice of a career. Thinking herself sure of possessing a talent for teaching, she had spoken of it to several friends who had come to see her, and who each and all exclaimed that they would like some lessons, a delicate way of helping her quite understood by Jacqueline. Pupils like Belle Ray and Yvonne d'Etaples, who wanted her to come twice a week to play duets with them or to read over new music, were not nearly so interesting as those in her little class who had hardly more than learned their scales! Besides this, Madame d'Avrigny begged her to come and dine with her, when there would be only themselves, on Mondays, and then practise with Dolly, who had not another moment in which she could take a lesson. She should be sent home scrupulously before ten o'clock, that being the hour at the convent when every one must be in. Jacqueline accepted all these kindnesses gratefully. By Giselle's advice she hid her slight figure under a loose cloak and put on her head a bonnet fit for a grandmother, a closed hat with long

strings, which, when she first put it on her head, made
her burst out laughing. She imagined herself to be going forth in disguise. To walk the streets thus masked
she thought would be amusing, so amusing that the moment she set foot on the street pavement she felt that the
joy of living was yet strong in her. With a roll of music
in her hand, she walked on rather hesitatingly, a little
afraid, like a bird just escaped from the cage where it
was born; her heart beat, but it was with pleasure;
she fancied every one was looking at her, and in fact
one old gentleman, not deceived by the cloak, did follow her till she got into an omnibus for the first time in
her life—a new experience and a new pleasure. Once
seated, and a little out of breath, she remembered Madame Saville's letter, which she had slipped into her
pocket. It was sealed and had a stamp on it; it was
too highly scented to be in good taste, and it was addressed to a lieutenant of *chasseurs* with an aristocratic
name, in a garrison at Fontainebleau.

Then Jacqueline began vaguely to comprehend that
Madame Saville's husband might have had serious reasons for commending his wife to the *surveillance* of the
nuns, and that there might have been some excuse for
their endeavoring to hinder all intimacy between herself and the little blonde.

This office of messenger, thrust upon her without
asking permission, was not agreeable to Jacqueline, and
she resolved as she dropped the missive, which, even
on the outside, looked compromising, into the nearest
post-box, to be more reserved in future. For which
reason she responded coldly to a sign Madame Saville

made her when, in the evening, she returned from giving her lessons.

Those lessons—those excursions which took her abroad in all weathers, though with praiseworthy and serious motives, into the fashionable parts of Paris, from which she had exiled herself by her own will—were greatly enjoyed by Jacqueline. Everything amused her, being seen from a point of view in which she had never before contemplated it. She seemed to be at a play, all personal interests forgotten for the moment, looking at the world of which she was no longer a part with a lively, critical curiosity, without regrets but without cynicism. The world did not seem to her bad—only man's higher instincts had little part in it. Such, at least, was what she thought, so long as people praised her for her courage, so long as the houses in which another Jacqueline de Nailles had been once so brilliant, received her with affection as before, though she had to leave in an anteroom her modest waterproof or wet umbrella. They were even more kind and cordial to her than ever, unless an exaggerated cordiality be one form of impertinence. But the enthusiasm bestowed on splendid instances of energy in certain circles, to which after all such energy is a reproach, is superficial, and not being genuine is sure not to last long. Some people said that Jacqueline's staid manners were put on for effect, and that she was only attempting to play a difficult part to which she was not suited; others blamed her for not being up to concert-pitch in matters of social interest. The first time she felt the pang of exclusion was at Madame d'Avrigny's, who was at the same moment overwhelming her with expressions of regard. In the first place, she could see that the little family dinner to which she had been so kindly invited was attended by so many guests that her deep mourning seemed out of place among them. Then Madame d'Avrigny would make whispered explanations, which Jacqueline was conscious of, and which were very painful to her. Such words as: "Old friend of the family;" "Is giving music lessons to my daughter;" fell more than once upon her ear, followed by exclamations of: "Poor thing!" "So courageous!" "Chivalric sentiments!" Of course, everyone added that they excused her toilette. Then when she tried to escape such remarks by wearing a new gown, Dolly, who was always a little fool (there is no cure for that infirmity) cried out in a tone such as she never would have dared to use in the days when Jacqueline was a model of elegance: "Oh, how fine you are!" Then again, Madame d'Avrigny, notwithstanding the good manners on which she prided herself, could not conceal that the obligation of sending home the recluse to the ends of the earth, at a certain hour, made trouble with her servants, who were put out of their way. Jacqueline seized on this pretext to propose to give up the Monday music-lesson, and after some polite hesitation her offer was accepted, evidently to Madame d'Avrigny's relief.

In this case she had the satisfaction of being the one to propose the discontinuance of the lessons. At Madame Ray's she was simply dismissed. About the close of winter she was told that as Isabelle was soon to be married she would have no time for music till her wedding was over, and about the same time the d'Etaples told her much the same thing. This was not to be wondered at, for Mademoiselle Ray was engaged to an officer of dragoons, the same Marcel d'Etaples who had acted with her in *Scylla and Charybdis*, and Madame Ray, being a watchful mother, was not long in perceiving that Marcel came to pay court to Isabelle too frequently at the hour for her music-lesson. Madame d'Etaples on her part had made a similar discovery, and both judged that the presence of so beautiful a girl, in Jacqueline's position, might not be desirable in these interviews between lovers.

When Giselle, as she was about to leave town for the country in July, begged Jacqueline, who seemed run down and out of spirits, to come and stay with her, the poor child was very glad to accept the invitation. Her pupils were leaving her one after another, she could not understand why, and she was bored to death in the convent, whose strict rules were drawn tighter on her than before, for the nuns had begun to understand her better, and to discover the real worldliness of her character. At the same time, that retreat within these pious walls no longer seemed like paradise to Jacqueline; her transition from the deepest crape to the softer tints of half mourning, seemed to make her less of an angel in their eyes. They said to each other that Mademoiselle de Nailles was fanciful, and fancies are the very last things wanted in a convent, for fancies can brave bolts, and make their escape beyond stone walls, whatever means may be taken to clip their wings.

"She does not seem like the same person," cried the

good sisters, who had been greatly edified at first by her behavior, and who were almost ready now to be shocked at her.

The course of things was coming back rapidly into its natural channel; in obedience to the law which makes a tree, apparently dead, put forth shoots in springtime. And that inevitable re-budding and re-blossoming was beautiful to see in this young human plant. M. de Talbrun, Jacqueline's host, could not fail to perceive it. At first he had been annoyed with Giselle for giving the invitation, having a habit of finding fault with everything he had not ordered or suggested, by virtue of his marital authority, and also because he hated above all things, as he said, to have people in his house who were "wobegones." But in a week he was quite reconciled to the idea of keeping Mademoiselle de Nailles all the summer at the Château de Fresne. Never had Giselle known him to take so much trouble to be amiable, and indeed Jacqueline saw him much more to advantage at home than in Paris, where, as she had often said, he diffused too strong an odor of the stables. At Fresne, it was more easy to forgive him for talking always of his stud and of his kennel, and then he was so obliging! Every day he proposed some new jaunt, an excursion to see some view, to visit all the ruined *châteaux* or abbeys in the neighborhood. And, with surprising delicacy, M. de Talbrun refrained from inviting too many of his country neighbors, who might perhaps have scared Jacqueline and arrested her gradual return to gayety. They might also have interrupted his *tête-à-tête* with his wife's guest,

for they had many such conversations. Giselle was
absorbed in the duty of teaching her son his a, b, c.
Besides, being very timid, she had never ridden on
horseback, and, naturally, riding was delightful to her
cousin. Jacqueline was never tired of it; while she
paid as little attention to the absurd remarks Oscar
made to her between their gallops as a girl does at a
ball to the idle words of her partner. She supposed it
was his custom to talk in that manner—a sort of rough
gallantry—but with the best intentions. Jacqueline
was disposed to look upon her life at Fresne as a feast
after a long famine. Everything was to her taste, the
whole appearance of this lordly *château* of the time of
Louis XIII, the splendid trees in the home park, the
gardens laid out *à la Française*, decorated with art and
kept up carefully. Everything, indeed, that pertained
to that high life which to Giselle had so little importance, was to her delightful. Giselle's taste was so
simple that it was a constant subject of reproach from
her husband. To be sure, it was with him a general
rule to find fault with her about everything. He did
not spare her his reproaches on a multitude of subjects;
all day long he was worrying her about small trifles
with which he should have had nothing to do. It is a
mistake to suppose that a man can not be brutal and
fussy at the same time. M. de Talbrun was proof to
the contrary.

"You are too patient," said Jacqueline often to
Giselle. "You ought to answer him back—to defend
yourself. I am sure if you did so you would have him,
by-and-bye, at your beck and call."

JACQUELINE

"Perhaps so. I dare say you could have managed better than I do," replied Giselle, with a sad smile, but without a spark of jealousy. "Oh, you are in high favor. He gave up this week the races at Deauville, the great race week from which he has never before been absent, since our marriage. But you see my ambition has become limited; I am satisfied if he lets me alone." Giselle spoke these words with emphasis, and then she added: "and lets me bring up his son my own way. That is all I ask."

Jacqueline thought in her heart that it was wrong to ask so little, that poor Giselle did not know how to make the best of her husband, and, curious to find out what line of conduct would serve best to subjugate M. de Talbrun, she became *herself*—that is to say, a born coquette—venturing from one thing to another, like a child playing fearlessly with a bulldog, who is gentle only with him, or a fly buzzing round a spider's web, while the spider lies quietly within.

She would tease him, contradict him, and make him listen to long pieces of scientific music as she played them on the piano, when she knew he always said that music to him was nothing but a disagreeable noise; she would laugh at his thanks when a final chord, struck with her utmost force, roused him from a brief slumber; in short, it amused her to prove that this coarse, rough man was to her alone no object of fear. She would have done better had she been afraid.

Thus it came to pass that, as they rode together through some of the prettiest roads in the most beautiful part of Normandy, M. de Talbrun began to talk, with an ever-increasing vivacity, of the days when they first met at Tréport, relating a thousand little incidents which Jacqueline had forgotten, and from which it was easy to see that he had watched her narrowly, though he was on the eve of his own marriage. With unnecessary persistence, and stammering as he was apt to do when moved by any emotion, he repeated over and over again, that from the first moment he had seen her he had been struck by her—devilishly struck by her—he had been, indeed! And one day when she answered, in order not to appear to attach any importance to this declaration, that she was very glad of it, he took an opportunity, as their horses stopped side by side before a beautiful sunset, to put his arm suddenly round her waist, and give her a kiss, so abrupt, so violent, so outrageous, that she screamed aloud. He did not remove his arm from her, his coarse, red face drew near her own again with an expression that filled her with horror. She struggled to free herself, her horse began to rear, she screamed for help with all her might, but nothing answered her save an echo. The situation seemed critical for Jacqueline. As to M. de Talbrun, he was quite at his ease, as if he were accustomed to make love like a centaur; while the girl felt herself in peril of being thrown at any moment, and trampled under his horse's feet. At last she succeeded in striking her aggressor a sharp blow across the face with her riding-whip. Blinded for a moment, he let her go, and she took advantage of her release to put her horse to its full speed. He galloped after her, beside himself with wrath and agitation; it was a mad but silent race, until they reached the gate of the Château de Fresne, which they entered at the same moment, their horses covered with foam.

"How foolish!" cried Giselle, coming to meet them. "Just see in what a state you have brought home your poor horses."

Jacqueline, pale and trembling, made no answer. M. de Talbrun, as he helped her to dismount, whispered, savagely: "Not a word of this!"

At dinner, his wife remarked that some branch must have struck him on the cheek, there was a red mark right across his face like a blow.

"We were riding through the woods," he answered, shortly.

Then Giselle began to suspect something, and remarked that nobody was talking that evening, asking, with a half-smile, whether they had been quarrelling.

"We did have a little difference," Oscar replied, quietly.

"Oh, it did not amount to anything," he said, lighting his cigar; "let us make friends again, won't you?" he added, holding out his hand to Jacqueline. She was obliged to give him the tips of her fingers, as she said in her turn, with audacity equal to his own:

"Oh, it was less than nothing. Only, Giselle, I told your husband that I had had some bad news, and shall have to go back to Paris, and he tried to persuade me not to go."

"I beg you not to go," said Oscar, vehemently.

"Bad news?" repeated Giselle, "you did not say a word to me about it!"

"I did not have a chance. My old Modeste is very
ill and asks me to come to her. I should never forgive
myself if I did not go."

"What, Modeste? So very ill? Is it really so serious? What a pity! But you will come back again?"

"If I can. But I must leave Fresne to-morrow
morning."

"Oh, I defy you to leave Fresne!" said M. de
Talbrun.

Jacqueline leaned toward him, and said firmly, but
in a low voice: "If you attempt to hinder me, I swear
I will tell everything."

All that evening she did not leave Giselle's side for a
moment, and at night she locked herself into her chamber and barricaded the door, as if a mad dog or a mur-
derer were at large in the *château*.

Giselle came into her room at an early hour.

"Is what you said yesterday the truth, Jacqueline?
Is Modeste really ill? Are you sure you have had no
reason to complain of anybody in this place?—of any
one?"

Then, after a pause, she added:

"Oh, my darling, how hard it is to do good even to
those whom we most dearly love."

"I don't understand you," said Jacqueline, with an
effort. "Everybody has been kind to me."

They kissed each other with effusion, but M. de Talbrun's leave-taking was icy in the extreme. Jacqueline had made a mortal enemy.

The grand outline of the *château*, built of brick and
stone with its wings flanked by towers, the green turf

of the great park in which it stood, passed from her sight as she drove away, like some vision in a dream.

"I shall never come back—never come back!" thought Jacqueline. She felt as if she had been thrust out everywhere. For one moment she thought of seeking refuge at Lizerolles, which was not very many miles from the railroad station, and when there of telling Madame d'Argy of her difficulties, and asking her advice; but false pride kept her from doing so—the same false pride which had made her write coldly, in answer to the letters full of feeling and sympathy Fred had written to her on receiving news of her father's death.

CHAPTER XV

HE experience through which Jacqueline had just passed was not calculated to fortify her or to elevate her soul. She felt for the first time that her unprotected situation and her poverty exposed her to insult, for what other name could she give to the outrageous behavior of M. de Talbrun, which had degraded her in her own eyes?

What right had that man to treat her as his plaything? Her pride and all her womanly instincts rose up in rebellion. Her nerves had been so shaken that she sobbed behind her veil ail the way to her destination. Paris, when she reached it, offered her almost nothing that could comfort or amuse her. That city is always empty and dull in August, more so than at any other season. Even the poor occupation of teaching her little class of music pupils had been taken away by the holidays. Her sole resource was in Modeste's society. Modeste—who, by the way, had never been ill, and who suffered from nothing but old age—was delighted to receive her dear young lady in her little room far up under the roof, where, though quite infirm, she lived comfortably, on her savings. Jacqueline, sitting beside her as she sewed, was soothed by her old nursery tales, or by anecdotes of former days. Her own relatives were often the old woman's theme. She knew the history of Jacqueline's family from beginning to end; but, wherever her story began, it invariably wound up with:

"If only your poor papa had not made away with all your money!"

And Jacqueline always answered:

"He was quite at liberty to do what he pleased with what belonged to him."

"Belonged to him! Yes, but what belonged to you? And how does it happen that your stepmother seems so well off? Why doesn't some family council interfere? My little pet, to think of your having to work for your living. It's enough to kill me!"

"Bah! Modeste, there are worse things than being poor."

"Maybe so," answered the old nurse, doubtfully, "but when one has money troubles along with the rest, the money troubles make other things harder to bear; whereas, if you have money enough you can bear anything, and you would have had enough, after all, if you had married Monsieur Fred."

At which point Jacqueline insisted that Modeste should be silent, and answered, resolutely: "I mean never to marry at all."

To this Modeste made answer: "That's another of your notions. The worst husband is always better than none; and I know, for I never married."

"That's why you talk such nonsense, my poor dear Modeste! You know nothing about it."

One day, after one of these visits to the only friend, as she believed, who remained to her in the world—for her intimacy with Giselle was spoiled forever—she saw, as she walked with a heavy heart toward her convent in a distant quarter, an open *fiacre* pull up, in obedience to a sudden cry from a passenger who was sitting inside. The person sprang out, and rushed toward Jacqueline with loud exclamations of joy.

"Madame Strahlberg!"

"Dear Jacqueline! What a pleasure to meet you!" And, the street being nearly empty, Madame Strahlberg heartily embraced her friend.

"I have thought of you so often, darling, for months past—they seem like years, like centuries! Where have you been all that long time?"

In point of fact, Jacqueline had no proof that the three Odinska ladies had ever remembered her existence, but that might have been partly her own fault, or rather the fault of Giselle, who had made her promise to have as little as possible to do with such compromising personages. She was seized with a kind of remorse when she found such warmth of recognition from the amiable Wanda. Had she not shown herself ungrateful and cowardly? People about whom the world talks, are they not sometimes quite as good as those who have not lost their standing in society, like M. de Talbrun? It seemed to her that, go where she would, she ran risks.

The cynicism that is the result of sad experience was beginning to show itself in Jacqueline.

"Oh, forgive me!" she said, feeling contrite.

JACQUELINE

"Forgive you for what, you beautiful creature?" asked Madame Strahlberg, with sincere astonishment.

She had the excellent custom of never observing when people neglected her, or at least, of never showing that she did so, partly because her life was so full of varied interests that she cared little for such trifles, and secondly because, having endured several affronts of that nature, she had ceased to be very sensitive.

"I knew, through the d'Avrignys," she said, "that you were still at the convent. You are not going to take the veil there, are you? It would be a great pity. No? You wish to lead the life of an intelligent woman who is free and independent? That is well; but it was rather an odd idea to begin by going into a cloister. Oh!—I see, public opinion?" And Madame Strahlberg made a little face, expressive of her contempt for public opinion.

"It does not pay to consult other people's opinions—it is useless, believe me. The more we sacrifice to public opinion, the more it asks of us. I cut that matter short long ago. But how glad I am to hear that you don't intend to hide that lovely face in a convent. You are looking better than ever —a little too pale, still, perhaps—a little too interesting. Colette will be so glad to see you, for you must let me take you home with me. I shall carry you off, whether you will or not, now I have caught you. We will have a little music just among ourselves, as we had in the good old times—you know, our dear music; you will feel like yourself again. Ah, art—there is nothing to compare with art in this world, my darling!"

THÉO BENTZON

Jacqueline yielded without hesitation, only too glad of the unhoped-for good fortune which relieved her from her *ennui* and her depression. And soon the hired victoria was on its way to that quarter of the city which is made up of streets with geographical names, and seems as if it were intended to lodge all the nations under heaven. It stopped in the Rue de Naples, before a house that was somewhat showy, but which showed from its outside, that it was not inhabited by high-bred people. There were pink linings to lace curtains at the windows, and quantities of green vines drooped from the balconies, as if to attract attention from the passers-by. Madame Strahlberg, with her ostentatious and undulating walk, which caused men to turn and notice her as she went by, went swiftly up the stairs to the second story. She put one finger on the electric bell, which caused two or three little dogs inside to begin barking, and pushed Jacqueline in before her, crying: "Colette! Mamma! See whom I have brought back to you!" Meantime doors were hurriedly opened, quick steps resounded in the ante-chamber, and the newcomer found herself received with a torrent of affectionate and delighted exclamations, pressed to the ample bosom of Madame Odinska, covered with kisses by Colette, and fawned upon by the three toy terriers, the most sociable of their kind in all Paris, their mistresses declared.

Jacqueline was passing through one of those moments when one is at the mercy of chance, when the heart which has been closed by sorrow suddenly revives, expands, and softens under the influence of a ray of sunshine. Tears came into her eyes, and she murmured:

"My friends—my kind friends!"

"Yes, your friends, whatever happens, now and always," said Colette, eagerly, though she had probably barely given a thought to Jacqueline for eighteen months. Nevertheless, on seeing her, Colette really thought she had not for a moment ceased to be fond of her. "How you have suffered, you poor pussy! We must set to work and make you feel a little gay, at any price. You see, it is our duty. How lucky you came to-day——"

A sign from her sister stopped her.

They carried Jacqueline into a large and handsome salon, full of dust and without curtains, with all the furniture covered up as if the family were on the eve of going to the country. Madame Strahlberg, nevertheless, was not about to leave Paris, her habit being to remain there in the summer, sometimes for months, picnicking as it were, in her own apartment. What was curious, too, was that the chandelier and all the side-lights had fresh wax candles, and seats were arranged as if in preparation for a play, while near the grand piano was a sort of stage, shut off from the rest of the room by screens.

Colette sat down on one of the front row of chairs and cried: "I am the audience—I am all ears." Her sister hurriedly explained all this to Jacqueline, without waiting to be questioned: "We have been giving some little summer entertainments of late, of which you see the remains." She went at once to the piano,

and incited Jacqueline to sing by beginning one of
their favorite duets, and Jacqueline, once more in her
native element, followed her lead. They went on
from one song to another, from the light to the severe,
from scientific music to mere tunes and airs, turning
over the old music-books together.

"Yes, you are a little out of practice, but all you have
to do is to rub off the rust. Your voice is finer than
ever—just like velvet." And Madame Strahlberg pretended that she envied the fine mezzo-soprano, speaking disparagingly of her own little thread of a voice,
which, however, she managed so skilfully. "What a
shame to take up your time teaching, with such a voice
as that!" she cried; "you are out of your senses, my
dear, you are raving mad. It would be sinful to keep
your gifts to yourself! I am very sorry to discourage
you, but you have none of the requisites for a teacher.
The stage would be best for you—*Mon Dieu!* why
not? You will see La Rochette this evening; she is a
person who would give you good advice. I wish she
could hear you!"

"But my dear friend, I can not stay," murmured
Jacqueline, for those unexpected words "the stage,
why not?" rang in her head, made her heart beat
fast, and made lights dance before her eyes. "They
are expecting me to dine at home."

"At your convent? I beg your pardon, I'll take
care of that. Don't you know me? My claws seldom let go of a prize, especially when that prize is
worth the keeping. A little telegram has already been
sent, with your excuses. The telegraph is good

for that, if not for anything else: it facilitates impromptus."

"Long live impromptus," cried out Colette, "there is nothing like them for fun!" And while Jacqueline was trying to get away, not knowing exactly what she was saying, but frightened, pleased, and much excited, Colette went on: "Oh! I am so glad, so glad you came to-day; now you can see the pantomime! I dreamed, wasn't it odd, only last night, that you were acting it with us. How can one help believing in presentiments? Mine are always delightful—and yours?"

"The pantomime?" repeated Jacqueline in bewilderment, "but I thought your sister told me you were all alone."

"How could we have anything like company in August?" said Madame Strahlberg, interrupting her; "why, it would be impossible, there are not four cats in Paris. No, no, we sha'n't have anybody. A few friends possibly may drop in—people passing through Paris—in their travelling-dresses. Nothing that need alarm you. The pantomime Colette talks about is only a pretext that they may hear Monsieur Szmera."

And who was M. Szmera?

Jacqueline soon learned that he was a Hungarian, second half-cousin of a friend of Kossuth, the most wonderful violinist of the day, who had apparently superseded the famous Polish pianist in these ladies' interest and esteem. As for the latter, they had almost forgotten his name, he had behaved so badly.

"But," said Jacqueline, anxiously, "you know I am obliged to be home by ten o'clock."

"Ah! that's like Cinderella," laughed Wanda. "Will the stroke of the clock change all the carriages in Paris into pumpkins? One can get *fiacres* at any hour."

"But it is a fixed rule: I *must* be in," repeated Jacqueline, growing very uneasy.

"Must you really? Madame Saville says it is very easy to manage those nuns——"

"What? Do you know Madame Saville, who was boarding at the convent last winter?"

"Yes, indeed; she is a countrywoman of ours, a friend, the most charming of women. You will see her here this evening. She has gained her divorce suit——"

"You are mistaken," said Colette, "she has lost it. But that makes no difference. She has got tired of her husband. Come, say 'Yes,' Jacqueline—a nice, dear 'Yes'—you will stay, will you not? Oh, you darling!"

They dined without much ceremony, on the pretext that the cook had been turned off that morning for impertinence, but immediately after dinner there was a procession of boys from a restaurant, bringing whipped creams, iced drinks, fruits, sweetmeats, and champagne —more than would have been wanted at the buffet of a ball. The Prince, they said, had sent these things. What Prince?

As Jacqueline was asking this question, a gentleman came in whose age it would have been impossible to guess, so disguised was he by his black wig, his dyed whiskers, and the soft bloom on his cheeks, all of which were entirely out of keeping with those parts

of his face that he could not change. In one of his
eyes was stuck a monocle. He was bedizened with
several orders, he bowed with military stiffness, and
kissed with much devotion the ladies' hands, calling
them by titles, whether they had them or not. His
foreign accent made it as hard to detect his nationality
as it was to know his age. Two or three other gentlemen, not less decorated and not less foreign, afterward
came in. Colette named them in a whisper to Jacqueline, but their names were too hard for her to pronounce, much less to remember. One of them, a
man of handsome presence, came accompanied by
a sort of female ruin, an old lady leaning on a cane,
whose head, every time she moved, glittered with jew-
els, placed in a very lofty erection of curled hair.

"That gentleman's mother is awfully ugly," Jacqueline could not help saying.

"His mother? What, the Countess? She is neither
his mother nor his wife. He is her gentleman-in-wait-
ing—that's all. Don't you understand? Well, imagine a man who is a sort of "gentleman-companion";
he keeps her accounts, he escorts her to the theatre,
he gives her his arm. It is a very satisfactory arrangement."

"The gentleman receives a salary, in such a case?"
inquired Jacqueline, much amused.

"Why, what do you find in it so extraordinary?"
said Colette. "She adores cards, and there he is,
always ready to be her partner. Oh, here comes dear
Madame Saville!"

There were fresh cries of welcome, fresh exchanges

of affectionate diminutives and kisses, which seemed to make the Prince's mouth water. Jacqueline discovered, to her great surprise, that she, too, was a dear friend of Madame Saville's, who called her her good angel, in reference, no doubt, to the letter she had secretly put into the post. At last she said, trying to make her escape from the party: "But it must be nine o'clock."

"Oh! but you must hear Szmera."

A handsome young fellow, stoutly built, with heavy eyebrows, a hooked nose, a quantity of hair growing low upon his forehead, and lips that were too red, the perfect type of a Hungarian gypsy, began a piece of his own composition, which had all the ardor of a mild galopade and a Satanic hunt, with intervals of dying sweetness, during which the painted skeleton they called the Countess declared that she certainly heard a nightingale warbling in the moonlight.

This charming speech was forthwith repeated by her "umbra" in all parts of the room, which was now nearly filled with people, a mixed multitude, some of whom were frantic about music, others frantic about Wanda Strahlberg. There were artists and amateurs present, and even respectable women, for Madame d'Avrigny, attracted by the odor of a species of Bohemianism, had come to breathe it with delight, under cover of a wish to glean ideas for her next winter's receptions.

Then again there were women who had been dropped out of society, like Madame de Versanne, who, with her sunken eyes and faded face, was not likely again to pick up in the street a bracelet worth ten thousand francs. There was a literary woman who signed herself Fraisiline, and wrote papers on fashion —she was so painted and bedizened that some one remarked that the principal establishments she praised in print probably paid her in their merchandise. There was a dowager whose aristocratic name appeared daily on the fourth page of the newspapers, attesting the merits of some kind of quack medicine; and a retired opera-singer, who, having been called Zenaïde Rochet till she grew up in Montmartre, where she was born, had had a brilliant career as a star in Italy under the name of Zina Rochette. La Rochette's name, alas! is unknown to the present generation.

In all, there were about twenty persons, who made more noise with their applause than a hundred ordinary guests, for enthusiasm was exacted by Madame Strahlberg. Profiting by the ovation to the Hungarian musician, Jacqueline made a movement toward the door, but just as she reached it she had the misfortune of falling in with her old acquaintance, Nora Sparks, who was at that moment entering with her father. She was forced to sit down again and hear all about Kate's marriage. Kate had gone back to New York, her husband being an American, but Nora said she had made up her mind not to leave Europe till she had found a satisfactory match.

"You had better make haste about it, if you expect to keep me here," said Mr. Sparks, with a peculiar expression in his eye. He was eager to get home, having important business to attend to in the West.

"Oh, papa, be quiet! I shall find somebody at Bellagio. Why, darling, are you still in mourning?"

She had forgotten that Jacqueline had lost her father. Probably she would not have thought it necessary to wear black so long for Mr. Sparks. Meantime, Madame Strahlberg and her sister had left the room.

"When are they coming back?" said Jacqueline, growing very nervous. "It seems to me this clock must be wrong. It says half-past nine. I am sure it must be later than that."

"Half-past nine!—why, it is past eleven," replied Miss Nora, with a giggle. "Do you suppose they pay any attention to clocks in this house? Everything here is topsy-turvy."

"Oh! what shall I do?" sighed poor Jacqueline, on the verge of tears.

"Why, do they keep you such a prisoner as that? Can't you come in a little late——"

"They wouldn't open the doors—they never open the doors on any pretext after ten o'clock," cried Jacqueline, beside herself.

"Then your nuns must be savages? You should teach them better."

"Don't be worried, dear little one, you can sleep on this sofa," said Madame Odinska, kindly.

To whom had she not offered that useful sofa? Wanda and Colette were just as ready to propose that others should spend the night with them as, on the smallest pretext, to accept the same hospitality from others. Wanda, indeed, always slept curled up like a cat on a divan, in a fur wrapper, which she put on early in

JACQUELINE

the evening when she wanted to smoke cigarettes. She went to sleep at no regular hour. A bear's skin was placed always within her reach, so that if she were cold she could draw it over her. Jacqueline, not being accustomed to these Polish fashions, did not seem to be much attracted by the offer of the sofa. She blamed herself bitterly for her own folly in having got herself into a scrape which might lead to serious consequences.

But this was neither time nor place for expressions of anxiety; it would be absurd to trouble every one present with her regrets. Besides, the harm was done —it was irreparable—and while she was turning over in her mind in what manner she could explain to the Mother Superior that the mistake about the hour had been no fault of hers—and the Mother Superior, alas! would be sure to make inquiries as to the friends whom she had visited—the magic violin of M. Szmera played its first notes, accompanied by Madame Odinska on the piano, and by a delicious little flute. They played an overture, the dreamy sweetness of which extorted cries of admiration from all the women.

Suddenly, the screens parted, and upon the little platform that represented a stage bounded a sort of anomalous being, supple and charming, in the traditional dress of Pierrot, whom the English vulgarize and call Harlequin. He had white camellias instead of buttons on his loose white jacket, and the bright eyes of Wanda shone out from his red- and-white face. He held a mandolin, and imitated the most charming of serenades, before a make-believe window, which, being opened by a white, round arm, revealed Colette, dressed as Colombine.

The little pantomime piece was called *Pierrot in Love.* It consisted of a series of dainty coquetries, sudden quarrels, fits of jealousy, and tender reconciliations, played by the two sisters. Colette with her beauty, Wanda with her talent, her impishness, her graceful and voluptuous attitudes, electrified the spectators, especially in a long monologue, in which Pierrot contemplated suicide, made more effective by the passionate and heart-piercing strains of the Hungarian's violin, so that old Rochette cried out: "What a pity such a wonder should not be upon the stage!" La Rochette, now retired into private life, wearing an old dress, with her gray hair and her black eyes, like those of a watchful crocodile, took the pleasure in the pantomime that all actors do to the very last in everything connected with the theatre. She cried *brava* in tones that might reach Italy; she blew kisses to the actors in default of flowers.

Madame d'Avrigny was also transported to the sixth heaven, but Jacqueline's presence somewhat marred her pleasure. When she first perceived her she had shown great surprise. "You here, my dear?" she cried, "I thought you safe with our own excellent Giselle."

"Safe, Madame? It seems to me one can be safe anywhere," Jacqueline answered, though she was tempted to say "safe nowhere;" but instead she inquired for Dolly.

Dolly's mother bit her lips and then replied: "You

JACQUELINE

see I have not brought her. Oh, yes, this house is very amusing—but rather too much so. The play was very pretty, and I am sorry it would not do at my house. It is too—too *risque*, you know;" and she rehearsed her usual speech about the great difficulties encountered by a lady who wished to give entertainments and provide amusement for her friends.

Meantime Pierrot, or rather Madame Strahlberg, had leaped over an imaginary barrier and came dancing toward the company, shaking her large sleeves and settling her little snake-like head in her large quilled collar, dragging after her the Hungarian, who seemed not very willing. She presented him to Madame d'Avrigny, hoping that so fashionable a woman might want him to play at her receptions during the winter, and to a journalist who promised to give him a notice in his paper, provided—and here he whispered something to Pierrot, who, smiling, answered neither yes nor no. The sisters kept on their costumes; Colette was enchanting with her bare neck, her long-waisted black velvet corsage, her very short skirt, and a sort of three-cornered hat upon her head. All the men paid court to her, and she accepted their homage, becoming gayer and gayer at every compliment, laughing loudly, possibly that her laugh might exhibit her beautiful teeth.

Wanda, as Pierrot, sang, with her hands in her pockets, a Russian village song: *"Ah! Dounaï-li moy Dounaï"* ("Oh! thou, my Danube"). Then she imperiously called Jacqueline to the piano: "It is your turn now," she said, "most humble violet."

THÉO BENTZON

Up to that moment, Jacqueline's deep mourning had kept the gentlemen present from addressing her, though she had been much stared at. Although she did not wish to sing, for her heart was heavy as she thought of the troubles that awaited her the next day at the convent, she sang what was asked of her without resistance or pretension. Then, for the first time, she experienced the pride of triumph. Szmera, though he was furious at not being the sole lion of the evening, complimented her, bowing almost to the ground, with one hand on his heart; Madame Rochette assured her that she had a fortune in her throat whenever she chose to seek it; persons she had never seen and who did not know her name, pressed her hands fervently, saying that her singing was adorable. All cried "Encore," "Encore!" and, yielding to the pleasure of applause, she thought no more of the flight of time. Dawn was peeping through the windows when the party broke up.

"What kind people!" thought the *débutante*, whom they had encouraged and applauded; "some perhaps are a little odd, but how much cordiality and warmth there is among them! It is catching. This is the sort of atmosphere in which talent should live."

Being very much fatigued, she fell asleep upon the offered sofa, half-pleased, half-frightened, but with two prominent convictions: one, that she was beginning to return to life; the other, that she stood on the edge of a precipice. In her dreams old Rochette appeared to her, her face like that of an affable frog, her dress the dress of Pierrot, and she croaked out, in a variety of tones: "The stage! Why not? Applauded every night—it would be glorious!" Then she seemed in her dream to be falling, falling down from a great height, as one falls from fairyland into stern reality. She opened her eyes: it was noon. Madame Odinska was waiting for her: she intended herself to take her to the convent, and for that purpose had assumed the imposing air of a noble matron.

Alas! it was in vain! Jacqueline, was made to understand that such an infraction of the rules could not be overlooked. To pass the night without leave out of the convent, and not with her own family, was cause for expulsion. Neither the prayers nor the anger of Madame Odinska had any power to change the sentence. While the Mother Superior calmly pronounced her decree, she was taking the measure of this stout foreigner who appeared in behalf of Jacqueline, a woman overdressed, yet at the same time shabby, who had a far from well-bred or aristocratic air. "Out of consideration for Madame de Talbrun," she said, "the convent consents to keep Mademoiselle de Nailles a few days longer—a few weeks perhaps, until she can find some other place to go. That is all we can do for her."

Jacqueline listened to this sentence as she might have watched a game of dice when her fate hung on the result, but she showed no emotion. "Now," she thought, "my fate has been decided; respectable people will have nothing more to do with me. I will go with the others, who, perhaps, after all are not worse, and who most certainly are more amusing."

A fortnight after this, Madame de Nailles, having

come back to Paris, from some watering-place, was telling Marien that Jacqueline had started for Bellagio with Mr. and Miss Sparks, the latter having taken a notion that she wanted that kind of chaperon who is called a *companion* in England and America.

"But they are of the same age," said Marien.

"That is just what Miss Sparks wants. She does not wish to be hampered by an elderly chaperon, but to be accompanied, as she would have been by her sister."

"Jacqueline will be exposed to see strange things; how could you have consented——"

"Consented? As if she cared for my consent! And then she manages to say such irritating things as soon as one attempts to blame her or advise her. For example, this is one of them: 'Don't you suppose,' she said to me, 'that every one will take the most agreeable chance that offers for a visit to Italy?' What do you think of that allusion? It closed my lips absolutely."

"Perhaps she did not mean what you think she meant."

"Do you think so? And when I warned her against Madame Strahlberg, saying that she might set her a very bad example, she answered: 'I may have had worse.' I suppose *that* was not meant for impertinence either!"

"I don't know," said Hubert Marien, biting his lips doubtfully, "but——"

He was silent a few moments, his head drooped on his breast, he was in some painful reverie.

JACQUELINE

"Go on. What are you thinking about?" asked Madame de Nailles, impatiently.

"I beg your pardon. I was only thinking that a certain responsibility might rest on those who have made that young girl what she is."

"I don't understand you," said the stepmother, with an impatient gesture. "Who can do anything to counteract a bad disposition? You don't deny that hers is bad? She is a very devil for pride and obstinacy—she has no affection—she has proved it. I have no inclination to get myself wounded by trying to control her."

"Then you prefer to let her ruin herself?"

"I should prefer not to give the world a chance to talk, by coming to an open rupture with her, which would certainly be the case if I tried to contradict her. After all, the Sparks and Madame Odinska are not yet put out of the pale of good society, and she knew them long ago. An early intimacy may be a good explanation if people blame her for going too far——"

"So be it, then; if you are satisfied it is not for me to say anything," replied Marien, coldly.

"Satisfied? I am not satisfied with anything or anybody," said Madame de Nailles, indignantly. "How could I be satisfied; I never have met with anything but ingratitude."

CHAPTER XVI

ADAME D'ARGY did not leave her son in ignorance of all the freaks and follies of Jacqueline. He knew every particular of the wrong-doings and the imprudences of his early friend, and even the additions made to them by calumny, ever since the fit of independence which, after her father's death, had led her to throw off all control. She told of her sudden departure from Fresne, where she might have found so safe a refuge with her friend and cousin. Then had not her own imprudence and coquetry led to a rupture with the families of d'Etaples and Ray?

She told of the scandalous intimacy with Madame Strahlberg; of her expulsion from the convent, where they had discovered, even before she left, that she had been in the habit of visiting undesirable persons; and finally she informed him that Jacqueline had gone to Italy with an old Yankee and his daughter—he being a man, it was said, who had laid the foundation of his colossal fortune by keeping a bar-room in a mining-camp in California. This last was no fiction, the cut of Mr. Sparks's beard and his unpolished manners left no doubt on the subject; and she wound up by saying that

JACQUELINE

Madame d'Avrigny, whom no one could accuse of ill-nature, had been grieved at meeting this unhappy girl in very improper company, among which she seemed quite in her element, like a fish in water.

It was said also that she was thinking of studying for the stage with La Rochette—M. de Talbrun had heard it talked about in the *foyer* of the Opera by an old Prince from some foreign country—she could not remember his name, but he was praising Madame Strahlberg without any reserve as the most delightful of *Parisiennes*. Thereupon Talbrun had naturally forbidden his wife to have anything to do with Jacqueline, or even to write to her. Fat Oscar, though he was not all that he ought to be himself, had some very strict notions of propriety. No one was more particular about family relations, and really in this case no one could blame him; but Giselle had been very unhappy, and to the very last had tried to stand up for her unhappy friend. Having told him all this, she added, she would say no more on the subject.

Giselle was a model woman in everything, in tact, in goodness, in good sense, and she was very attentive to the poor old mother of Fred, who but for her must have died long ago of loneliness and sorrow. Thereupon ensued the poor lady's usual lamentations over the long, long absence of her beloved son; as usual, she told him she did not think she should live to see him back again; she gave him a full account of her maladies, caused, or at least aggravated, by her mortal, constant, incurable sorrow; and she told how Giselle had been nursing her with all the patience and devotion of a Sister of Charity. Through all Madame d'Argy's letters at this period the angelic figure of Giselle was contrasted with the very different one of that young and incorrigible little devil of a Jacqueline.

Fred at first believed his mother's stories were all exaggeration, but the facts were there, corroborated by the continued silence of the person concerned. He knew his mother to be too good wilfully to blacken the character of one whom for years she had hoped would be her daughter-in-law, the only child of her best friend, the early love of her son. But by degrees he fancied that the love so long living at the bottom of his heart was slowly dying, that it had been extinguished, that nothing remained of it but remembrance, such remembrance as we retain for dead things, a remembrance without hope, whose weight added to the homesickness which with him was increasing every day.

There was no active service to enable him to endure exile. The heroic period of the war had passed. Since a treaty of peace had been signed with China, the fleet, which had distinguished itself in so many small engagements and bombardments, had had nothing to do but to mount guard, as it were, along a conquered coast. All round it in the bay, where it lay at anchor, rose mountains of strange shapes, which seemed to shut it into a kind of prison. This feeling of nothing to be done—of nothing likely to be done, worked in Fred's head like a nightmare. The only thing he thought of was how he could escape, when could he once more kiss the faded cheeks of his mother, who often, when he slept or lay wakeful during the long hours of the *siesta*, he saw beside him in tears. Hers was the only face that he recalled distinctly; to her and to her only were devoted his long reveries when on watch; that time when he formerly composed his love verses, tender or angry, or full of despair. That was all over! A sort of mournful resignation had succeeded his bursts of excited feeling, his revolt against his fate.

This was Fred's state of mind when he received orders to return home—orders as unexpected as everything seems to be in the life of a naval man. "I am going back to her!" he cried. *Her* was his mother, *her* was France. All the rest had disappeared as if into a fog. Jacqueline was a phantom of the past; so many things had happened since the old times when he had loved her. He had crossed the Indian Ocean and the China Sea; he had seen long stretches of interminable coast-line; he had beheld misery, and glory, and all the painful scenes that wait on warfare; he had seen pestilence, and death in every shape, and all this had wrought in him a sort of stoicism, the result of long acquaintance with solitude and danger. He remembered his old love as a flower he had once admired as he passed it, a treacherous flower, with thorns that had wounded him. There are flowers that are beneficent, and flowers that are poisonous, and the last are sometimes the most beautiful. They should not be blamed, he thought; it was their nature to be hurtful; but it was well to pass them by and not to gather them.

By the time he had debarked Fred had made up his mind to let his mother choose a wife for him, a daughter-in-law suited to herself, who would give her the delight of grandchildren, who would bring them up well, and who would not weary of Lizerolles. But a week later the idea of this kind of marriage had gone out of his head, and this change of feeling was partly owing to Giselle. Giselle gave him a smile of welcome that went to his heart, for that poor heart, after all, was only waiting for a chance again to give itself away. She was with Madame d'Argy, who had not been well enough to go to the sea-coast to meet her son, and he saw at the same moment the pale and aged face which had visited him at Tonquin in his dreams, and a fair face that he had never before thought so beautiful, more oval than he remembered it, with blue eyes soft and tender, and a mouth with a sweet infantine expression of sincerity and goodness. His mother stretched out her trembling arms, gave a great cry, and fainted away.

"Don't be alarmed; it is only joy," said Giselle, in her soft voice.

And when Madame d'Argy proved her to be right by recovering very quickly, overwhelming her son with rapid questions and covering him with kisses, Giselle held out her hand to him and said:

"I, too, am very glad you have come home."

"Oh!" cried the sick woman in her excitement, "you must kiss your old playfellow!"

Giselle blushed a little, and Fred, more embarrassed than she, lightly touched with his lips her pretty smooth hair which shone upon her head like a helmet of gold. Perhaps it was this new style of hairdressing which made her seem so much more beautiful than he remembered her, but it seemed to him he saw her for the first time; while, with the greatest eagerness, notwithstanding Giselle's attempts to interrupt her, Madame d'Argy repeated to her son all she owed to that dear friend—"her own daughter, the best of daughters, the most patient, the most devoted of daughters, could not have done more! Ah! if there only could be found another one like her!"

Whereupon the object of all these praises made her escape, disclaiming everything.

Why, after this, should she have hesitated to come back to Lizerolles every day, as of late had been her custom? Men know so little about taking care of sick people. So she came, and was present at all the rejoicings and all the talks that followed Fred's return. She took her part in the discussions about Fred's future. "Help me, my pet," said Madame d'Argy, "help me to find a wife for him: all we ask is that she should be like you."

In answer to which Fred declared, half-laughing and half-seriously, that *that* was his ideal.

She did not believe much of this, but, following her natural instinct, she assumed the dangerous task of consolation, until, as Madame d'Argy grew better, she discontinued her daily visits, and Fred, in his turn, took a habit of going over to Fresne without being invited, and spending there a good deal of his time.

"Don't send me away. You who are always charitable," he said. "If you only knew what a pleasure a Parisian conversation is after coming from Tonquin!"

THÉO BENTZON

"But I am so little of a *Parisienne*, or at least what you mean by that term, and my conversation is not worth coming for," objected Giselle.

In her extreme modesty she did not realize how much she had gained in intellectual culture. Women left to themselves have time to read, and Giselle had done this all the more because she had considered it a duty. Must she not know enough to instruct and superintend the education of her son? With much strong feeling, yet with much simplicity, she spoke to Fred of this great task, which sometimes frightened her; he gave her his advice, and both discussed together the things that make up a good man. Giselle brought up frequently the subject of heredity: she named no one, but Fred could see that she had a secret terror lest Enguerrand, who in person was very like his father, might also inherit his character. Fears on this subject, however, appeared unfounded. There was nothing about the child that was not good; his tastes were those of his mother. He was passionately fond of Fred, climbing on his lap as soon as the latter arrived and always maintaining that he, too, wanted a pretty red ribbon to wear in his buttonhole, a ribbon only to be got by sailing far away over the seas, like sailors.

"A sailor! Heaven forbid!" cried Madame de Talbrun.

"Oh! sailors come back again. He has come back. Couldn't he take me away with him soon? I have some stories about cabin-boys who were not much older than I."

"Let us hope that your friend Fred won't go away,"

said Giselle. "But why do you wish to be a cabin-boy?"

"Because I want to go away with him, if he does not stay here—because I like him," answered Enguer-rand in a tone of decision.

Hereupon Giselle kissed her boy with more than usual tenderness. *He* would not take to the hunting-field, she thought, the *boulevard*, and the *corps de ballet*. She would not lose him. "But, oh, Fred!" she cried, "it is not to be wondered at that he is so fond of you! You spoil him! You will be a devoted father some day; your vocation is evidently for marriage."

She thought, in thus speaking, that she was saying what Madame d'Argy would like her to say.

"In the matter of children, I think your son is enough for me," he said, one day; "and as for marriage, you would not believe how all women—I mean all the young girls among whom I should have to make a choice—are indifferent to me. My feeling almost amounts to antipathy."

For the first time she ventured to say: "Do you still care for Jacqueline?"

"About as much as she cares for me," he answered, dryly. "No, I made a mistake once, and that has made me cautious for the future."

Another day he said:

"I know now who was the woman I ought to have loved."

Giselle did not look up; she was devoting all her attention to Enguerrand.

Fred held certain theories which he used to talk

about. He believed in a high, spiritual, disinterested affection which would raise a man above himself, making him more noble, inspiring a disgust for all ignoble pleasures. The woman willing to accept such homage might do anything she pleased with a heart that would be hers alone. She would be the lady who presided over his life, for whose sake all good deeds and generous actions would be done, the idol, higher than a wife or any object of earthly passion, the White Angel whom poets have sung.

Giselle pretended that she did not understand him, but she was divinely happy. This, then, was the reward of her spotless life! She was the object of a worship no less tender than respectful. Fred spoke of the woman he ought to have loved as if he meant to say, "I love you;" he pressed his lips on the auburn curls of little Enguerrand where his mother had just kissed him. Day after day he seemed more attracted to that salon where, dressed with more care than she had ever dressed before, she expected him. Then awoke in her the wish to please, and she was beautiful with that beauty which is not the insipid beauty of St. Agnes, but that which, superior to all other, is seen when the face reflects the soul. All that winter there was a new Giselle—a Giselle who passed away again among the shadows, a Giselle of whom everybody said, even her husband, "*Ma foi!* but she is beautiful!" Oscar de Talbrun, as he made this remark, never thought of wondering *why* she was more beautiful. He was ready to take offense and was jealous by nature, but he was perfectly sure of his wife, as he had often said. As to

[260]

JACQUELINE

Fred, the idea of being jealous of him would never have entered his mind. Fred was a relative and was admitted to all the privileges of a cousin or a brother; besides, he was a fellow of no consequence in any way.

While this platonic attachment grew stronger and stronger between Fred and Giselle, assisted by the innocent complicity of little Enguerrand, Jacqueline was discovering how hard it is for a girl of good birth, if she is poor, to carry out her plans of honest independence. Possibly she had allowed herself to be too easily misled by the title of "companion," which, apparently more cordial than that of *demoiselle de compagnie*, means in reality the same thing—a sort of half-servile position.

Money is a touchstone which influences all social relations, especially when on one side there is a somewhat morbid susceptibility, and on the other a lack of good breeding and education. The Sparks, father and daughter, Americans of the lower class, though willing to spend any number of dollars for their own pleasure, expected that every penny they disbursed should receive its full equivalent in service; the place therefore offered so gracefully and spontaneously to Mademoiselle de Nailles was far from being a sinecure. Jacqueline received her salary on the same footing as Justine, the Parisian maid, received her wages, for, although her position was apparently one of much greater importance and consideration than Justine's, she was really at the beck and call of a girl who, while she called her "darling," gave her orders and paid her for her services. Very often Miss Nora asked her to sew, on the plea that she was as skilful with her fingers as a fairy, but in reality that her employer might feel the superiority of her own position.

Hitherto Miss Nora had been delighted to meet at watering-places a friend of whom she could say proudly, "She is a representative of the old nobility of France" (which was not true, by the way, for the title of Baron borne by M. de Nailles went no farther back than the days of Louis XVIII); and she was still more proud to think that she was now waited on by this same daughter of a nobleman, when her own father had kept a drinking-saloon. She did not acknowledge this feeling to herself, and would certainly have maintained that she never had had such an idea, but it existed all the same, and she was under its influence, being very vain and rather foolish. And, indeed, Jacqueline, would have been very willing to plan trimmings and alter finery from morning to night in her own chamber in a hotel, exactly as Mademoiselle Justine did, if she could by this means have escaped the special duties of her difficult position, which duties were to follow Miss Nora everywhere, like her own shadow, to be her confidant and to act sometimes as her screen, or even as her accomplice, in matters that occasionally involved risks, and were never to her liking.

The young American girl had already said to her father, when he asked her to give up her search for an entirely satisfactory European suitor, which search he feared might drag on forever without any results: "Oh! I shall be sure to find him at Bellagio!" And she made up her mind that there he was to be sought and found at any price. Hotel life offered her opportunities to exercise her instincts for flirtation, for there she met many specimens of men she called *chic*, with a funny little foreign accent, which seemed to put new life into the worn-out word. Twenty times a day she baited her hook, and twenty times a day some fish would bite, or at least nibble, according as he was a fortune-hunter or a dilettante. Miss Nora, being incapable of knowing the difference, was ready to capture good or bad, and went about dragging her slaves at her chariot-wheels.

Sometimes she took them rowing, with the Stars and Stripes floating over her boat, by moonlight; sometimes she drove them recklessly in a drag through roads bordered by olive-groves and vineyards; all these expeditions being undertaken under pretence of admiring the romantic scenery. Her father was not disposed to interfere with what he called "a little harmless dissipation." He was confident his daughter's "companion" must know what was proper, she being, as he said, accustomed to good society. Were not all Italian ladies attended by gentlemen? Who could blame a young girl for amusing herself? Meantime Mr. Sparks amused himself after his own fashion, which was to sit comfortably, with his feet up on the piazza rail of the hotel, imbibing strong iced drinks through straws. But in reality Jacqueline had no power whatever to preserve propriety, and only compromised herself by her associations, though her own conduct was irreproachable. Indeed she was considered quite prudish, and the rest of the mad crowd laughed at her for having the manners of a governess. In vain she tried to say words of warning to Nora; what she said was laughed at or resented in a tone that told her that a paid companion had not the right to speak as frankly as a friend.

Her business, she was plainly told one day, was to be on the spot in case any impertinent suitor should venture too far in a *tête-à-tête*, but short of that she was not to "spoil sport." "I am not doing anything wrong; it is allowable in America," was Miss Nora's regular speech on such occasions, and Jacqueline could not dispute the double argument. Nora's conduct was not wicked, and in America such things might be allowed. Yet Jacqueline tried to demonstrate that a young girl can not pass unscathed through certain adventures, even if they are innocent in the strict sense of the word; which made Nora cry out that all she said was subterfuge and that she had no patience with prejudices.

In vain her young companion pointed out to her charge that other Americans at Bellagio seemed far from approving her conduct. American ladies of a very different class, who were staying at the hotel, held aloof from her, and treated her with marked coldness whenever they met; declaring that her manners would be as objectionable in her own country, in good society, as they were in Italy.

But Miss Sparks was not to be put down by any argument. "Bah! they are stuck-up Bostonians. And do you know, Jacqueline, you are getting very tiresome? You were faster yourself than I when we were the Blue Band at Tréport."

Nora's admirers, sometimes encouraged, sometimes snubbed, when treated cavalierly by this young lady, would occasionally pay court to the *demoiselle de compagnie*, who indeed was well worth their pains; but, to their surprise, the subordinate received their attentions with great coldness. Having entered her protest against what was going on, and having resisted the contagion of example, it was natural she should somewhat exaggerate her prudery, for it is hard to hit just the right point in such reaction. The result was, she made herself so disagreeable to Miss Sparks that the latter determined on getting rid of her as tactfully as possible.

Their parting took place on the day after an excursion to the Villa Sommariva, where Miss Sparks and her little court had behaved with their usual noise and rudeness. They had gone there ostensibly to see the pictures, about which none of them cared anything, for Nora, wherever she was, never liked any one to pay attention to anybody or to look at anything but her own noisy, all-pervading self.

It so happened that at the most riotous moment of the picnic an old gentleman passed near the lively crowd. He was quite inoffensive, pleasant-mannered, and walked leaning on his cane, yet, had the statue of the Commander in Don Juan suddenly appeared it could not have produced such consternation as his presence did on Jacqueline, when, after a moment's hesitation, he bowed to her. She recognized in him a friend of Madame d'Argy, M. Martel, whom she had often met at her house in Paris and at Lizerolles. When he recognized her, she fancied she had seen pass over his face a look of painful surprise. He would surely tell how he had met her; what would her old friends think of her? What would Fred? For some time past she had thought more than ever before of what Fred would think of her. The more she grew disgusted with the men she met, the more she appreciated his good qualities, and the more she thought of the honest, faithful love he had offered her—love that she had so madly thrown away. She never should meet such love again, she thought. It was the idea of how Fred would blame her when he heard what she pictured to herself the old gentleman would say of her, that suddenly decided her to leave Bellagio.

She told Mr. Sparks that evening that she was not strong enough for such duties as were required of a companion.

He looked at her with pity and annoyance.

"I should have thought you had more energy. How do you expect to live by work if you are not strong enough for pleasure?"

"Pleasure needs strength as well as labor," she said, smiling; "I would rather work in the fields than go on amusing myself as I have been doing."

"My dear, you must not be so difficult to please. When people have to earn their bread, it is a bad plan. I am afraid you will find out before long that there are harder ways of making a living than lunching, dancing, walking, and driving from morning to night in a pretty country——"

Here Mr. Sparks began to laugh as he thought of all he had had to do, without making objections, in the Far West, in the heroic days of his youthful vigor. He

was rather fond of recalling how he had carried his
pick on his shoulder and his knife in his belt, with two
Yankee sayings in his head, and little besides for bag-
gage: "Muscle and pluck!—Muscle and pluck!" and
"Go ahead for ever!" That was the sort of thing to be
done when a man or a woman had not a cent.

And now, what was Jacqueline to do next? She reflected that in a very short time she had attempted
many things. It seemed to her that all she could do
now was to follow the advice which, when first given
her by Madame Strahlberg, had frightened her, though
she had found it so attractive. She would study
with Madame Rochette; she would go to the Milan
Conservatory, and as soon as she came of age she
would go upon the stage, under a feigned name,
of course, and in a foreign country. She would
prove to the world, she said to herself, that the career
of an actress is compatible with self-respect. This
resolve that she would never be found wanting in self-
respect held a prominent place in all her plans, as she
began to understand better those dangers in life which
are for the most part unknown to young girls born
in her social position. Jacqueline's character, far from
being injured by her trials and experiences, had gained
in strength. She grew firmer as she gained in knowledge. Never had she been so worthy of regard and
interest as at the very time when her friends were
saying sadly to themselves, "She is going to the bad,"
and when, from all appearances, they were right in
this conclusion.

CHAPTER XVII

ACQUELINE came to the conclusion that she had better seriously consult Madame Strahlberg. She therefore stopped at Monaco, where this friend, whom she intended to honor with the strange office of Mentor, was passing the winter in a little villa in the Condamine quarter—a cottage surrounded by roses and laurel-bushes, painted in soft colors and looking like a plaything.

Madame Strahlberg had already urged Jacqueline to come and make acquaintance with her "paradise," without giving her any hint of the delights of that paradise, from which that of gambling was not excluded, for Madame Strahlberg was eager for any kind of excitement. Roulette now occupied with her a large part of every night—indeed, her nights had been rarely given to slumber, for her creed was that morning is the time for sleep, for which reason they never took breakfast in the pink villa, but tea, cakes, and confectionery were eaten instead at all hours until the evening. Thus it happened very often that they had no dinner, and guests had to accommodate themselves to the strange ways of the family. Jacqueline, however, did not stay long enough to know much of those ways.

JACQUELINE

She arrived, poor thing, with weary wing, like some bird, who, escaping from the fowler's net, where it has left its feathers, flies straight to the spot where a sportsman lies ready to shoot it. She was received with the same cries of joy, the same kisses, the same demonstrations of affection, as those which, the summer before, had welcomed her to the Rue de Naples. They told her she could sleep on a sofa, exactly like the one on which she had passed that terrible night which had resulted in her expulsion from the convent; and it was decided that she must stay several days, at least, before she went on to Paris, to begin the life of hard study and courageous work which would make of her a great singer.

Tired?—No, she was hardly tired at all. The journey over the enchanting road of the Corniche had awakened in her a fervor of admiration which prevented her from feeling any bodily needs, and now she seemed to have reached fairyland, where the verdure of the tropics was like the hanging gardens of Babylon, only those had never had a mirror to reflect back their ancient, far-famed splendor, like that before her eyes, as she looked down upon the Mediterranean, with the sun setting in the west in a sky all crimson and gold.

Notwithstanding the disorder of her travelling-dress, Jacqueline allowed her friend to take her straight from the railway station to the Terrace of Monte Carlo. She fell into ecstasies at sight of the African cacti, the century plants, and the fig-trees of Barbary, covering the low walls whence they looked down into the water; at the fragrance of the evergreens that surrounded the beautiful palace with its balustrades, dedicated to all the worst passions of the human race; with the sharp rocky outline of Turbia; with an almost invisible speck on the horizon which they said was Corsica; with everything, which, whether mirage or reality, lifted her out of herself, and plunged her into that state of excited happiness and indescribable sense of bodily comfort, which exterior impressions so easily produce upon the young.

After exhausting her vocabulary in exclamations and in questions, she stood silent, watching the sun as it sank beneath the waters, thinking that life is well worth living if it can give us such glorious spectacles, notwithstanding all the difficulties that may have to be passed through. Several minutes elapsed before she turned her radiant face and dazzled eyes toward Wanda, or rather toward the spot where Wanda had been standing beside her. "Oh! my dear—how beautiful!" she murmured with a long sigh.

The sigh was echoed by a man, who for a few moments had looked at her with as much admiration as she had looked at the landscape. He answered her by saying, in a low voice, the tones of which made her tremble from head to foot:

"Jacqueline!"

"Monsieur de Cymier!"

The words slipped through her lips as they suddenly turned pale. She had an instinctive, sudden persuasion that she had been led into a snare. If not, why was Madame Strahlberg now absorbed in conversation with three other persons at some little distance.

"Forgive me—you did not expect to see me—you

seem quite startled," said the young man, drawing near her. With an effort she commanded herself and looked full in his face. Her anger rose. She had seen the same look in the ugly, brutal face of Oscar de Talbrun. From the Terrace of Monte Carlo her memory flew back to a country road in Normandy, and she clenched her hand round an imaginary riding-whip. She needed coolness and she needed courage. They came as if by miracle.

"It is certain, Monsieur," she answered, slowly, "that I did not expect to meet you here."

"Chance has had pity on me," he replied, bowing low, as she had set him the example of ceremony.

But he had no idea of losing time in commonplace remarks—he wished to take up their intimacy on the terms it had been formerly, to resume the romance he himself had interrupted.

"I knew," he said in the same low voice, full of persuasion, which gave especial meaning to his words, "I knew that, after all, we should meet again."

"I did not expect it," said Jacqueline, haughtily.

"Because you do not believe in the magnetism of a fixed desire."

"No, I do not believe any such thing, when, opposed to such a desire, there is a strong, firm will," said Jacqueline, her eyes burning.

"Ah!" he murmured, and he might have been supposed to be really moved, so much his look changed, "do not abuse your power over me—do not make me wretched; if you could only understand——"

She made a swift movement to rejoin Madame Strahlberg, but that lady was already coming toward them with the same careless ease with which she had left them together.

"Well! you have each found an old acquaintance," she said, gayly. "I beg your pardon, my loveliest, but I had to speak to some old friends, and ask them to join us to-morrow evening. We shall sup at the restaurant of the Grand Hotel, after the opera—for, I did not tell you before, you will have the good luck to hear Patti. Monsieur de Cymier, we shall expect you. *Au revoir*."

He had been on the point of asking leave to walk home with them. But there was something in Jacqueline's look, and in her stubborn silence, that deterred him. He thought it best to leave a skilful advocate to plead his cause before he continued a conversation which had not begun satisfactorily. Not that Gérard de Cymier was discouraged by the behavior of Jacqueline. He had expected her to be angry at his defection, and that she would make him pay for it; but a little skill on his part, and a little credulity on hers, backed by the intervention of a third party, might set things right.

One moment he lingered to look at her, admiring her as she stood in the light of the dying sun, as beautiful in her plain dress and her indignant paleness, while she looked far out to sea, that she might not be obliged to look at him, as she had been when he had known her in prosperity.

At that moment he knew she hated him, but it would be an additional delight to overcome that feeling.

JACQUELINE

The two women, when he left them, continued walking on the terrace side by side, without a word. Wanda watched her companion out of the corners of her eyes, and hummed an air to herself to break the silence. She saw a storm gathering under Jacqueline's black eyebrows, and knew that sharp arrows were likely to shoot forth from those lips which several times had opened, though not a word had been uttered, probably through fear of saying too little or too much.

At last she made some trifling comment on the view, explaining something about pigeon-shooting.

"Wanda," interrupted Jacqueline, "did you not know what happened once?"

"Happened, how? About what?" asked Madame Strahlberg, with an air of innocence.

"I am speaking of the way Monsieur de Cymier treated me."

"Bah! He was in love with you. Who didn't know it? Every one could see that. It was all the more reason why you should have been glad to meet him."

"He did not act as if he were much in love," said Jacqueline.

"Because he went away when your family thought he was about to make his formal proposal? Not all men are marrying men, my dear, nor have all women that vocation. Men fall in love all the same."

"Do you think, then, that when a man knows he has no intention of marrying he should pay court to a young girl? I think I told you at the time that he had paid court to me, and that he afterward—how shall I say it?—basely deserted me."

THÉO BENTZON

The sharp and thrilling tone in which Jacqueline said this amused Madame Strahlberg.

"What big words, my dear! No, I don't remember that you ever said anything of the sort to me before. But you are wrong. As we grow older we lay aside harsh judgments and sharp words. They do no good. In your place I should be touched by the thought that a man so charming had been faithful to me."

"Faithful!" cried Jacqueline, her dark eyes flashing into the cat-like eyes of Madame Strahlberg.

Wanda looked down, and fastened a ribbon at her waist.

"Ever since we have been here," she said, "he has been talking of you."

"Really—for how long?"

"Oh, if you must know, for the last two weeks."

"It is just a fortnight since you wrote and asked me to stay with you," said Jacqueline, coldly and reproachfully.

"Oh, well—what's the harm? Suppose I did think your presence would increase the attractions of Monaco?"

"Why did you not tell me?"

"Because I never write a word more than is necessary; you know how lazy I am. And also because, I may as well confess, it might have scared you off, you are so sensitive."

"Then you meant to take me by surprise?" said Jacqueline, in the same tone.

"Oh! my dear, why do you try to quarrel with me?" replied Madame Strahlberg, stopping suddenly and looking at her through her eyeglass. "We may as well understand what you mean by a free and independent life."

And thereupon ensued an address to which Jacqueline listened, leaning one hand on a balustrade of that enchanted garden, while the voice of the serpent, as she thought, was ringing in her ears. Her limbs shook under her—her brain reeled. All her hopes of success as a singer on the stage Madame Strahlberg swept away, as not worth a thought. She told her that, in her position, had she meant to be too scrupulous, she should have stayed in the convent. Everything to Jacqueline seemed to dance before her eyes. The evening closed around them, the light died out, the landscape, like her life, had lost its glow. She uttered a brief prayer for help, such a prayer as she had prayed in infancy. She whispered it in terror, like a cry in extreme danger. She was more frightened by Wanda's wicked words than she had been by M. de Talbrun or by M. de Cymier. She ceased to know what she was saying till the last words, "You have good sense and you will think about it," met her ear.

Jacqueline said not a word.

Wanda took her arm. "You may be sure," she said, "that I am thinking only of your good. Come! Would you like to go into the Casino and look at the pictures? No, you are tired? You can see them some evening. The ballroom holds a thousand persons. Yes, if you prefer, we will go home. You can take a nap till dinner-time. We shall dine at eight o'clock."

Conversation languished till they reached the Villa

Rosa. Notwithstanding Jacqueline's efforts to appear natural, her own voice rang in her ears in tones quite new to her, a laugh that she uttered without any occasion, and which came near resulting in hysterics. Yet she had power enough over her nerves to notice the surroundings as she entered the house. At the door of the room in which she was to sleep, and which was on the first story, Madame Strahlberg kissed her with one of those equivocal smiles which so long had imposed on her simplicity.

"Till eight o'clock, then."

"Till eight o'clock," repeated Jacqueline, passively.

But when eight o'clock came she sent word that she had a severe headache, and would try to sleep it off.

Suppose, she thought, M. de Cymier should have been asked to dinner; suppose she should be placed next to him at table? Anything in that house seemed possible now.

They brought her a cup of tea. Up to a late hour she heard a confused noise of music and laughter. She did not try to sleep. All her faculties were on the alert, like those of a prisoner who is thinking of escape. She knew what time the night trains left the station, and, abandoning her trunk and everything else that she had with her, she furtively—but ready, if need were, to fight for her liberty with the strength of desperation — slipped down the broad stairs over their thick carpet and pushed open a little glass door. Thank heaven! people came in and went out of that house as if it had been a mill. No one discovered her flight till the next morning, when she was far on her way to Paris in an express train.

Modeste, quite unprepared for her young mistress's arrival, was amazed to see her drop down upon her, feverish and excited, like some poor hunted animal, with strength exhausted. Jacqueline flung herself into her nurse's arms as she used to do when, as a little girl, she was in what she fancied some great trouble, and she cried: "Oh, take me in—pray take me in! Keep me safe! Hide me!" And then she told Modeste everything, speaking rapidly and disconnectedly, thankful to have some one to whom she could open her heart. In default of Modeste she would have spoken to stone walls.

"And what will you do now, my poor darling?" asked the old nurse, as soon as she understood that her young lady had come back to her, "with weary foot and broken wing," from what she had assured her on her departure would be a brilliant excursion.

"Oh! I don't know," answered Jacqueline, in utter discouragement; "I am too worn out to think or to do anything. Let me rest; that is all."

"Why don't you go to see your stepmother?"

"My stepmother? Oh, no! She is at the bottom of all that has happened to me."

"Or Madame d'Argy? Or Madame de Talbrun? Madame de Talbrun is the one who would give you good advice."

Jacqueline shook her head with a sad smile.

"Let me stay here. Don't you remember—years ago—but it seems like yesterday—all the rest is like a nightmare—how I used to hide myself under your petticoats, and you would say, going on with your knitting: 'You see she is not here; I can't think where she can be.' Hide me now just like that, dear old Modeste. Only hide me."

And Modeste, full of heartfelt pity, promised to hide her "dear child" from every one, which promise, however, did not prevent her, for she was very self-willed, from going, without Jacqueline's knowledge, to see Madame de Talbrun and tell her all that had taken place. She was hurt and amazed at her reception by Giselle, and at her saying, without any offer of help or words of sympathy, "She has only reaped what she has sown." Giselle would have been more than woman had not Fred, and a remembrance of the wrongs that he had suffered through Jacqueline, now stood between them. For months he had been the prime object in her life; her mission of comforter had brought her the greatest happiness she had ever known. She tried to make him turn his attention to some serious work in life; she wanted to keep him at home, for his mother's sake, she thought; she fancied she had inspired him with a taste for home life. If she had examined herself she might have discovered that the task she had undertaken of doing good to this young man was not wholly for his sake but partly for her own. She wanted to see him nearly every day and to occupy a place in his life ever larger and larger. But for some time past the conscientious Giselle had neglected the duty of strict self-examination. She was thankful to be happy—and though Fred was a man little given to self-flattery in his relations with women, he could not but be pleased at the change produced in her by her intercourse with him.

But while Fred and Giselle considered themselves as two friends trying to console each other, people had begun to talk about them. Even Madame d'Argy asked herself whether her son might not have escaped from the cruel claws of a young coquette of the new school to fall into a worse scrape with a married woman. She imagined what might happen if the jealousy of "that wild boar of an Oscar de Talbrun" were aroused; the dangers, far more terrible than the perils of the sea, that might in such a case await her only son, the child for whose safety her mother-love caused her to suffer perpetual torments. "O mothers! mothers!" she often said to herself, "how much they are to be pitied. And they are very blind. If Fred must get into danger and difficulty for any woman, it should not have been for Giselle de Talbrun."

CHAPTER XVIII

A MEETING took place yesterday at Vésinet between the Vicomte de Cymier, secretary of Embassy at Vienna, and M. Frédéric d'Argy, ensign in the navy. The parties fought with swords. The seconds of M. de Cymier were the Prince de Moelk and M. d'Etaples, captain in the —th Hussars; those of M. d'Argy were M. Edmond Lavour, of the navy, and Hubert Marien, the painter. M. d'Argy was wounded in the right arm, and for the present the affair is terminated, but it is said it will be resumed on M. d'Argy's recovery, although this seems hardly probable, considering the very slight cause of the quarrel—an altercation at the Cercle de la Rue Boissy d'Anglas, which took place over the card-table.

Such was the announcement in a daily paper that met the eyes of Jacqueline, as she lay hidden in Modeste's lodging, like a fawn in its covert, her eyes and ears on the alert, watching for the least sign of alarm, in fear and trembling. She expected something, she knew not what; she felt that her sad adventure at Monaco could not fail to have its epilogue; but this was one of which she never had dreamed.

"Modeste, give me my hat! Get me a carriage! Quick! Oh, my God, it is my fault!—I have killed him!"

JACQUELINE

These incoherent cries came from her lips while Modeste, in alarm, picked up the newspaper and adjusted her silver spectacles upon her nose to read the paragraph. "Monsieur Fred wounded! Holy Virgin! His poor mother! That is a new trouble fallen on her, to be sure. But this quarrel had nothing to do with you, my pet; you see they say it was about cards."

And folding up the *Figaro*, while Jacqueline in all haste was wrapping her head in a veil, Modeste, with the best intentions, went on to say: "Nobody ever dies of a sword-thrust in the arm."

"But you see it says that they are going to fight all over again—don't you understand? You are so stupid! What could they have had to quarrel about but me? O God! Thou art just! This is indeed punishment —too much punishment for me!"

So saying, she ran down the many stairs that led up to Modeste's little lodging in the roof, her feet hardly touching them as she ran, while Modeste followed her more slowly, crying: "Wait for me! Wait for me, Mademoiselle!"

Calling a *fiacre*, Jacqueline, almost roughly, pushed the old woman into it, and gave the coachman the address of Madame d'Argy, having, in her excitement, first given him that of their old house in the Parc Monceau, so much was she possessed by the idea that this was a repetition of that dreadful day, when with Modeste, just as now, she went to meet an irreparable loss. She seemed to see before her her dead father— he looked like Fred, and now, as before, Marien had his part in the tragedy. Could he not have prevented the duel? Could he not have done something to prevent Fred from exposing himself? The wound might be no worse than it was said to be in the newspaper— but then a second meeting was to take place. No!— it should not, she would stop it at any price!

And yet, as the coach drew nearer to the Rue de Varenne, where Madame d'Argy had her winter residence, a little calm, a little sense returned to Jacqueline. She did not see how she could dare to enter that house, where probably they cursed her very name. She would wait in the street with the carriage-blinds pulled down, and Modeste should go in and ask for information. Five minutes passed—ten minutes passed —they seemed ages. How slow Modeste was, slow as a tortoise! How could she leave her there when she knew she was so anxious? What could she be doing? All she had to do was to ask news of M. Fred in just two words!

At last, Jacqueline could bear suspense no longer. She opened the coach-door and jumped out on the pavement. Just at that moment Modeste appeared, brandishing the umbrella that she carried instead of a stick, in a manner that meant something. It might be bad news, she would know in a moment; anything was better than suspense. She sprang forward.

"What did they say, Modeste? Speak!—Why have you been such a time?"

"Because the servants had something else to do than to attend to me. I wasn't the only person there—they were writing in a register. Get back into the carriage, Mademoiselle, or somebody will see you—There are lots of people there who know you—Monsieur and Madame d'Etaples——"

"What do I care?—The truth! Tell me the truth——"

"But didn't you understand my signals? He is going on well. It was only a scratch—Ah! *dame!* that's only my way of talking. He will be laid up for a fortnight. The doctor was there—he has some fever, but he is not in any danger."

"Oh! what a blessing! Kiss me, Modeste. We have a fortnight in which we may interfere—But how—Oh, how?—Ah! there is Giselle! We will go to Giselle at once!"

And the *fiacre* was ordered to go as fast as possible to the Rue Barbet-de-Jouy. This time Jacqueline herself spoke to the concierge.

"Madame la Comtesse is out."

"But she never goes out at this hour. I wish to see her on important business. I must see her."

And Jacqueline passed the concierge, only to encounter another refusal from a footman, who insisted that Madame la Comtesse was at home to no one.

"But me, she will see me. Go and tell her it is Mademoiselle de Nailles."

Moved by her persistence, the footman went in to inquire, and came back immediately with the answer:

"Madame la Comtesse can not see Mademoiselle."

"Ah!" thought Jacqueline, "she, too, throws me off, and it is natural. I have no friends left. No one will tell me anything!—I think it will drive me mad?"

THÉO BENTZON

She was half-mad already. She stopped at a news-
stand and bought all the evening journals; then, up in
her garret, in her poor little nest under the roof—which,
as she felt bitterly, was her only refuge, she began to
look over those printed papers in which she might possibly find out the true cause of the duel. Nearly all
related the event in almost the exact terms used by the
Figaro. Ah!—here was a different one! A reporter who
knew something more added, in *Gil Blas:* "We have
stated the cause of the dispute as it has been given to
the public, but in affairs of this nature more than in any
others, it is safe to remember the old proverb: 'Look
for the woman.' The woman could doubtless have
been found enjoying herself on the sunny shores of the
Mediterranean, while men were drawing swords in her
defense."

Jacqueline went on looking through the newspapers,
crumpling up the sheets as she laid them down. The
last she opened had the reputation of being a repository
of scandals, never to be depended on, as she well knew.
Several times it had come to her hand and she had not
opened it, remembering what her father had always
said of its reputation. But where would she be more
likely to find what she wanted than in the columns of a
journal whose reporters listened behind doors and
peeped through keyholes? Under the heading of *Les
Dessous Parisiens,* she read on the first page:

"Two hens lived in peace; a cock came
And strife soon succeeded to joy;
E'en as love, they say, kindled the flame
That destroyed the proud city of Troy.

JACQUELINE

"This quarrel was the outcome of a violent rupture between the two hens in question, ending in the flight of one of them, a young and tender pullet, whose voice we trust soon to hear warbling on the boards at one of our theatres. This was the subject of conversation in a low voice at the Cercle, at the hour when it is customary to tell such little scandals. M. de C—— was enlarging on the somewhat Bohemian character of the establishment of a lovely foreign lady, who possesses the secret of being always surrounded by delightful friends, young ladies who are self-emancipated, quasi-widows who, by divorce suits, have regained their liberty, etc. He was speaking of one of the beauties who are friends of his friend Madame S——, as men speak of women who have proved themselves careless of public opinion; when M. d'A——, in a loud voice, interrupted him; the lie was given in terms that of course led to the hostile meeting of which the press has spoken, attributing it to a dispute about the Queen of Spades, when it really concerned the Queen of Hearts."

Then she had made no mistake; it had been her flight from Madame Strahlberg's which had led to her being attacked by one man, and defended by the other! Jacqueline found it hard to recognize herself in this tissue of lies, insinuations, and half-truths. What did the paper mean its readers to understand by its account? Was it a jealous rivalry between herself and Madame Strahlberg?—Was M. de Cymier meant by the cock?— And Fred had heard all this—he had drawn his sword to refute the calumny. Brave Fred! Alas! he had been prompted only by chivalric generosity. Doubtless he, also, looked upon her as an adventuress.

All night poor Jacqueline wept with such distress that she wished that she might die. She was dropping off to sleep at last, overpowered by fatigue, when a ring

THÉO BENTZON

at the bell in the early morning roused her. Then she
heard whispering:

"Do you think she is so unhappy?"

It was the voice of Giselle.

"Come in—come in quickly!" she cried, springing
out of bed. Wrapped in a dressing-gown, with bare
feet, her face pale, her eyelids red, her complexion
clouded, she rushed to meet her friend, who was almost
as much disordered as herself. It seemed as if Madame
de Talbrun might also have passed a night of sleeplessness and tears.

"You have come! Oh! you have come at last!"
cried Jacqueline, throwing her arms around her, but
Giselle repelled her with a gesture so severe that the
poor child could not but understand its meaning. She
murmured, pointing to the pile of newspapers: "Is it
possible?—Can you have believed all those dreadful
things?"

"What things? I have read nothing," said Giselle,
harshly. "I only know that a man who was neither
your husband nor your brother, and who consequently
was under no obligation to defend you, has been foolish
enough to be nearly killed for your sake. Is not that a
proof of your downfall? Don't you know it?"

"Downfall?" repeated Jacqueline, as if she did not
understand her. Then, seizing her friend's hand, she
forcibly raised it to her lips: "Ah! what can anything
matter to me," she cried, "if only you remain my
friend; and he has never doubted me!"

"Women like you can always find defenders," said
Giselle, tearing her hand from her cousin's grasp.

JACQUELINE

Giselle was not herself at that moment. "But, for your own sake, it would have been better he should have abstained from such an act of Quixotism."

"Giselle! can it be that you think me guilty?"

"Guilty!" cried Madame de Talbrun, her pale face aflame. "A little more and Monsieur de Cymier's sword-point would have pierced his lungs."

"Good heavens!" cried Jacqueline, hiding her faee in her hands. "But I have done nothing to——"

"Nothing except to set two men against each other; to make them suffer, or to make fools of them, and to be loved by them all the same."

"I have not been a coquette," said Jacqueline, with indignation.

"You must have been, to authorize the boasts of Monsieur de Cymier. He had seen Fred so seldom, and Tonquin had so changed him that he spoke in his presence—without supposing any one would interfere. I dare not tell you what he said——"

"Whatever spite or revenge suggested to him, no doubt," said Jacqueline. "Listen, Giselle—Oh, you must listen. I shall not be long."

She forced her to sit down; she crouched on a footstool at her feet, holding her hands in hers so tightly that Giselle could not draw them away, and began her story, with all its details, of what had happened to her since she left Fresne. She told of her meeting with Wanda; of the fatal evening which had resulted in her expulsion from the convent; her disgust at the Sparks family; the snare prepared for her by Madame Strahlberg. "And I can not tell you all," she added, "I can not tell you what drove me away from my true friends, and threw me among these people——"

Giselle's sad smile seemed to answer, "No need—I am aware of it—I know my husband." Encouraged by this, Jacqueline went on with her confession, hiding nothing that was wrong, showing herself just as she had been, a poor, proud child who had set out to battle for herself in a dangerous world. At every step she had been more and more conscious of her own imprudence, of her own weakness, and of an ever-increasing desire to be done with independence; to submit to law, to be subject to any rules which would deliver her from the necessity of obeying no will but her own.

"Ah!" she cried, "I am so disgusted with independence, with amusement, and amusing people! Tell me what to do in future—I am weary of taking charge of myself. I said so the other day to the Abbé Bardin. He is the only person I have seen since my return. It seems to me I am coming back to my old ideas—you remember how I once wished to end my days in the cell of a Carmelite? You might love me again then, perhaps, and Fred and poor Madame d'Argy, who must feel so bitterly against me since her son was wounded, might forgive me. No one feels bitterly against the dead, and it is the same as being dead to be a Carmelite nun. You would all speak of me sometimes to each other as one who had been very unhappy, who had been guilty of great foolishness, but who had repaired her faults as best she could."

Poor Jacqueline! She was no longer a girl of the period; in her grief and humiliation she belonged to the past. Old - fashioned forms of penitence attracted her.

"And what did the Abbé Bardin tell you?" asked Giselle, with a slight movement of her shoulders.

"He only told me that he could not say at present whether that were my vocation."

"Nor can I," said Giselle.

Jacqueline lifted up her face, wet with tears, which she had been leaning on the lap of Giselle.

"I do not see what else I can do, unless you would get me a place as governess somewhere at the ends of the earth," she said. "I could teach children their letters. I should not mind doing anything. I never should complain. Ah! if you lived all by yourself, Giselle, how I should implore you to take me to teach little Enguerrand!"

"I think you might do better than that," said Giselle, wiping her friend's eyes almost as a mother might have done, "if you would only listen to Fred."

Jacqueline's cheeks became crimson.

"Don't mock me—it is cruel—I am too unworthy— it would pain me to see him. Shame—regret—you understand! But I can tell you one thing, Giselle— only you. You may tell it to him when he is quite old, when he has been long married, and when everything concerning me is a thing of the past. I never had loved any one with all my heart up to the moment when I read in that paper that he had fought for me, that his blood had flowed for me, that after all that had passed he still thought me worthy of being defended by him."

Her tears flowed fast, and she added: "I shall be proud of that all the rest of my life! If only you, too, would forgive me."

The heart of Giselle was melted by these words.

"Forgive you, my dear little girl? Ah! you have been better than I. I forgot our old friendship for a moment—I was harsh to you; and I have so little right to blame you! But come! Providence may have arranged all for the best, though one of us may have to suffer. Pray for that some one. Good-by—*au revoir!*"

She kissed Jacqueline's forehead and was gone, before her cousin had seized the meaning of her last words. But joy and peace came back to Jacqueline. She had recovered her best friend, and had convinced her of her innocence.

CHAPTER XIX

EFORE Giselle went home to her own house she called on the Abbé Bardin, whom a rather surly servant was not disposed to disturb, as he was just eating his breakfast. The Abbé Bardin was Jacqueline's confessor, and he held the same relation to a number of other young girls who were among her particular friends. He was thoroughly acquainted with all that concerned their delicate and generally childish little souls. He kept them in the right way, had often a share in their marriages, and in general kept an eye upon them all their lives. Even when they escaped from him, as had happened in the case of Jacqueline, he did not give them up. He commended them to God, and looked forward to the time of their repentance with the patience of a father. The Abbé Bardin had never been willing to exercise any function but that of catechist; he had grown old in the humble rank of third assistant in a great parish, when, with a little ambition, he might have been its rector. "Suffer little children to come unto me" had been his motto. These words of his Divine Master seemed more often than any others on his lips—lips so expressive of loving-

kindness, though sometimes a shrewd smile would pass over them and seem to say: "I know, I can divine." But when this smile, the result of long experience, did not light up his features, the good Abbé Bardin looked like an elderly child; he was short, his walk was a trot, his face was round and ruddy, his eyes, which were short-sighted, were large, wide-open, and blue, and his heavy crop of white hair, which curled and crinkled above his forehead, made him look like a sixty-year-old angel, crowned with a silvery aureole.

Rubbing his hands affably, he came into the little parlor where Madame de Talbrun was waiting for him. There was probably no ecclesiastic in all Paris who had a salon so full of worked cushions, each of which was a keepsake—a souvenir of some first communion. The Abbé did not know his visitor, but the name Talbrun seemed to him connected with an honorable and well-meaning family. The lady was probably a mother who had come to put her child into his hands for religious instruction. He received visits from dozens of such mothers, some of whom were a little tiresome, from a wish to teach him what he knew better than they, and at one time he had set apart Wednesday as his day for receiving such visits, that he might not be too greatly disturbed, as seemed likely to happen to him that day. Not that he cared very much whether he ate his cutlet hot or cold, but his housekeeper cared a great deal. A man may be a very experienced director, and yet be subject to direction in other ways.

The youth of Giselle took him by surprise.

JACQUELINE

"Monsieur l'Abbé," she said, without any preamble, while he begged her to sit down, "I have come to speak to you of a person in whom you take an interest, Jacqueline de Nailles."

He passed the back of his hand over his brow and said, with a sigh: "Poor little thing!"

"She is even more to be pitied than you think. You have not seen her, I believe, since last week."

"Yes—she came. She has kept up, thank God, some of her religious duties."

"For all that, she has played a leading part in a recent scandal."

The Abbé sprang up from his chair.

"A duel has taken place because of her, and her name is in all men's mouths—whispered, of course—but the quarrel took place at the Club. You know what it is to be talked of at the Club."

"The poison of asps," growled the Abbé; "oh! those clubs—think of all the evil reports concocted in them, of which women are the victims!"

"In the present case the evil report was pure calumny. It was taken up by some one whom you also know—Frédéric d'Argy."

"I have had profound respect these many years for his excellent and pious mother."

"I thought so. In that case, Monsieur l'Abbé, you would not object to going to Madame d'Argy's house and asking how her son is."

"No, of course not; but—it is my duty to disapprove——"

"You will tell her that when a young man has compromised a young girl by defending her reputation in a manner too public, there is but one thing he can do afterward—marry her."

"Wait one moment," said the Abbé, who was greatly surprised; "it is certain that a good marriage would be the best thing for Jacqueline. I have been thinking of it. But I do not think I could so suddenly—so soon after——"

"To-day at four o'clock, Monsieur l'Abbé. Time presses. You can add that such a marriage is the only way to stop a second duel, which will otherwise take place."

"Is it possible?"

"And it is also the only way to bring Frédéric to decide on sending in his resignation. Don't forget that —it is important."

"But how do you know——"

The poor Abbé stammered out his words, and counted on his fingers the arguments he was desired to make use of.

"And you will solemnly assure them that Jacqueline is innocent."

"Oh! as to that, there are wolves in sheeps' clothing, as the Bible tells us; but believe me, when such poor young things are in question, it is more often the sheep which has put on the appearance of a wolf—to seem in the fashion," added the Abbé, "just to seem in the fashion. Fashion will authorize any kind of counterfeiting."

"Well, you will say all that, will you not, to Madame d'Argy? It will be very good of you if you will. She will make no difficulties about money. All she wants is a quietly disposed daughter-in-law who will be willing to pass nine months of the year at Lizerolles, and Jacqueline is quite cured of her Paris fever."

"A fever too often mortal," murmured the Abbé; "oh, for the simplicity of nature! A priest whose lot is cast in the country is fortunate, Madame, but we can not choose our vocation. We may do good anywhere, especially in cities. Are you sure, however, that Jacqueline——"

"She loves Monsieur d'Argy."

"Well, if that is so, we are all right. The great misfortune with many of these poor girls is that they have never learned to love anything; they know nothing but agitations, excitements, curiosities, and fancies. All that sort of thing runs through their heads."

"You are speaking of a Jacqueline before the duel. I can assure you that ever since yesterday, if not before, she has loved Monsieur d'Argy, who on his part for a long time—a very long time—has been in love with her."

Giselle spoke eagerly, as if she forced herself to say the words that cost her pain. Her cheeks were flushed under her veil. The Abbé, who was keen-sighted, observed these signs.

"But," continued Giselle, "if he is forced to forget her he may try to expend elsewhere the affection he feels for her; he may trouble the peace of others, while deceiving himself. He might make in the world one of those attachments— Do not fail to represent all these dangers to Madame d'Argy when you plead the cause of Jacqueline."

"Humph! You are evidently much attached, Madame, to Mademoiselle de Nailles."

"Very much, indeed," she answered, bravely, "very much attached to her, and still more to *him;* therefore you understand that this marriage must—absolutely *must* take place."

She had risen and was folding her cloak round her, looking straight into the Abbé's eyes. Small as she was, their height was almost the same; she wanted him to understand thoroughly why this marriage must take place.

He bowed. Up to that time he had not been quite sure that he had not to do with one of those wolves dressed in fleece whose appearance is as misleading as that of sheep disguised as wolves: now his opinion was settled.

"*Mon Dieu!* Madame," he said, "your reasons seem to me excellent—a duel to be prevented, a son to be kept by the side of his sick mother, two young people who love each other to be married, the saving, possibly, of two souls——"

"Say three souls, Monsieur l'Abbé!"

He did not ask whose was the third, nor even why she had insisted that this delicate commission must be executed that same day. He only bowed when she said again: "At four o'clock: Madame d'Argy will be prepared to see you. Thank you, Monsieur l'Abbé." And then, as she descended the staircase, he bestowed upon her silently his most earnest benediction, before returning to the cold cutlet that was on his breakfast-table.

JACQUELINE

Giselle did not breakfast much better than he. In truth, M. de Talbrun being absent, she sat looking at her son, who was eating with a good appetite, while she drank only a cup of tea; after which, she dressed herself, with more than usual care, hiding by rice-powder the trace of recent tears on her complexion, and arranging her fair hair in the way that was most becoming to her, under a charming little bonnet covered with gold net-work which corresponded with the embroidery on an entirely new costume.

When she went into the dining-room Enguerrand, who was there with his nurse finishing his dessert, cried out: "Oh! mamma, how pretty you are!" which went to her heart. She kissed him two or three times —one kiss after another.

"I try to be pretty for your sake, my darling."

"Will you take me with you?"

"No, but I will come back for you, and take you out."

She walked a few steps, and then turned to give him such a kiss as astonished him, for he said:

"Is it really going to be long?"

"What?"

"Before you come back? You kiss me as if you were going for a long time, far away."

"I kissed you to give myself courage."

Enguerrand, who, when he had a hard lesson to learn, always did the same thing, appeared to understand her.

"You are going to do some thing you don't like."

[297]

"Yes, but I have to do it, because you see it is my duty."

"Do grown people have duties?"

"Even more than children."

"But it isn't your duty to write a copy—your writing is so pretty. Oh! that's what I hate most. And you always say it is my duty to write my copy. I'll go and do it while you do your duty. So that will seem as if we were both together doing something we don't like—won't it, mamma?"

She kissed him again, even more passionately.

"We shall be always together, we two, my love!"

This word love struck the little ear of Enguerrand as having a new accent, a new meaning, and, boy-like, he tried to turn this excess of tenderness to advantage.

"Since you love me so much, will you take me to see the puppet-show?"

"Anywhere you like—when I come back. Goodby!"

CHAPTER XX

A CHIVALROUS SOUL

ADAME D'ARGY sat knitting by the window in Fred's chamber, with that resigned but saddened air that mothers wear when they are occupied in repairing the consequences of some rash folly. Fred had seen her in his boyhood knitting in the same way with the same look on her face, when he had been thrown from his pony, or had fallen from his velocipede. He himself looked ill at ease and worried, as he lay on a sofa with his arm in a sling. He was yawning and counting the hours. From time to time his mother glanced at him. Her look was curious, and anxious, and loving, all at the same time. He pretended to be asleep. He did not like to see her watching him. His handsome masculine face, tanned that pale brown which tropical climates give to fair complexions, looked odd as it rose above a light-blue cape, a very feminine garment which, as it had no sleeves, had been tied round his neck to keep him from being cold. He felt himself, with some impatience, at the mercy of the most tender, but the most sharp-eyed of nurses, a prisoner to her devotion, and made conscious of her power every mo-

[299]

ment. Her attentions worried him; he knew that they
all meant "It is your own fault, my poor boy, that you
are in this state, and that your mother is so unhappy."
He felt it. He knew as well as if she had spoken that
she was asking him to return to reason, to marry, without more delay, their little neighbor in Normandy,
Mademoiselle d'Argeville, a niece of M. Martel, whom
he persisted in not thinking of as a wife, always calling
her a "cider apple," in allusion to her red cheeks.

A servant came in, and said to Madame d'Argy that
Madame de Talbrun was in the salon.

"I am coming," she said, rolling up her knitting.

But Fred suddenly woke up:

"Why not ask her to come here?"

"Very good," said his mother, with hesitation. She
was distracted between her various anxieties; ex-
asperated against the fatal influence of Jacqueline,
alarmed by the increasing intimacy with Giselle, desirous that all such complications should be put an
end to by his marriage, but terribly afraid that her
"cider apple" would not be sufficient to accomplish it.

"Beg Madame de Talbrun to come in here," she
said, repeating the order after her son; but she settled
herself in her chair with an air more patient, more
resigned than ever, and her lips were firmly closed.

Giselle entered in her charming new gown, and
Fred's first words, like those of Enguerrand, were:
"How pretty you are! It is charity," he added, smiling, "to present such a spectacle to the eyes of a sick
man; it is enough to set him up again."

"Isn't it?" said Giselle, kissing Madame d'Argy on

the forehead. The poor mother had resumed her
knitting with a sigh, hardly glancing at the pretty
walking-costume, nor at the bonnet with its network
of gold.

"Isn't it pretty?" repeated Giselle. "I am delighted with this costume. It is made after one of
Réjane's. Oscar fell in love with it at a first representation of a vaudeville, and he gave me over into the
hands of the same dressmaker, who indeed was named
in the play. That kind of advertising seems very
effective."

She went on chattering thus to put off what she had
really come to say. Her heart was beating so fast
that its throbs could be seen under the embroidered
front of the bodice which fitted her so smoothly. She
wondered how Madame d'Argy would receive the suggestion she was about to make.

She went on: "I dressed myself in my best to-day
because I am so happy."

Madame d'Argy's long tortoiseshell knitting-needles
stopped.

"I am glad to hear it, my dear," she said, coldly,
"I am glad anybody can be happy. There are so
many of us who are sad."

"But why are you pleased?" asked Fred, looking at
her, as if by some instinct he understood that he had
something to do with it.

"Our prodigal has returned," answered Giselle,
with a little air of satisfaction, very artificial, however,
for she could hardly breathe, so great was her fear and
her emotion. "My house is in the garb of rejoicing."

"The prodigal? Do you mean your husband?" said Madame d'Argy, maliciously.

"Oh! I despair of him," replied Giselle, lightly. "No, I speak of a prodigal who did not go far, and who made haste to repent. I am speaking of Jacqueline."

There was complete silence. The knitting-needles ticked rapidly, a slight flush rose on the dark cheeks of Fred.

"All I beg," said Madame d'Argy, "is that you will not ask me to eat the fatted calf in her honor. The comings and going of Mademoiselle de Nailles have long ceased to have the slightest interest for me."

"They have for Fred at any rate; he has just proved it, I should say," replied Giselle.

By this time the others were as much embarrassed as Giselle. She saw it, and went on quickly:

"Their names are together in everybody's mouth; you can not hinder it."

"I regret it deeply—and allow me to make one remark: it seems to me you, show a want of tact such as I should never have imagined in you, my dear, in telling us——"

Giselle read in Fred's eyes, which were steadily fixed on her, that he was, on that point, of his mother's opinion. She went on, however, still pretending to blunder.

"Forgive me—but I have been so anxious about you ever since I heard there was to be a second meeting——"

"A second meeting!" screamed Madame d'Argy,

who, as she read no paper but the *Gazette de France*, or occasionally the *Débats*, knew nothing of all the rumors that find their echo in the daily papers.

"Oh, *mon Dieu!* I thought you knew——"

"You need not frighten my mother," said Fred, almost angrily; "Monsieur de Cymier has written a letter which puts an end to our quarrel. It is the letter of a man of honor apologizing for having spoken lightly, for having repeated false rumors without verifying them—in short, retracting all that he had said that reflected in any way on Mademoiselle de Nailles, and authorizing me, if I think best, to make public his retraction. After that we can have nothing more to say to each other."

"He who makes himself the champion to defend a young girl's character," said Madame d'Argy, sententiously, "injures her as much as those who have spoken evil of her."

"That is exactly what I think," said Giselle. "The self-constituted champion has given the evil rumor circulation."

There was again a painful silence. Then the intrepid little woman resumed: "This step on the part of Monsieur de Cymier seems to have rendered my errand unnecessary. I had thought of a way to end this sad affair; a very simple way, much better, most certainly, than men cutting their own throats or those of other people. But since peace has been made over the ruins of Jacqueline's reputation, I had better say nothing and go away."

"No—no! Let us hear what you had to propose,"

said Fred, getting up from his couch so quickly that he jarred his bandaged arm, and uttered a cry of pain, which seemed very much like an oath, too.

Giselle was silent. Standing before the hearth, she was warming her small feet, watching, as she did so, Madame d'Argy's profile, which was reflected in the mirror. It was severe—impenetrable. It was Fred who spoke first.

"In the first place," he said, hesitating, "are you sure that Mademoiselle de Nailles has not just arrived from Monaco?"

"I am certain that for a week she has been living quietly with Modeste, and that, though she passed through Monaco, she did not stay there twenty-four hours, finding that the air of that place did not agree with her."

"But what do you say to what Monsieur Martel saw with his own eyes, and which is confirmed by public rumor?" cried Madame d'Argy, as if she were giving a challenge.

"Monsieur Martel saw Jacqueline in bad company. She was not there of her own will. As to public rumor, we may feel sure that to make it as flattering to her tomorrow as it is otherwise to-day only a marriage is necessary. Yes, a marriage! That is the way I had thought of to settle everything and make everybody happy."

"What man would marry a girl who had compromised herself?" said Madame d'Argy, indignantly.

"He who has done his part to compromise her."

"Then go and propose it to Monsieur de Cymier!"

"No. It is not Monsieur de Cymier whom she loves."

"Ah!" Madame d'Argy was on her feet at once. "Indeed, Giselle, you are losing your senses. If I were not afraid of agitating Fred——"

He was, in truth, greatly agitated. The only hand that he could use was pulling and tearing at the little blue cape crossed on his breast, in which his mother had wrapped him; and this unsuitable garment formed such a queer contrast to the expression of his face that Giselle, in her nervous excitement, burst out laughing, an explosion of merriment which completed the exasperation of Madame d'Argy.

"Never!" she cried, beside herself. "You hear me —never will I consent, whatever happens!"

At that moment the door was partly opened, and a servant announced "Monsieur l'Abbé Bardin."

Madame d'Argy made a gesture which was anything but reverential.

"Well, to be sure—this is the right moment with a vengeance! What does he want! Does he wish me to assist in some good work—or to undertake to collect money, which I hate——"

"Above all, mother," cried Fred, "don't expose me to the fatigue of receiving his visit. Go and see him yourself. Giselle will take care of your patient while you are gone. Won't you, Giselle?"

His voice was soft, and very affectionate. He evidently was not angry at what she had dared to say, and she acknowledged this to herself with an aching heart.

THÉO BENTZON

"I don't exactly trust your kind of care," said Madame d'Argy, with a smile that was not gay, and certainly not amiable.

She went, however, because Fred repeated:

"But go and see the Abbé Bardin."

Hardly had she left the room when Fred got up from his sofa and approached Giselle with passionate eagerness.

"Are you sure I am not dreaming," said he. "Is it you—really you who advise me to marry Jacqueline?"

"Who else should it be?" she answered, very calm to all appearance. "Who can know better than I? But first you must oblige me by lying down again, or else I will not say one word more. That is right. Now keep still. Your mother is furiously displeased with me—I am sorry—but she will get over it. I know that in Jacqueline you would have a good wife—a wife far better than the Jacqueline you would have married formerly. She has paid dearly for her experience of life, and has profited by its lessons, so that she is now worthy of you, and sincerely repentant for her childish peccadilloes."

"Giselle," said Fred, "look me full in the face—yes, look into my eyes frankly and hide nothing. Your eyes never told anything but the truth. Why do you turn them away? Do you really and truly wish this marriage?"

She looked at him steadily as long as he would, and let him hold her hand, which was burning inside her glove, and which with a great effort she prevented from trembling. Then her nerves gave way under his long and silent gaze, which seemed to question her, and she laughed, a laugh that sounded to herself very unnatural.

"My poor, dear friend," she cried, "how easily you men are duped! You are trying to find out, to discover whether, in case you decide upon an honest act, a perfectly sensible act, to which you are strongly inclined —don't tell me you are not—whether, in short, you marry Jacqueline, I shall be really as glad of it as I pretend. But have you not found out what I have aimed at all along? Do you think I did not know from the very first what it was that made you seek me? I was not the rose, but I had lived near the rose; I reminded you of her continually. We two loved her; each of us felt we did. Even when you said harm of her, I knew it was merely because you longed to utter her name, and repeat to yourself her perfections. I laughed, yes, I laughed to myself, and I was careful how I contradicted you. I tried to keep you safe for her, to prevent your going elsewhere and forming attachments which might have resulted in your forgetting her. I did my best—do me justice—I did my best; perhaps sometimes I pushed things a little far— in her interest, in that of your mother, but in yours more than all; in yours, for God knows I am all for you," said Giselle, with sudden and involuntary fervor. "Yes, I am all yours as a friend, a faithful friend," she resumed, almost frightened by the tones of her own voice; "but as to the slightest feeling of love between us, love the most spiritual, the most platonic—yes, all men, I fancy, have a little of that kind of self-conceit.

THÉO BENTZON

Dear Fred, don't imagine it—Enguerrand would never have allowed it."

She was smiling, half laughing, and he looked at her with astonishment, asking himself whether he could believe what she was saying, when he could recollect what seemed to him so many proofs to the contrary. Yet in what she said there was no hesitation, no incoherence, no false note. Pride, noble pride, upheld her to the end. The first falsehood of her life was a masterpiece.

"Ah, Giselle!" he said at last, not knowing what to think, "I adore you! I revere you!"

"Yes," she replied, with a smile, gracious, yet with a touch of sadness, "I know you do. But *her* you love!"

Might it not have been sweet to her had he answered: "No, I loved her once, and remembered that old love enough to risk my life for her, but in reality I now love only you—all the more at this moment when I see you love me more than yourself." But, instead, he murmured only, like a man and a lover: "And Jacqueline —do you think she loves me?" His anxiety, a thrill that ran through all his frame, the light in his eyes, his sudden pallor, told more than his words.

If Giselle could have doubted his love for Jacqueline before, she would have now been convinced of it. The conviction stabbed her to the heart. Death is not that last sleep in which all our faculties, weakened and exhausted, fail us; it is the blow which annihilates our supreme illusion and leaves us disabused in a cold and empty world. People walk, talk, and smile after this death—another ghost is added to the drama played on the stage of the world; but the real self is dead.

Giselle was too much of a woman, angelic as she was, to have any courage left to say: "Yes, I know she loves you."

She said instead, in a low voice: "That is a question you must ask of her."

Meantime, in the next room they could hear Madame d'Argy vehemently repeating: "Never! No, I never will consent! Is it a plot between you?"

They heard also a rumbling monotone preceding each of these vehement interruptions. The Abbé Bardin was pointing out to her that, unmarried, her son would return to Tonquin, that Lizerolles would be left deserted, her house would be desolate without daughter-in-law or grandchildren; and, as he drew these pictures, he came back, again and again, to his main argument:

"I will answer for their happiness: I will answer for the future."

His authority as a priest gave weight to this assurance, at least Madame d'Argy felt it so. She went on saying *never*, but less and less emphatically, and apparently she ceased to say it at last, for three months later the d'Etaples, the Rays, the d'Avrignys and the rest, received two wedding announcements in these words:

"Madame d'Argy has the honor to inform you of the marriage of her son, M. Frédéric d'Argy, Chevalier of the Legion of Honor, to Mademoiselle de Nailles."

THÉO BENTZON

The accompanying card ran thus:

"The Baroness de Nailles has the honor to inform you of the marriage of Mademoiselle Jacqueline de Nailles, her stepdaughter, to M. Frédéric d'Argy."

Congratulations showered down on both mother and stepmother. A love-match is nowadays so rare! It turned out that every one had always wished all kinds of good fortune to young Madame d'Argy, and every one seemed to take a sincere part in the joy that was expressed on the occasion, even Dolly, who, it was said, had in secret set her heart on Fred for herself; even Nora Sparks, who, not having carried out her plans, had gone back to New York, whence she sent a superb wedding present. Madame de Nailles apparently experienced at the wedding all the emotions of a real mother.

The roses at Lizerolles bloomed that year with unusual beauty, as if to welcome the young pair. Modeste sang *Nunc Dimittis*. The least demonstrative of all those interested in the event was Giselle.